ONE CRIED MURDER

ONE CRIED MURDER

DAVID COOPER WALL

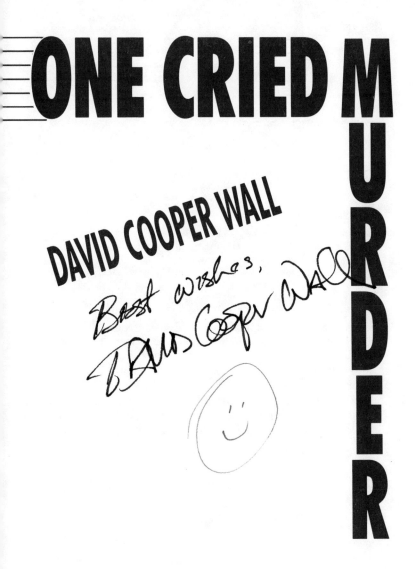

Best wishes,
David Cooper Wall

D E M B N E R   B O O K S
New York

DEMBNER BOOKS
Published by Red Dembner Enterprises Corp.,
80 Eighth Avenue, New York, N.Y. 10011
Distributed by W. W. Norton & Company, Inc.,
500 Fifth Avenue, New York, N.Y. 10110

Copyright © 1990 by David Cooper Wall

Library of Congress Cataloging-in-Publication Data
Wall, David Cooper.
   One cried murder / David Cooper Wall.
     p. cm.
   ISBN 0-942637-21-6 : $16.95
   I. Title.
PS3573.A425540S   1990   89-27652
813'.54—dc20   CIP

Designed by Antler & Baldwin, Inc.

This book is in memory of my friend
Frances L. Phillips.
I think she would have liked it.

A special word of thanks goes to
Dr. Norman Einstein,
Captain Phillip Borneman, and
Detective Lieutenant Steve Reid
for their patient advice, influence,
and expertise.

There's one did laugh in's sleep, and one cried
    "Murder!"
That they did wake each other: I stood and heard
    them:
But they did say their prayers, and address'd them
    Again to sleep.

—Macbeth

CHAPTER ONE

Fifty bucks for gin martinis and stuffed cabbage leaves would be hard to justify when I got up in the morning, but as the heavy ornate door slipped quietly shut behind me, closing out the clatter, chat, and aroma of dinner, I felt as though I'd just bought the best used car in America; expansive, available, everybody's best friend. Christ, I love gin. All those pine trees stuffed in a bottle. Amazing, absolutely amazing.

A three-day rain had reduced itself to a cool September mist that drifted horizontally through the luminous arcs of the streetlights along East 57th Street. The moisture felt good against my skin after the warmth and cigarette smoke of the restaurant, but it had rained too long for me. Goddamn stuff's OK out in Iowa somewhere, but in New York rain is inconvenient, filthy before it hits the ground, and qualifies as hazardous waste after it does. Tonight it had emptied the streets early, and only occasionally a lone automobile bounced into view on First Avenue, spraying water in five directions as it headed north.

It was after eleven, so a taxi was probably out of the question. First sign of bad weather and cabbies disappear into that looking-glass world where every fare is a trip to Westchester. A walk would do me good.

I got as far as 67th Street before the rain began again in earnest, so I cut across to Lexington, double-timed it half a block, and took the steps into the 67th Street precinct house two at a time. There was a chance Florio was still in his office and I could stay dry and do some incidental politicking at the same time. With permission from the desk sergeant, I dripped across the green linoleum lobby, climbed a flight of stairs, and stuck my head in the first office on the left.

Marc Florio is a big man even by John Wayne standards, but what strikes you first about him is his clothes. The man likes to dress well, and does, which isn't easy on a captain's salary with three children. His bulk, style, and freight-train personality make an imposing combination, kind of like walking head-on into a life-size Giorgio Armani ad.

At the moment, though, I found myself staring into his broad, open, forty-two-year-old face wondering why he looked different. His mustache was still in place, no nicks, no missing teeth. Shit! I couldn't place it.

"The mole," Florio said reading the confusion on my face and pointing to his chin.

"Huh?"

"The mole," he repeated, standing. "I had it removed."

"That's it, that's it," I said, mentally reapplying the small brown bump to the left side of his chin. "I knew there was something. It looks good, Marc. You can't even tell it was ever there."

"Yeah, I'm pleased, really am," he said, letting his finger run lightly over his face as he laid my coat on a straightback chair before coming to rest behind his desk. "So what's new with you, Ham?"

"Nothing really. I was on my way home and got caught in the rain. Actually, I'm a little surprised that you're here—it's late."

Florio rose again, squeezed himself into a closet behind his

2

desk, and reappeared with two sodas. He tossed one can in my direction and I dropped the goddamn thing.

"Technically, I'm on vacation," he said, sitting down and opening his soda, "but Joni and two of the kids have a virus, my mother decided the South America trip was 'more dangerous than her heart could stand,' plus I've got four bodies I can't identify, which is, as you know, the easy part." He let the end of his explanation slide as he lifted his soda. I was waiting patiently for him to continue when a young man in his late twenties strolled into the office.

"Hi, John," Florio said, without coming to his feet. "This is David Hamilton. David, Lieutenant John Marston." Florio turned his attention back to me, leaving Marston leaning against the far wall like a bad painting at Sotheby's. It looked as though he wasn't going to offer him a soda.

Marston was about five feet ten and trim, probably 165 pounds, wearing a double-breasted blue blazer that hadn't come off a rack at 25th and Fifth. Silk tie, pleated wool slacks, and Bally tassels finished out the look, and I realized that Florio's well-dressed ego was probably in a sling and for more than material reasons. Marston had future administration written all over him. Oh, he was a cop all right, but as soon as his street time was finished he was going upstairs. Florio must have hated his guts.

"What I need," Florio began, "is to have you on my staff. Honest. Don't give me that sheepish grin shit. We cover a lot of the same ground. Hell, you're already a good detective; you'd just have to learn the cop part."

"I'm flattered," I said and decided this was a performance for Marston's benefit. "But pay in the private sector is a lot better, as are the hours, so I'll respectfully decline, thank you."

I turned my full attention to the soda that was dripping foam down my pants leg thanks to my earlier display of manual dexterity. I was busy wiping up but had my mind on how best to ease this awkwardness of egos. I decided on Florio's children.

"Aside from having a virus, how are Jane and Michael?" I asked.

3

"The children!" Florio announced, placing both hands against his temples and rocking back in his chair—it was not a Norman Rockwell image of proud fatherhood. "They fight, they cry, they yell, they whine, and what they don't break they spill. Does that give you a general idea?"

"Roughly," I said, getting a kick out of his exaggerated show of inner torment. "Was this all before breakfast today or cumulative over the course of a week?"

"You bet your ass it was all before breakfast," he said, bringing his elbows back to the desktop. "I'm talking six A.M."

There was distress written all over his face, but it might just have been lack of sleep. If he hadn't looked so earnest, I would have laughed out loud and risked hurting his feelings. Not having had kids, I couldn't speak firsthand, but I also didn't have to read Dr. Spock to know that raising three children aged six, four, and two was no day at the beach. I didn't question that he was a good father. There were plenty of times I'd seen him in the office on weekends with his oldest son Michael, and he could literally glow when talking about how Jane had learned to walk or talk or read Milton "way ahead of other four-year-olds in the neighborhood." So it wasn't a matter of not loving his kids but rather, as he told me one day over a beer, the dynamics of having three was such that you almost always had one in tears, and usually two. "You don't know what hell is," he'd said, "until you've had a couple of kids with ear infections." I believed him.

"It's incredible what those little monsters get into when they're stuck in the house sick," Florio continued, glancing up to include Marston now, who was starting to smile. Florio showed no reaction, he just kept on with his story. "This morning I tried to do what the books say, be the boss, set the limits, all that shit? So the three of them snuck around to Joni and told her what an ogre I was. Daddy won't let us do this, Daddy won't let us do that, he just doesn't love us and he's a real meaniac."

"Meaniac?" Marston repeated before I could, and this time he laughed.

"Yeah, that's Jane's heaviest verbal condemnation, to date. I can't fucking win." By this time Florio was laughing himself, and we were starting to get really friendly when the phone rang and Florio answered it. The pitch of his voice immediately went hard and flat. I looked up to see that his eyes matched his tone, and I knew it was business, probably body number five.

"Listen guys," I said as the phone hit its cradle, "I'll get out of your way."

"Come on, Ham, this could be interesting, just like old times," Florio said. "Marston, blow out the troops, 125 East 82nd Street—and wipe your feet before you go through the door. Hey, it's a nice neighborhood," he said in my direction, moving toward the hall.

"Well, I could use a ride," I said, remembering the rain, "but don't be insulted if I leave early. This isn't a suicide, is it?"

"Shit no," he yelled back from the stairwell. "Would I take you to a fucking suicide? This is the real ditchdigger."

Ditchdigger? Jesus, where did that come from? But he was already out the door.

I used to think that riding in a cavalry charge with George Custer must have been like being in a squad car with Marc Florio; lots of bluster, noise, and motion tinged with anticipation and the onrush of danger. It's easy to get caught up in the excitement. I hadn't tagged along like this in a while. The first time I went was soon after signing on as a cop reporter for the *Times*. The experience hadn't changed. Sirens scream, the radio cracks and blares unintelligibly, the car literally careens up the avenue, and everybody shouts to be heard over the commotion. Constancy in life is comforting.

"You know anything about this, Florio," I shouted from the backseat, ducking my head to keep from hitting the roof as we caught a pothole, "or is this just another attempt to impress me with your bravado?"

"Could be the Coalition of Gay Parking Lot Attendants trapped in a Jacuzzi for all I know," he threw back over his shoulder. "Gunshots for sure, possibly a body."

We turned the corner off Park Avenue, and as the car rolled

5

up to No. 125 Florio swung out, barking orders in a classic take-off of Broderick Crawford in "Highway Patrol." I made a mental note to ask him if it was intentional or just an unconscious imitation.

"Marston, send a man through the lobby to the back and have the basement checked," Florio barked, "and take the doorman with you. Hey, Pops, which elevator?"

"On the right, Penthouse A, the Craigs'," the old man said before Marston dragged him away through the door. Florio and I stood elbow to elbow, stunned by the revelation that whatever the incident responsible for bringing us here, it had happened in the home of one of New York's best-known families.

"Leonard Craig," I muttered. "Christ Almighty."

We both ran across the lobby to the elevators.

On the way up, I didn't even try to speculate what the situation might be. The only thing I knew for certain was that I was early. Realistically, I'd probably be the third or fourth person to arrive at this event. Nothing would have been touched, nothing removed, nothing covered up; and depending on the brutality of preceding events, there was a good chance I was going to throw up those cabbage leaves.

I'd spent three years chasing homicide squads through Manhattan, and I'd developed a self-protective timing that kept me from arriving too soon at whatever blood-splattered bedroom or deserted side street was the scene of man's most recent, blunt, and debased declaration of affection for his fellow being. To the discerning professional, it was a matter of getting there in time to talk to the numb eyewitness or still-sobbing relative, but not before the medical examiner had released the body and most of the gore had been cleaned up. There were some guys who took the candid color snapshots of disemboweled call girls and head-less depressives to show at the Wednesday-night poker game, but reasonable journalists, with an appreciation for the last meal they ate, paced the event. I knew I did. Yet time and disuse dull all senses, and here I was about to walk into the familiar unknown.

The elevator opened directly into the penthouse with barely enough room for an umbrella stand and two pairs of rubber boots. The front door stood open, showing an empty foyer. We passed through, turned left into a living room the size of Madison Square Garden, and stopped. Two paramedics worked with precision and speed over a body lying face up on a very beautiful, and no doubt expensive, Persian rug.

I stepped around the couch to get a better look: young, thirty-two or -three would be my guess, which wasn't Leonard Craig—he was wrinkled and in his seventies. The kid on the floor had light blond hair and didn't look so good. His eyes were rolled back and bulging. A tongue depressor was jammed into his mouth and an IV connected his right arm to a 1,000 cc plasma bag. His left arm was stuffed into the front of his pants to keep it from flapping around and his entire body quivered with small irregular spasms: a marionette with no strings.

I doubted he was going to make it to Lenox Hill. He'd been shot once in the right temple and his skull was a little asymmetrical. I didn't see an exit wound. Out of the corner of my eye I caught Florio bending over to pick up a silver-plated .38-caliber snubnose and I dropped my odds. I wasn't going to give this kid as far as the downstairs lobby.

The place was starting to fill up with personnel. I watched a uniformed officer on the far side of the room ease behind a large potted fern and light a cigarette, dropping the match into the base of the plant. Where do they get these guys? Better yet, what do they teach them? Florio crossed over to me after a brief chat with one of the medical attendants. We stood together, looking down at the frantic activity on the floor in front of us. It was an exquisite rug.

"Any flash burns on the skin?" I asked quietly.

"Too soon to tell and no chance to look," he answered. "They're just trying to keep him alive."

I nodded and became a spectator again. A lot of things run through your mind at times like these, and none of them are funny. The more time I spent around human carnage, the more my mind drifted from reality to abstract. A natural protective reflex, I suppose. Stifle the emotion and think about statistics or nothing at all. Stay detached. Stick to your job. Remember that emotion gets in the way of performance. It brings down your efficiency rating and makes you waste time pondering your relationship to God, your place in the universe, and the inhuman nature of child molestation. When you have a job that presents you with a daily ration of homicide, the armor of programed activity becomes necessary to assure safe passage through evenings like this. It also allows for the intellectual freedom to make cold calculating comments about the body at your feet. Most important, it lets you sleep at night.

"I think somebody shot him, Florio," I said without looking up.

"Hmmmmmmm," was his only response.

Florio's nonverbal rumble destroyed my rising self-confidence and I quickly added, "I don't mean it was cold-blooded premeditation, but I'll bet this is pussy, drugs, or money."

This time I got an affirmative nod along with a mumbled "What isn't?" Then he added, "The statistics give you better than a seventy to thirty chance of being right."

"So it wasn't a major prediction," I said, starting to see the numbers in my head. "But there were roughly twenty-four thousand murders nationwide last year, making homicide the eleventh leading cause of death. Of those deaths, forty-two percent involved an argument, usually with a relative or close acquaintance. If you factor in the statistic that half your killings involve handguns used within a distance of three feet, and inside a two-second time frame, there's a good chance we can pigeonhole this one before we leave."

"What are you, a fucking book?" Florio asked.

"Hey, I remember things."

"Yeah, I'd forgotten."

The kid on the floor died and everything came to rest for a moment—not so much in respect for the dead, but because

8

everyone's job was finished and there was a natural lapse. The pause stretched. Florio was the first to speak.

"OK guys," he said in an undertone to the paramedics, "unhook him and let's get everything out into the hall. Is this pretty much where you found him when you got here?"

"Almost exactly," said one medic, coming to his feet and adjusting his glasses. "Almost exactly."

"Thanks, just make a lane for traffic," Florio told him and looked to Marston, who was coming in through the kitchen door. "John, call the medical examiner's office and make sure they're on the way, and send up the photo team as soon as they arrive. Also, get Peoples, Fredrick, and Norse out of bed and moving this way. I want prints, interviews—the whole works."

"I agree with you it's no suicide," Florio said, coming back to me. "There was nobody here when the ambulance arrived, the doorman's got liquor on his breath, and we don't even know who called it in. It's all cursory at this point, but you're probably right."

"Anything you pick up on right away?" I asked him.

"Nothing much. Maybe something in the kitchen." He wasn't enthusiastic.

"I guess you know Leonard Craig and my boss, Roseman, are close friends," I said. He didn't respond. "I just hope we don't end up working against each other on this. I'd like to go make a phone call and then hang around if I'm told to."

Florio was quiet for a moment, then said, "I've always liked you, Ham. We'll let it ride as far as it goes." He paused and then added, "Use a phone outside the apartment and don't get underfoot. Got it?"

"Got it."

Six men and a half ton of equipment rolled past me in the foyer as I got into the elevator and headed for the street. A light drizzle dampened my face as I came out of the building, took a left at the uniformed officer, and found a pay phone on the corner. I glanced at my watch as I diddled for a quarter among a handful of pocket change; eleven-fifty, way past Roseman's bedtime, but it was important.

At sixty-two, Arthur Roseman was arguably the best trial lawyer in the city. He was certainly the most successful, though less celebrated than some because he was less flamboyant. His English childhood kept him in bow ties and wool vests, and, to some colleagues, he was overrefined to the point of being a snobby old snot. He could be, and on frequent occasions he was, but his natural inclination, and I knew him well, was respectful aloofness. Roseman was a very private, very smart gentleman with a strong sense of personal commitment to his clients and friends. After two years of employment, I liked to think of myself as a member of the latter group, and he offered every indication that I was.

Roseman was also a person of strong habits. Midnight on a Tuesday in September usually found him sound asleep in his bed under a blaze of lights with his lap full of cracker crumbs and magazines. Reading material ranged from the previous day's London *Times* to the most recent issue of *Better Homes and Gardens*. He'd been a widower for eight years, and told me one night, almost in tears, that he just couldn't bring himself to cancel his wife's magazine subscriptions. Couldn't throw them out either, so he read them, or at least thumbed the pages. When he answered the phone on the first ring, I knew that I wasn't the only one who'd had an unusual evening.

"Hi, it's me. A little late for you to be up isn't it?"

"Precisely my thought on the matter, but it is, nonetheless, a fact and the circumstances surrounding it are rather disturbing. Can you talk? It sounds as if you're in a tunnel."

"A pay phone outside Leonard Craig's apartment. I'm here with Florio and it's not a pretty sight. He'll never get the rug clean."

"He's here."

"Who?"

"Leonard."

10

"No shit, does he know what's happened? Was he there? I can think of about six hundred questions I want to ask him."

"At the moment he is not making much sense," Roseman said slowly, "but unfortunately, the answer to most of your inquiries would be yes. I also imagine that at this juncture I know a great deal more than anyone."

"Can you identify the body?"

"Yes," he said, and paused.

"So tell me!"

"Lane Peters. An actor. Rather a good one I believe, if I remember my reviews correctly, though I've never seen him in performance. He is currently playing the lead in *Macbeth* at an off-Broadway house . . ."

"Arthur, I don't need the guy's résumé, OK?" His silence was wounded and I immediately regretted my sharpness. "Sorry, Arthur, but this guy isn't going to be playing the lead in anything because dead men can't act."

"Oh Lord, that's not good," he said and sighed. "Not good at all."

"Yeah, you should have been there. Do you know why Peters was in Leonard's apartment?"

"It seems this young man, Peters, and Leonard's wife have been seeing each other for . . ." the pause was agonizing, "some time."

"Great motive," I said.

"Yes, a great motive indeed. Your Captain Florio should not need much more I'm afraid."

"Listen, I thought I was going to be the messenger with this story, so I got a reinvite before I left upstairs. Do you still want me to hang around?"

"Without question," he said and paused again. "I'll need you here in the morning, early, and preferably without the police. I need some time, but I will bend to your discretion there. . . ."

"The guy's dead, Arthur. This is a murder case."

"I am sorry, David, but my mind is on Leonard. He is my dearest, oldest friend, and he's virtually in pieces on my library couch at this moment. I don't think he shot this young man, though I know he had more than enough motive and even, occasionally, the frame of mind. But for him to actually kill someone. . . . That is a difficult reality for me to grasp. I desperately need more time."

"OK, OK, it hasn't been an easy night for either of us," I told him. "Get Craig quiet and pump him for as much as possible. I'm going back upstairs. I'll do what I can about Florio, but I hate to lie to him."

"I understand perfectly, David. Do as you think best." I thought he was gone and was about to hang up when his voice broke in again. "Before you ring off, was Samantha there? In the apartment, I mean?"

"No, the place was empty. Just the body."

"That vile, maneuvering bitch," he said, spitting out the words as you would a bad taste.

I wasn't used to such unrestrained emotion from Roseman, but if anyone could elicit that kind of response it would be Samantha. I didn't know the new Mrs. Craig well, and I knew even less about Roseman's relationship with her. What I did know I read on page six of the *Post* along with the rest of Manhattan's commuting public.

Leonard had been to Roseman's often since the death of his first wife. Sometimes he came as one of the invited guests for dinner, other times as a single friend and associate widower to share a drink and an evening cigar. The visits had dropped off considerably once Samantha arrived.

I'd met her briefly just after she and Leonard became acquainted. They were at Roseman's, ostensibly for pre-theater drinks, but I had the feeling Leonard was looking more for his friend's stamp of approval than for a scotch. He didn't get it.

Samantha rubbed Roseman like nails across a blackboard. She strutted, stormed around, and displayed a general arrogance that was both insulting and offensive. Maybe she was nervous, who knows? I'm sure Leonard told her what a wonderful, important, and powerful man Roseman was, enhancing his own

12

stature by the association; yet he also must have told her that he was gentle, genuine, and kind.

Regardless of the preambles, Samantha came out like glass from a cannon barrel, and the evening ended in bruised feelings, sideways glances, and raised eyebrows. The two were never back in the apartment after that evening. As Leonard moved from infatuation to matrimony, Roseman advised against the union, but Leonard wasn't listening. I think having his advice ignored hurt Roseman's feelings more than any discomfort Samantha's uncensored tongue could inflict. He despised the woman and she never did anything after the marriage to dispel his first impressions. To Roseman, she was a good-looking hard-roller with money on her mind.

"So you think she's involved?" I suggested weakly.

"Of course she's involved," he snapped. "I imagine she is responsible. Mere speculation, mind you, and a tendency on my part to think the worst of people I detest."

"Don't let it get under your skin, Arthur. You said everything you could before he married her. It was his choice and you came to terms with it. Don't start second-guessing yourself now. I'll see you in the morning. OK?"

"Yes, you're right, of course," he said with resignation. "Good-bye."

I hung up and dropped another quarter in the box. The phone only rang once.

"Burlington," said a voice.

"Jordan there?"

"Yeah, hang on." Business was heavy, judging from the noise in the background. Nothing made Jordan's smile spread more than a full house early in the week. Jordan was from New Jersey, in his mid-fifties, maybe five feet four, Jewish, and the owner of an extremely successful restaurant on West 18th Street. His success was tied directly to his personal appearance from the moment The Burlington opened till the last customer ambled out. Hell, he knew practically everyone who walked in the door by name, occupation, social profile, and sexual preference. If he

13

didn't, and thought you were interesting, he found out. In addition to biographical information, Jordan also knew what his customers liked to eat, and I had to admit, nothing can make you feel more comfortable in this city than a small personalized production—complete with lights, choreography, and the occasional costume. It made you want to walk in more often, which was, I suppose, his main intention.

Sometimes Jordan would break into song and come spinning toward you the instant you hit the door. He'd take you by the hand, lead you to the bar, and ask if you were planning to stay for dinner or just have a drink. A first-timer, hearing Jordan's strong baritone lofting an a cappella version of "Getting to Know You," might take a step backward and scrutinize the crowd. Jordan was also an accomplished mimic and, on special occasions, if you got enough booze in him, his Maggie Smith brought double-takes from across the room—Jordan seldom spoke, or performed, in undertones. The Burlington was his stage. His customers were his loving audience, and he put on the best show in town. I'd been attending for years.

"Helloooooo, this is Jordan."

"How you doing? This is Ham."

"Hear that crowd? Hear those orders? Hear that register ring, ring, ring?" I could feel him smiling. "I'm doing very well thank you. How about yourself?"

"I'm OK, but not great," I said truthfully. "Are you going to be there late? I'm working and in need of a drink."

"Working? What are you working?" His voice became his own.

"Somebody just died."

"Forget the time, you come see Uncle Jordan. If the crowd leaves, the door will be open. Can you tell me anything?"

"Not yet, but I hope to have the basics before I get there. See ya."

I hung up, pulled out another quarter, took a deep breath, and dropped it in. This time the phone at the other end rang a while before the receiver was picked up.

14

"Yes?"

"Hi, Marilyn. It's David. I hope . . ." was as far as I got before she slammed the phone down, hard. I couldn't believe she was still pissed. I stared at the black box in front of me for a moment, shrugged, and dropped the receiver into place.

CHAPTER TWO

The atmosphere in Penthouse A had changed from controlled hysteria to the scientifically casual as Homicide's specialists filled the apartment. Marston caught my eye as I came in the door and stepped around the couch to meet me.

"The Captain went out for a moment," he said in a friendly manner. "He asked me to keep you entertained till he got back."

That was expected. I never thought Florio would let me wander around unattended, but I was unsure about Marston. I didn't have a good gauge on him yet, and I never knew how much to relax with police officers I didn't know personally. Marston seemed straightforward enough, but my inclination was to be pleasant and accommodating without giving anything away—a little something I learned from a girl I used to date. Then I realized what it was that bothered me about him. There was no character in his face. It was flat, smooth, and empty. A little too attractive. No hard work and worry in his life—yet. But if he didn't watch his step, Florio was going to rout a few furrows across his brow.

"How long ago did you leave the *Times*?" Marston probed.

"About three years ago," I answered, wondering if he wore

those round, rimless spectacles to help take the edge off his $1,000 wardrobe. I kicked myself for not giving the guy more of a chance.

"Did you get tired of chasing Florio around the east side of Manhattan, or did the daily grind and gore finally get to you?"

"Neither really, though I think I was in the early stages of burnout. I just got a better offer."

"Roseman?"

I nodded and watched some guy from the forensics lab gingerly lift a cigarette butt and match out of the potted plant where the uniformed cop had stood earlier. He dropped them into a plastic bag and carefully marked it. Christ Almighty, it's the Keystone Kops.

"You know," Marston threw himself into the breach again, "we had an entire course devoted to him in law school. The man's a living legend."

"Which one?"

"What?"

"Law school."

"Oh, Yale. Is he the paragon we were taught to believe?"

"Faster than a speeding bullet."

Marston gave me a "that's cute" look over the top of his glasses and added, "More powerful than a locomotive, too, huh?" Pulling a filterless Pall Mall from his coat pocket, Marston turned his attention to the room's activity. I was starting to warm to him.

"My work for Roseman is pretty much what I did at the *Times*, investigative legwork with a license," I offered, taking a cigarette from him. "I try to reach the client before the subpoena does; find a witness, lose a witness, and occasionally, when Sandra's busy, I even make the coffee."

We both smoked in silence as the plastic bag with the incriminating cigarette butt was safely stowed in the evidence box. The elevator arrived and Pete Damich, an assistant medical examiner, walked in.

Pete was one of the newcomers down at First Avenue and

18

30th Street. I barely knew him and we exchanged nothing but glances as he passed.

I had gone to work for Tim Ellerton at the ME's office when I first came to New York. The job was basically typing transcripts of autopsy findings dictated by the pathologists during surgery. I'd done the same thing in college to cover expenses; the position was posted on the job board at the journalism school for months and nobody would touch it. I finally did because the work was mostly at night and I liked the quiet. Then, after graduation, when I decided to come to the city, one of the doctors who'd recently transferred to Chapel Hill from Ellerton's staff made a phone call for me.

Though the primary purpose of a coroner's office is not forensic, the influx of bodies into the New York ME's office related to homicide investigations was dizzying. Autopsies were performed in about 93 percent of these cases and in about 50 percent of suicides. We stayed busy.

After a couple of years spent either at the tables in the basement or the offices on the third floor, I knew all the reporters and most of the detectives in town. So when an opening came up for a cop reporter at the *Times*, I applied and got some great recommendations. I also got the job. I tried to stay in touch, but it wasn't easy. Working for a newspaper, I was on the outside looking in. The information I now wanted for publication was the information I had once guarded so carefully. It was OK, just different, and there were times when I was given preferential treatment. That was OK, too. Damich had joined the staff about a month before I changed jobs and I just never got to know him.

Nodding to Pete, who was on his way over to the sheet on the floor, Marston asked me, "You been around dead bodies much?"

"All my life it seems," I said, looking at him. I wanted to say more, explain myself, but as he walked over to join Damich, there was no way I could tell him about the knot in my stomach, the tightness in my throat.

I crushed my cigarette in one of the glass Petri dishes set out by guys from the forensic lab for heavy smokers who couldn't control themselves. With my personal surveillance lifted for the moment, I started showing myself around. The living room fed into three doorways: one, directly past the body, opened into a formal dining area and then out to a rooftop patio facing south; another door led to a short hall that doglegged right, I assumed to the bedrooms; and the third went straight into the kitchen. Bedrooms have always fascinated me, so I decided to see how the Craigs' taste in bedsheets ran. I was angling toward the dogleg when I pulled up short next to a narrow rectangular brass table with a glass top.

The table stood against one wall of the living room and supported, between two glass bookends, a neatly arranged row of books pyramiding in height to a center point occupied by Alistair Cook's *America*. There were also matching plants on each end of the table. They were attractive, but what had caught my eye was an envelope lying face down on the rug next to the wall. It was small, like a child's birthday invitation, and cream colored, matching the fringe on the rug. It was virtually invisible, and if I hadn't been standing directly above it, I might never have taken notice.

A quick glance around told me that I could squat without being seen and I soon had the envelope safely in my pocket. I stepped around to one of Florio's men and said I needed to take a piss.

"We're using the toilet off the master bedroom," he said, pointing back down the hallway I'd just left. "Keep your hands off the furniture and don't shake it more than twice."

"Thanks, I'll try."

The door clicked shut behind me and I pushed in the lock with my thumb. Two light switches gave me operating-room illumination and the pleasant hum of a distant ventilator fan. I hadn't seen so much marble since Florence. The envelope was unmarked and contained a single sheet of Leonard Craig's personal stationery. The message was in blue ink, addressed to one Randall Bergman, and brief.

I've paid enough. There will be no more money for you or Peters. This is the last of it. You can both go to hell.

Oh Christ, I thought, not only is this guy slamming Leonard's wife, but he's also blackmailing him. I looked back at the note. It wasn't signed, but I had no doubt the script was Leonard's. Which thing to do? If I turned this note over to Florio, Roseman's friend goes straight to jail, just what I'm not supposed to let happen. If I don't turn it over, then I'm withholding evidence, and that is not, I reminded myself, a misdemeanor offense, especially in a murder investigation.

I couldn't show the note to Roseman either. His position would be compromised, not to mention his ethics. Flush it down the toilet! Now there's an idea, if I could find the thing in here. But I had to consider that Leonard could be guilty. I stuffed the paper into my pocket, located the john, gave it a whirl, and started back down the hall. My decision was to not do anything immediately. In twenty-four to thirty-six hours, I'd have a much better idea of how the case might unfold, and besides, Leonard wasn't going anywhere. If murder as the result of blackmail was indeed the real story, I could turn over the note later and say it got sent to the cleaners with my suit.

In the meantime, all I had to do was lie to a friend, mislead my employer, and go on with my job as if I didn't possess the single most important piece of evidence in the case. No problem, right? To be truthful, I didn't know if I could make myself do it.

Coming back into the living room, I passed the plainclothesman I'd asked for directions.

"That's not a bathroom," I told him. "It's an efficiency apartment."

"If you think that's something," he said, laughing, "take a look at the kitchen."

"I will, thanks," I said, and with childhood instincts, I gave a polite "Hi ya," to the cop at the door and walked right in. It was a sprawling kitchen with a massive gas stove, two stainless-steel

21

iceboxes, and a walk-in freezer. I didn't get to peek into the refrigerators because sitting on the counter nearest the stove were two brown bags filled with Chinese takeout. The tops were stapled shut with the restaurant menu still attached. A quick feel told me the food was still warm, so I checked the address on the menu: Panda Garden East, 84th and Third. So that's where Florio disappeared to, I said to myself, heading out the door. I was planning a quick trip to 84th Street for a chat with their delivery staff myself, and maybe an eggroll, when I walked into Florio.

"What the fuck you doing in there?" he demanded in his official pissed off voice.

"Looking for a beer. They're out."

"Funny. You said you'd stay out of the way, not take inventory. Where's Marston?" he snapped, taking in the room quickly.

"He got busy and I didn't know what to do with myself, honest, I was just poking around."

"Forget it," he said, not wanting to make a big deal of my solo wanderings. "What can you tell me about Craig's personal life?"

"A lot. What can you tell me about where you've been for the last half-hour?"

"Jesus Christ, Ham, that's department stuff," he said, giving the general impression of being a hassled cop.

"Fine," I said, giving the general impression of having my feelings hurt. "It shouldn't take your people long to pull a bio together. Lunchtime tomorrow at the latest."

He gave his best hangdog look and then offered me a smoke.

"No thanks, I just finished one of Marston's chest busters." I held the pause a little longer and asked him. "You want to chat, or what?"

"All right, you first." He shook the pack again and I pulled one out; at least these had filters. I hadn't smoked this much in months.

"Leonard Craig inherited his father's shipping business

22

about thirty-five years ago when he was in his mid-thirties. He's since doubled its size and was recently negotiating the company's sale to a Japanese group. He ships some kind of cane product or alfalfa to the Orient from Central America: owns the farms and everything.

"Anyway, he was married to his childhood sweetheart for most of his life until she died three years ago. Cancer. After a decent interval, he increased his social appointments and reentered the world. Craig was always active with the symphony, the Metropolitan, and a variety of philanthropic projects. As you might imagine, he was pretty desirable property and attracted a lot of attention. He courted some, dated a lot, and finally married Samantha Reyes."

"What do you know about her?" Florio asked through a cloud of cigarette smoke.

"A tawdry little whore in my opinion," I said bluntly. "She does whoever, whenever, and in whatever fashion it takes to stay center stage. Craig got a lot of advice from his friends before the marriage, Roseman included, but he was taken with her and eventually by her as well."

"You want to spell that out for me?"

"She's beautiful, sexual, active, greedy, and if you can't fuck your husband's buddies who can you fuck?"

"Thanks," Florio said, "but he should have seen it coming. Are you talking fact or hearsay?"

"An informed source close to the investigation, who asked not to be identified, is my only attribution. Trust me. Now it's your turn. How are things at the Panda Garden?" I knew I'd overstepped myself the instant the words left my mouth. Florio exploded.

"What the fuck you asking me for, huh? You know so fucking much, you hurry on up there yourself. Shit, take a squad car for Christ sakes. Better yet," he yelled snatching up the telephone, "just call and have something delivered. You can use one of the bedrooms for your interview. Have some privacy. You fucking shithead."

23

I was moving toward the elevator as quickly as I could without seeming to run. The door was open and I stepped in and pushed the lobby button while 250 pounds of screaming Italian searched for something to throw. He grabbed a roll of white medical tape from an aid kit and hurled it through the closing doors. It rebounded twice and dropped to the floor.

"Smartassin' son of a bitch . . ." and his voice slowly faded as the elevator dropped. I hit the street and headed east for Third Avenue. The rain had turned heavy again and I broke into a trot keeping an eye out for a free cab. My suit was just starting to cling like knit on a fat lady when I turned north up Third. I'd only gone about half a block when I saw a delivery bike being pumped hard and heading my way.

The wire basket slung from the bike's handlebars was empty and the white-jacketed rider kept checking over his shoulder as if he were being chased or, maybe, were running from someone: a city detective with questions was what I figured. I judged his speed, set the angle, and cut across the avenue. He was hard on me before realizing I was trying to flag him down, and he tried to cut away, but hit a metal canopy support. The impact flipped him over the handlebars, his forearm catching me full in the chest, and we both went down into a pile of plastic garbage bags stacked on the curb. The bike, with one wheel still spinning, lay crumpled in the street. It took me a couple of gasps to get my breath before I could pull myself up. I was still working for air when I looked over and saw that my solitary cyclist and sometime Chinese delivery boy was no youngster. And no Chinaman either. He was over forty and rode hard. Just my luck to get some guy out on work release.

"Hey, you OK?" I asked, stepping over a bag of trash to help him up.

"Who's asking?" he said, wheezing.

"Listen, I'm not a cop, so relax. I've just got a couple of questions. Hell, you might not even be the person I'm looking for." A thought flashed over his face that I read as a desire to run

24

if he could only get his wind back. I decided to press. "You deliver for the Panda Garden up on Eighty-fourth and Third?"

Without answering he began to back away, and I pulled out a fifty-dollar bill. He stopped moving. "You deliver for the Panda Garden up on Eighty-fourth?" I repeated.

"Yeah. Yeah, I do." His fingers closed around the bill. He was just under six feet with thick, raw hands, and shoulders wide as a stack of south Georgia pulpwood. A two-day beard and hair that hadn't seen shampoo for weeks made his overall appearance pretty grubby. It was enough to make me wonder if he ever collected a tip.

He tugged on the fifty, but I held tight to my end. He looked me in the eye and I thought he was about to speak when his attention was diverted by something behind me. His pupils narrowed and fixed. His hand fell away from the bill just as the first bullet hit him under the chin. I flinched as the blood splattered across my face and a bone chip caught my lip. A second round hit him high in the chest and my stocky pulp-wooder staggered sideways. The blood was brilliant red against his white jacket, carnival red. It was horrible and it was everywhere. I grabbed the front of his coat and spun us both back to the pavement as a third bullet shattered the plate-glass storefront behind us. I still hadn't heard a gunshot and I didn't hear the next one either, but it tore through my right side like a red hot spit. A silencer meant preparation and premeditation. I couldn't fault his aim either. I rolled off the curb in time to see a dark-colored Buick speed by with all of its windows down and no headlights. The driver was hunched over the wheel wearing a hat so that an identification of any sort was impossible. Then it was gone, taking the turn at 86th, doing at least fifty, and sliding around the corner. The street was empty. The rain was coming down harder than ever and the burning in my side increased. But I was still among the living. The fixed stare and ashen face of the body next to me didn't offer the same hope.

"Ahhhhhhhh, shit, it hurts," I moaned, letting my forehead come to rest on the wet concrete sidewalk. My thoughts were

25

getting scattered and I felt dizzy, light. The sound of a siren reached me through the haze and rain. It seemed a long way off and I was tired, suddenly very tired. My shoulders sagged and I let go of consciousness.

CHAPTER THREE

Lights! Where'd all the lights come from? Everywhere lights, white walls and lights. As the sounds and images began to sort themselves, I recognized a familiar voice at high pitch and full bore.

"Goddamnit, he's only got a crease across his ass," Florio bellowed, showing no hesitation to express his limited knowledge of my injury. "How can you stand there and say I can't talk to him?"

"His ribs, Captain Florio, not his ass" was the firm, admonishing, feminine response. "The man's unconscious and in a state of shock."

"Unconscious? Fuck unconscious," snapped Florio. "You've never seen him drunk. He walks unconscious; he drives unconscious. Hell, he usually is unconscious."

"I'm sure you're right, Captain, but nonetheless you're not going to see him."

I pulled myself up on an elbow, then to a sitting position, and got so light-headed I almost fell off the gurney. I propped a steadying hand against the wall and peeked past my surgically separated shirt to view the damage. Couldn't see shit though, just bandages, tape, trace amounts of blood on the white cotton fabric, and some red, dotting through the gauze.

"Hey, doctor, I'm fine. Let him in."

The curtain zipped back immediately and there stood Roy Orbison's "pretty woman." It was August 1964 on Monument Records and this was the girl he was singing about: thick, full, raven-black hair brushed off her forehead; a thin, intelligent face with high cheekbones and fresh skin barely touched with makeup. At five foot five in flats, she moved with an easy professional grace and was exquisitely beautiful.

"You are not fine," she said taking my arm for a pulse reading. "I want you to lie back down. Now!"

"You're a bum is what you are," Florio said, bringing me back to reality.

"Listen . . ." I protested, but got cut short by the doctor.

"That's enough," she commanded, and pointing a finger at Florio's chest she added, "I want you out of here!"

Marston drifted into the room and gave a diplomatic tug on Florio's sleeve. As the two men turned to leave, Marston tossed a pack of cigarettes onto the sheet beside me and gave a thumbs-up. He'll be fine, I thought, he really will. I wonder how I'm going to tell him I don't smoke.

A sting of pain brought my attention back to the doctor and my right side. I bent a little to read her name tag: "Carlson, Rachel F., M.D."

"Am I all right, Dr. Carlson?"

"Yes, you seem to be," she said simply, glancing up at me. "I've admitted you for overnight observation."

"I don't think that'll stick. I want out of here and with the Captain just as eager, you haven't got a prayer. But I appreciate your not letting him jerk me off the table until I woke up."

Her smile became a laugh that showed a perfect set of teeth.

"Are you a Roy Orbison fan?" I asked.

"I'm not sure I follow your question, but you'd be foolish to leave here now. You've been shot and I advise against it."

"Thanks, but I can't stay."

28

She stepped back and looked at me hard as if I were a delinquent schoolboy. "It really is just a superficial wound, but it concerned me that you lost consciousness."

"So I pass out easily. What can I tell you, not everybody can be John Wayne. All those bullets flying around, I got a little frightened. And I was the lucky one, the other guy's dead."

It wasn't a joke, but it came out that way and she laughed harder this time. I felt my heart slip.

"Do you know a place on Eighteenth Street called The Burlington?" I asked.

"No, I don't believe I do."

"Well, I'm going there in a few minutes. It's a nice, comfortable place. . . . I'd take my mother there, you know? If you'd like a drink when you get off, or a little nosh maybe, it'd be my pleasure."

"I don't accept invitations after midnight and it's one-twenty in the morning," she said, glancing at her watch.

"Seriously, I'd like to see you without your lab coat. You can still take my pulse, check my temperature. I'll behave."

She seemed pleased with the invitation, but the best I could get was, "We'll see."

I slid off the stretcher to my feet and began buttoning up the remains of my shirt.

"Well, if I can't interest you in an early morning drink, how about I call you later and we can arrange something at a more reasonable hour. Breakfast, maybe, with candlelight."

"I go home for breakfast, thank you."

"OK. I can tell you're having a good time. You're just uncertain." She laughed. "I understand that. This is Manhattan; you don't know me too well, hell, you don't know my family at all and, I admit, I've just been in a gunfight." There was definitely a sparkle in her eye. "Why don't you give me your phone number and I'll call you for a date."

"I don't think that's possible."

"What's not possible? You won't see me again or you won't give me your phone number?"

29

"I won't give you my phone number," she said, busying herself with my chart, but her eyes were dancing. She was having fun.

"At least I'm making progress. Suppose you tell me what borough you live in, and I'll look you up in the phone book."

"Sorry." She started toward the door. "You can always reach me here or leave a message with the switchboard. Of course," she said, turning to face me, "if you stay for the twenty-four-hour observation period I recommended, it would be my professional obligation to check on your condition before you left."

"Think you got me, don't you," I said, thinking she almost did.

With a coquettish laugh and turn of the head, she said, "No, I don't think I've got you, but it was worth a try." She made a few additional notes on the chart, handed it to me to sign, and walked out. I slipped into wet shoes, a cold soggy suit coat, and squished out after her to meet the lions. Florio was gone. Only Marston waited for me. I handed back his cigarettes with thanks, but other words failed me.

"He wants to see you in his office first thing after sunrise," Marston said.

"That's not very convenient, John."

"Maybe not, but I wouldn't be late."

"I have a boss, too, and he also wants to see me first thing. I need some time, not to mention rest, a shower, and that doctor's home phone number."

"Cut the rhetoric," he said, trying to suppress a yawn, "and listen to me. Florio is pissed. It would be a mistake to stall him."

"I feel like shit," I said with emphasis. "I haven't seen a mirror, but I imagine I look like shit, too, and I really, really want a drink. Five hours from now I'm not going to feel like playing twenty questions with Captain Bly."

"Would you rather talk to me?"

"Only over a drink."

A smile broke across his face as he checked his watch. "I don't work completely around the clock."

"Done. I've got the place, the cab fare, and the inclination to talk." Ten minutes later we swung open the outer door of The Burlington. The place was half full and Jordan looked up from a conversation, slid his glasses down his nose, and said in a voice loud enough to carry easily across the room, "Death, you look like death."

"Mind if I have a drink before I stand inspection?" I asked, pulling up at the bar.

"A drink!" Jordan continued with added volume. "Since when have you needed a drink to talk to your Uncle Jordan? Herman," he said to the bartender, "let me have a bottle of Bombay and two lemons, sliced. Here, take these with you upstairs, get a shower and come back when you look better. The closets, take something, anything, it's yours. I'll entertain the friend," he said, turning to Marston. "He is your friend? You never introduce me to anybody. He has no manners," Jordan explained to the eighteen people closest to him.

I shook my head at Marston, who was taking in the performance with wide eyes, and introduced him. Then I headed for the stairs with a detour through the kitchen where I collected some baked chicken and vegetables on a plate. Two sets of stairs later I dumped the whole lot, bottle, lemons, plate, and utensils, on top of a dresser and stripped. Then I sat my bare ass down on the toilet seat and ate as though I'd missed four meals. I was a little concerned that Marston might think I'd slipped out, so I shoveled the food, drank the gin straight from the bottle, and hurried my shower. The hot water felt terrific and I sat on the tile floor letting it run over me. The bandage taped to my side became sodden and heavy and began to sag, so I jerked it off completely and jumped involuntarily at the sting of the water against my raw skin. It didn't bleed much though.

After toweling off, I settled on a pair of full-cut slacks, a T-shirt in case my side began to ooze, and a pull-over shirt with tennis shoes. I also took a navy blue overcoat. I'd need it on the way home to keep out what chill the gin didn't blunt. Clean, comfortable, and with the alcohol beginning to kick in, I felt as

31

though I could make my sunrise appointment with Roseman without benefit of sleep.

Downstairs, Marston was in the middle of an animated exchange with Jordan and seemed at ease despite my absence. The four empties in front of them told me I could relax.

"Is that a banana in your pocket or are you just glad to be alive?" Jordan said without humor.

"A lemon, Jordan," I answered. "It's a lemon and yes I am glad to be alive, so don't lecture me about self-defense. You know I don't carry a gun unless it's essential."

"Essential!" he exclaimed. "What's essential? You don't even look like Gary Cooper, so stay out of the streets. Let somebody else get shot."

"I did," I said, and flinched at the memory.

"Well, sit," Jordan ordered, "and you two can talk shop. I've heard more than I care to already. I'll send Martin with some drinks."

"He's a nice man," Marston remarked as Jordan walked away from the table. "He cares a lot for you."

"I know," I said, meeting Marston's gaze. "He's a good friend, but it's not what you're thinking."

"I wasn't thinking anything."

"Good," I said, and we took our drinks off Martin's tray. "Where do you want me to start? I assume you caught hell from Florio after he assaulted me at the elevator, am I right?"

"It was fairly unpleasant," he said wistfully, waving his scotch under his nose before tasting it. "Let's start with when you hit the lobby."

"Well, for you to really understand everything, we need to go a little farther back." And I told him, using the abbreviated version. I have a good mind for detail and there's not much I've read, seen, or heard that I can't bring back in one of two ways: verbatim, or just the basics.

Verbatim is everything from three-person conversations to the color of her stockings and the number of capped teeth. The basics are simply a verbal shorthand that conveys the essence of

32

what happened without belaboring the listener with details he doesn't want. Roseman usually wanted the whole schmear, and I was used to extended monologues with questions and answers at the end. It was a good system; Roseman got all the facts with no interpretations and I enjoyed the opportunity to make myself a little more invaluable to my employer.

Tonight was a different matter, though. It was late and I was tired and showing the stress of both shootings, so I did myself a favor by keeping it short, and Marston didn't seem to care. I started with dinner and hit the high spots till I got to the incident on Third Avenue. Marston took relatively few notes and the formal part of the interview was over quickly. It figured he was as tired as I was and would leave the rough stuff to Florio.

"That should do it," he said, slipping his pen into a jacket pocket and flipping his notebook shut. "I'm sure I can keep Florio occupied for a while, but I'm also sure he's going to want to see you."

"Let's deal with that as it happens," I told him and jotted Roseman's phone number down on a cocktail napkin. "You can reach me there after seven o'clock. Did you ever identify the body at Craig's?"

"No, we haven't. For that matter, Craig's wife hasn't shown either."

"How about the guy on the bike?"

"Matthew Harwood was his name, forty-two, lived in a halfway house for ex-cons and drug abusers up on Ninety-eighth Street; armed robbery, arson, and assault mostly. He'd been back in town about three months. Got the job through his parole officer." Marston tipped the last few amber drops from his glass, rattled the ice, and set his empty down with finality. "Thanks," he said, letting the length of his day show in his face for the first time. "I'm beat," he said, and he reached for his wallet. I stopped him.

"Jordan wouldn't hear of it."

"Thanks twice then." And he turned for the door. As it

closed behind him, Jordan came over carrying a small brown bag and wearing his best guardian angel face. I braced myself.

"Are you still drinking?" he asked.

"Are you pouring?"

"I'm pouring."

"Then I'm drinking."

"You would have made such a nice Jewish boy," he said, lightly slapping my cheek as he sat down. Once settled, he took an automatic out of the bag and motioned for Martin.

"So what's the gun for, Jordan?"

"After walking in here like you did an hour ago, how can you ask me such a question? Maybe I'd like to see you live to your next birthday, that's what it's for. Take it." He slid the gun across the table.

"I have one, thanks." I pushed it back to him.

"With you? Have you got it with you?"

"No, but I'll be fine. I'm just going home."

"Home, he says. I need this? A *goyisher* boy who bleeds all over my bathroom and then tells me not to worry, he's just going home. To use a phrase you'll understand, Christ!"

I looked down at the blue-steeled Mauser HSc automatic in front of Jordan. It was a good weapon; small, efficient, and dependable—I actually owned two, plus a Walther PPK. Both models are considered popguns by those in the know on such matters. When I took the small arms course offered by the police department, everybody was always telling me I needed a pistol that packed more punch or at least one that made more noise. They had a point because, when compared to the .44 Magnums and .9 mm automatics that populated the firing range, my Mauser sounded like a fart in a cathedral. I stuck with the Mauser, though, operating on the premise that at some point I'd want to talk to the guy I was exchanging potshots with, and that's hard to do if you take his head off or excavate half his chest with the first round.

The Mausers were my personal admission to the reality that life in New York as a quasi-detective for a noted criminal attorney

34

was, only occasionally, a dangerous profession. I owned the Walther because I grew up on James Bond movies. In fact, I like the Mauser because it has so much in common with the Walther: both weigh twenty-three ounces; are about six and a half inches long; have double-action, fixed sights; and carry seven .380 rounds. I bought one of the wartime models, which are inferior in workmanship to those made from 1929 to the early 1940s. It didn't matter though, because I never carried the Walther for business purposes. I just wanted to own a gun similar to 007's, not feel like a jerk for lugging a piece of nostalgia around under my arm. I put the pistol back inside the bag and left it on the table.

"Jordan, what can you tell me about Leonard Craig's wife?"

"She's like every other *alrightnikeh* I've ever known, only more so."

"You'll have to translate that for me."

"Nouveau riche, acquired not earned."

"Anything else come to mind?"

"An American Express card with faded numbers."

"Gotcha."

The bar was empty now; chairs topped the tables. I stretched as far as my side would let me and stood to leave. Jordan rose with me, picking up the gun. "Here," he said, offering the Mauser one more time.

"Jordan, having, or not having, that gun isn't going to make a bit of difference in whether I get home safely. It's just a pistol."

"You want it should sing, too?" He sighed with the depth of ages and said quietly, "David, you're my friend. I love you. I would feel much better if you were armed."

"Sure, Jordan," I said, giving in. He handed me the gun, I kissed him on the forehead and stuck the bag into my pocket. "Don't let me forget my clothes."

"Not to worry, Martin brought them down earlier," he said, and he headed for the bar.

"That Martin sure is Johnny-on-the-spot around here."

"My every desire," Jordan sang from the bar, and I thought

I saw a flash of color in his cheek, but he was too far away for me to be sure.

"Is this something permanent, or is that sparkle in your eye a reflection off the mirror?" I called.

"Permanent? What's permanent?" he said, coming back with a larger bag containing my clothes. "And you're a fine one to give me a hard time about permanency. You, the revolving door of heterosexual Fifth Avenue. The least you could do is be interesting enough to maintain a variety of partners instead of spinning round and around with the same woman."

"I hardly think of myself as a sexual Olympian, Jordan, but I get around, which, by the way, was a great song by the Beach Boys in 1964." He wasn't impressed.

"Olympian? You're not even Tidewater Farm Team these days. I, on the other hand, have known, and continue to enjoy, novices, jades, old men, and the clergy. Good table gossip is my stock-and-trade and I don't appreciate it when my sources start behaving themselves. Think about someone other than yourself for a change."

I laughed, a deep releasing laugh, said "Goodnight," and pushed open the door to the street. The morning had gone cold, the rain clouds hanging low and gray in the day's first light. Was it really just a few hours ago that I'd walked into Leonnard Craig's penthouse? God, it seemed longer, days. I hunched inside my borrowed overcoat and hurried to the corner where I dropped a quarter into the pay phone. As I punched in the numbers a long silver limo eased up next to me. I held the last two digits as the tinted driver's window slid down.

"You need a ride uptown?" asked the little man behind the mustache.

"How much to Sixty-First and Fifth?"

"Twenty bucks."

"Ten."

"Fifteen."

"Fifteen! A cab's half that."

"Listen, Jack," he said flashing me his watch, "it's almost five in the morning. You see a cab?"

"Good point, but ten bucks is my limit."

"You got it. Hop in."

I hung up the phone and waited for my quarter; I'd only have pissed her off again.

CHAPTER FOUR

It was 8:22 by the clock on Roseman's desk; three letters next to the minute hand said WED. and I'd been talking nonstop for an hour. Roseman's office is the forty-fourth floor of a high rise at the corner of Fifth Avenue and 61st Street. Roseman also owns the forty-third floor, which is where he lives. I'm on the next floor down. Not the entire place, but spacious rooms with the same view of Central Park and the boat pond.

Originally, all three floors had been part of Roseman's residence. But after being widowed, he found the place oppressively large and eventually withdrew to the more livable space of kitchen, den, bedroom, and library on the forty-third floor. He was, after all, "just a simple, overly domesticated man, prone to all manner of inactivity." Something he was fond of pointing out, especially to people who suggested he subdivide, sell, and move to Greenwich.

It came as no surprise, then, that Roseman moved his office and not himself, thus saving the daily commute downtown. Now he simply stepped aboard either of two elevators, which had been installed for his wife's convenience during the last years of her life, and took a short ride up—or down. That's where I come in.

My work for Roseman is about equally split between his personal life and his law practice. Consequently, I was forever in and out of the office and apartment at every conceivable hour of the day. In fact, it was often as convenient for me to sleep on his couch as go home. It was after one of these overnight campouts that Roseman suggested I move in downstairs.

So, we negotiated a lower than fair-market rent, and I gave up my boxcar flat on West 97th Street. It was a sacrifice, but I managed to come to terms with it. The only problem was that my furniture looked like cattle from the Sudan against the freshly painted plaster walls of East 61st Street. I figured the decorating could wait. If I wanted to eat in a place where the window appointments complimented the color of my date's dress, I'd make a reservation.

I'd arrived home around five-thirty and had taken a second hot shower, which had made the starched shirt and tie feel almost comfortable. Roseman was as crisp as the weather outside and strictly business. After two quick coffees, it was recital time, and I'd been going ever since. I called it quits after Marston's last drink and poured myself another cup of coffee.

"Yes, well," Roseman said, walking to the window, "that was clear, concise, and, as always, well presented. Thank you. The morning papers confirm that the young man on the floor at Leonard's was Lane Peters. There was no mention of the affair, which offers a momentary relief, though I am not foolish enough to believe that will remain the case for long. At least we're not faced with any undeniably damning evidence to implicate him."

I winced at the thought of Leonard's note buried among my BVDs downstairs. Initially, I thought I'd tell Roseman about the possible existence of just such a piece of evidence—top secret, very hush, hush, and Florio would have my license if he knew I let anything out—that type of thing. But I trashed the idea after realizing that if Roseman got interested, he'd keep after me until the whole story came out. His ethics were unshakable. Once he knew about the blackmail, he'd tell Florio, maybe not instantly, but within twenty-four hours. He'd give himself time to think things through and then pick up the phone. It was an admirable quality, he was known for it, but right now it was in my way so I kept my mouth shut. Besides, I suspected that my main reason for wanting to tell him was nothing more than a selfish desire for a little inner peace.

"Were you able to get a coherent story out of Leonard once he calmed down?" I asked.

"I was, and you should hear it for yourself," he said, suggesting we go downstairs. "I left him in the library."

We both squeezed into the small elevator concealed behind a sliding panel near his desk and dropped to the library below.

With a silent jolt, we came to rest and stepped through the bookcase to meet a sunken-eyed version of a Raggedy Andy doll folded into the back of a deep, overstuffed couch. He was still wearing his evening clothes from the night before.

"Leonard," Arthur said. He paused, waiting for a sign of recognition. "You remember David, don't you? David happened to be with the police when they arrived at the apartment last night. I want you to tell him what happened. Tell him what you remember. Everything. Do you think you can?"

The rag doll nodded a faint affirmative and I settled onto an ottoman facing him. Roseman propped himself against the fireplace mantel and didn't move again. The voice that finally came out of Craig was as broken as he looked.

"I knew the young man," he began slowly. "Peters was his name, Lane Peters. I had met him before, with Samantha. In time, I knew they were lovers. She took great pleasure in waving their relationship under my nose and she did so at every opportunity. Even in front of our friends. . . ."

"Leonard," I broke in, hoping to stop the digression, "was she with him last night? Do you know where she is now?"

"No." And he began mentally to drift. I threw a glance at Roseman, who met my gaze with a shrug of resignation. I leaned

41

forward a little and gripped Craig's knee, shaking him back to the present.

"We had a fight last night," he said weakly.

"Who had a fight?"

"Samantha and I."

"Where?" I prompted.

"At dinner. The Carlyle. I'm afraid it was very loud and very public. I said some things I shouldn't have." His lips began to tremble.

"That's OK, Leonard," I said easily. "It's OK, take a minute and calm down." I watched him breathe, this old man in front of me, and it was a tired, labored effort. Leonard was only ten years older than Roseman, but tonight he looked deflated and ancient. Even the gaiety of his dinner jacket and red tie seemed violently juxtaposed to the pallor of his face. He had taken an emotional gut punch and the fight was out of him. "Tell me, what did you argue about, Leonard?"

He lifted his head from his hands and whispered, "Money, always money. She'd been pouring tens of thousands into that production of *Macbeth*. She was always saying Lane had such great potential; well, I doubt he'll make his next entrance."

"Surely, considering the age difference, it occurred to you she would have a lover sometime," I offered.

"Lovers," he said quietly.

"Lovers? What do you mean, Leonard? Explain yourself."

"Lane Peters wasn't her only 'man'," he said, and he pronounced the last word with distaste. I waited. "She was also seeing Banks Reid."

"So who's Banks Reid?" I asked him.

"Oh, her latest man in tow," he said with exasperation.

"Was Reid at the table last night?"

"He was, along with Randall Bergman. Actually, it was Reid I went to see. I wanted him to know that Samantha was using him just as she had used me. All she wanted was his money, financing to support that goddamn play and her young stud."

"And how did Reid take that bit of news?"

42

"I don't know; blankly, I guess. I even went so far as to announce that I knew she was planning to meet Peters later that night. I was so angry I would have said anything. He didn't seem to react."

Maybe not then and there, I thought, but eight to five it ruined what was left of his appetite.

"How did you know she was going to meet Peters?"

"I overheard her on the telephone," he explained weakly.

"When did all of this take place?"

"Early, before the theater. She was going to see his stage performance this time, perhaps she's tired of his private one."

"Leonard, why weren't you part of the dinner party?"

"Oh, of course I was asked," he said derisively, showing some life for the first time, "but I couldn't bear another night of 'Lane this,' and 'Lane that'; she rubbed him in my face enough as it was. And then those two fawning, ridiculous 'escorts', she called them. God save me!" He fell silent, staring at the aged spotted hands in his lap.

I studied his face, collected my thoughts, and became aware of a strong feeling of sympathy for Roseman's friend. He must have been completely humiliated, standing at that table help-less, hopeless, confused, and angry; facing not only his faithless wife and her lover but also Randall Bergman. Sex and blackmail. Jesus. I wondered how much he had paid out, and for what.

"Did you know all this about Reid?" I asked, turning to Roseman.

"The first I've heard," he said without inflection. Roseman often spoke in monotones when his mind was preoccupied; it was as if he needed every available brain cell for thought.

"OK," I said, starting out again with Leonard, "let's try to keep this focused on Lane Peters. When Lane and Samantha got together, did they use his apartment?" Leonard either didn't want to answer or couldn't. "Your apartment?" I pressed.

"Yes, I think so," he said meekly.

I shook my head in wonder while Roseman studied the tile inlay above the mantel.

"Wasn't that a little awkward for you?"

"We live very separate lives, Samantha and I," Craig said sharply, getting his manhood pinched a little.

"I take that to mean you don't sleep together, right?" I could barely hear his mumbled answer.

"She has her own rooms," he said. "I never go into hers and she never comes into mine." He looked me straight in the eye for the first time. "That's the way it is."

I sidestepped his defiance with another question.

"Did you object to her supporting the show?"

"No, not at first. She seemed genuinely interested. But then, after the affair started—the one with Peters—I felt I needed to do something, strike back, take some kind of action, so I cut off the money." He let out a hard, curt laugh. "Obviously that didn't work." I held my tongue. "Then last night I noticed some checks missing from my private account book. I went to the Carlyle and confronted her. She just laughed. God, it was infuriating. I could have choked her then and there; to that I will admit."

This was one woman I could hardly wait to meet again. She seemed to have developed several new facets. Though, to her credit, a lot of women go through life and never inspire anywhere near this kind of passion. It's the kind that gets you throttled instead of married, but at least it's passion.

"After the fight, what did you do?" I asked.

"I went on to the Whitney Museum for an opening of primitive American Indian drawings."

"And what time did you get home?"

"It was sometime before midnight. Maybe eleven-thirty, maybe a little earlier."

"Tell me what happened after you got there."

"I went upstairs to the apartment and found the door wide open. I called out, but there no response. I became

44

concerned and took a pistol from the closet in the foyer—I keep several around the house."

"What caliber?"

"A .38 Colt." He stopped, drifted, but came back. "I entered the living room and immediately the lights went out. It frightened me and my gun went off."

"Where did the shot go, Leonard, can you place it?"

"Into the floor perhaps, I don't know, really."

"And then . . ."

"Then there was another shot. Someone screamed, I remember that, and then I was knocked down and I hit my head, here," he said, pulling back the hair on his forehead to show a good-sized lump with the skin broken. It looked recent.

"I must have lost consciousness, because it was several minutes before I got to my feet and was able to orient myself enough to find the light switch. That was when I saw the body. I couldn't think. It was unbelievable. I know I should have done something; called for help, tried to stop the bleeding, something, but I couldn't think. I ran. I came directly here to Arthur."

"You don't remember anything about the person who knocked you down? Size? Smell? An aftershave, perfume? Type of clothing?"

"No, nothing. It was completely dark."

"No light from the street?"

"The maid always pulls the curtains before she leaves."

"How about the scream? Was it male or female? Do you know?"

"Female, I think. I can't be sure. The gunshot was still ringing in my ears."

"Did they both come from the same direction?" He looked puzzled. "The scream and the gunshot," I said. He thought for a moment.

"No, the gunshot was over here"—he indicated his left—"and the scream came from over here," and his right hand fluttered in the air.

"So," I said, "there were at least two other people in the

room besides you and Peters. I didn't think he'd shot himself." I motioned Roseman toward the door. "Will you be all right here for a couple of minutes while I talk to Arthur?" I asked Craig. He didn't acknowledge the question, and from the look in his eyes, he was back out in the cosmos with Voyager 2. Roseman and I stepped out to the hallway.

"If we include Harwood the deliveryman, there were enough people up in Craig's apartment that night for a convention, which is good, because it makes for a lot of suspects besides your friend. But I'd bet good money the gun Florio found next to Peters' body was the one Leonard dropped in the hallway when he got shoved."

"Yes, I quite agree with you," Roseman said. "Regardless of who shot Peters, that gun will, undoubtedly, turn out to be Leonard's." Roseman and I were standing as close as two Arabs in a business transaction and I marveled at the smoothness of his morning shave. Polished jowls, silk tie, and the slight fragrance of a hair tonic that I couldn't place. "I believe him, David," he said turning to face me. "I simply have to."

"I know you do, but you've got to realize he may be guilty. Don't get your hopes up, OK?" Roseman looked at me quizzically. The question in his face made me nervous, like maybe he realized I knew something I wasn't telling him, so I plunged right ahead. "I'll start with Samantha and her dinner companions as soon as I check in with Florio. What do you want to do?"

"Concerning what?" he seemed surprised.

"Leonard."

"Oh yes, I see. Suggestions?"

"Let Florio know he's here. It's worth some Brownie points. Actually, it's a wonder he hasn't been here already."

"Trust, my dear boy. I imagine he puts more faith in you than you allow." My conscience did a full gainer at the thought. "If you think it best, call him and pray to God he doesn't make an arrest. Leonard's too pathetic. He's in no condition to be booked, arraigned, or held even for the shortest period of time. Do you agree?"

"I'd take him in if it were me." I looked at Roseman, watching him think. "I'll call from the kitchen. Maybe, if we're cooperative and get some medical mumbo jumbo stating Craig's delicate condition, Florio will be happy with a statement and the knowledge of where he can be found in a hurry. I'll do my best and see you back here tonight. OK?"

"She never loved him," Roseman said softly. "She never gave him anything warmer than indifference. She's vain, shallow, and vile." I let the silence stretch and then he was gone. Back to the library. Back to his friend.

A growl from my midsection reminded me of mortal necessities, and I set off in search of breakfast and the telephone, both of which were in the kitchen. Kripp Thomas was also to be found there and it was a good thing because breakfast depended on Kripp.

His mother had named him after Kripp Johnson of the Del Vikings, a group that recorded back in the fifties, but he looked more like a black Sal Mineo, only taller. He also couldn't sing worth a shit, which, thankfully, didn't affect his cooking. We were within months of being the same age and in the middle of our first handshake, three years ago, I said, "Did you know you've got the same first name as Kripp Johnson? One of the Del Vikings? Back in the fifties?" Well, it made his eyes go all startled. I guessed that kind of ethnic music trivia wasn't expected from a thirty-two-year-old white man in a bow tie. Kripp managed a stuttered, "You heard of him?"

"Sure," I said. "They were one of the few mixed race groups ever to have a national hit." To be truthful, I wasn't all that well versed on musical groups of the fifties. I'd read something about the Del Vikings and then forgotten it until the prick of a handshake brought it back. Since then he often grilled me, along with the breakfast sausage, all about things musical and black, so I started doing some off-hours research to stay ahead of him.

I came through the door with a "Hi ya, Kripp," checked in the fridge for orange juice, pulled up a stool, and reached for the telephone.

"Don't you ever use your own office?" he asked, looking up from his morning paper. "I know you've got one because I've seen it. Nice one, too, right up there with the boss, but no, you'd rather be down here taking up space and eating everything you can get your hands on. I don't know how you stay so thin. What you want this morning, Ham?" and he flashed a smile that lit up his black face like a neon beer sign.

"Captain Florio," I said into the phone. "Thanks, I'll hold." Kripp had folded his paper and laid it by the stove that took up most of one wall; it had eight burners and a thirty-six-inch grill. "What's available?" I asked.

"Got some fresh blueberries and the pancake mix is already made, sausage? coffee? leftover sweet potatoes from last night that I can slice and grill, plus eggs any way you like them."

"I'll have everything and lots of it, please." The phone clicked and Florio came on the line. "Marc, good morning, this is David. How's your day shaping up?"

"Not bad, how's your side?"

"OK but not great. It oozes a little and kind of sticks to my shirt, you know?"

"I know. You coming to see me?"

"Not unless it's absolutely necessary. Have you talked to Marston?"

"Yeah, it'll pass. What else is on your mind?"

"I wanted to know if you had issued any warrants." There was a pause while he thought about his answer.

"Warrants for Leonard Craig, you mean?"

"Yes."

"Not yet."

"So it is a possibility?"

"Maybe. We just finished talking to his wife. Fine lady. Very concerned. Terribly upset. If they made them in her size, she'd wear big, brass balls. Says she spent the night with her boyfriend Banks Reid at his corporate apartment on Fifty-eighth and Madison. She also says she doesn't know where her husband is. Do you?"

"That's why I called—provided you can talk to him without making an arrest."

"You're pushing it, Ham," he said, letting an edge creep into his voice.

"I know. I don't want to, but it's important."

"The official department statement is we are questioning a number of people about the circumstances surrounding the death of Lane Peters. As yet, no warrants have been issued. So is he there or not?"

"He is and you're expected. Kripp's just made some fresh coffee. I won't be here but Sandra will show you down. Roseman's with him."

"Be right there." And he hung up. I wandered over toward the stove and grazed on the blueberries until I got to Kripp's newspaper.

"Company coming, huh?"

"Yes, large hairy men with stained teeth and worn shoes," I said, turning to the sports page and pouring a cup of coffee. "Have you got a phone book in here?"

"Top drawer of my desk," he said as he eased over a golden brown pancake and poked the sausage. It smelled delicious. Taking the paper and coffee back to my stool, I picked up the phone again and dialed. "City desk, please, Ira Katz." After a short pause, the biggest, blackest, Southern Jew I knew answered. "Ira, this is David Hamilton, what's the lead story for tomorrow's front page?"

"Maybe your obit, if what I hear from Florio is correct."

"I believe he's recovered. At least he was civil on the phone a minute ago. Ira, I need a favor."

"I only owe you twenty, what is it?"

"Can I come down and go through your photo files? I need to put some names and faces together."

"That would be fine with me." Then he uncorked a question. "Are you working for a new client this morning?"

"Why would you ask such a question, Ira?"

"Well, since last night's shooting was at Leonard Craig's, that means Roseman is involved. Or were you coming down here because you've forgotten what last year's Miss America looks like?"

"You're right, Ira. I do have a new client, but I've just gotten started so there's nothing to tell. I'll be there before lunch. Thanks." Breakfast arrived. I reopened the paper and put my mind in neutral as Kripp topped-off our coffee mugs and sat down with the phone book.

"What number you want?"

"Schirmer's on Sixty-second," I said through a mouthful of sweet potato.

"Ah, shit, Ham. Not more sheet music. What happened this time?" he said with a half laugh as he flipped pages. "Naw, wait, I don't want to hear it."

"She plays the piano extremely well," I said, trying to keep from sounding too defensive.

"Yeah, Mr. Roseman said she's got a beautiful grand, but you need to stop sending her stuff every time you guys go at it," he said, giving me a sideways glance. "I was out driving Roseman yesterday and I saw her. She was coming down Madison right by Altman's with some slick piece lapping at her heels. I know this isn't news to you, Ham, but a woman with her kind of money and looks doesn't have to spend time with a private detective. I mean, you're probably the only guy she knows who draws a paycheck; her kind usually clip coupons."

"Laugh, go ahead and laugh," I said, jabbing an egg yoke with my fork and wishing it was his tongue. "Listen Kripp, I know I stand in line until she thinks she has the time to spend an evening with me . . ."

"That line sounds real familiar, Ham. What song is it from?"

I ignored him and concentrated on the egg. He gave first.

"OK, sorry, Ham, but you've got to admit your relationship with Marilyn has gotten to be a joke. It's like one of those soap opera things that goes on and on and on. Come to terms or get out. How's that for advice you never asked for?"

"Excellent. Really Kripp, excellent," I said, trying to show great interest in the Celtic's box score, and it was good advice, goddamn his black hide. I wiped up a fugitive drop of maple syrup with the last forkful of pancake, drained the coffee, and stuffed my napkin into his shirt pocket. "When you get the number at Schirmer's, call and ask them to deliver a copy of sheet music to 'Something Stupid.' They have the address."

"Is she a Sinatra fan?"

"Yes. In fact, she probably has the largest private collection of his tapes I've ever seen." Kripp's eyes widened in mock disbelief. "No shit, she's got cabinets filled, just crammed full." I started for the door.

"Hey, Ham," he said, snapping his fingers in recognition. I turned. "That's where I've heard that line before. Frank Sinatra."

"Well done, Kripp," and I started back out the door.

"Ham!" I stopped again. "Can you name the original members of the Chords?"

"Claude and Carl Feaster, James Keyes, Floyd McRae, and James Edwards, 1954 and their all-time classic, 'Sh-Boom' on Cat Records."

"Damn you're good," he exclaimed, slapping the table with the palm of his hand. "You're really good."

"And so was breakfast, Kripp, thanks. See you later."

I decided to walk to West 43rd Street. The weather was clear and I wanted some time to think. My chat with Leonard Craig had been a letdown. I guess I was hoping he would volunteer the news that he was being blackmailed by Bergman and Peters. I don't know why I was disappointed, most sane men would be hesitant to admit they had a motive for murder, especially after the fact. No, what I had wanted was a magnificent outpouring from the old man that would have gotten me off the hook with Florio. I didn't get it. I tried turning my thoughts to more immediate problems, like what I was going to do to keep Leonard out of the slammer, but my mind kept drifting back to Lane Peters. I couldn't shake the image of his twitching arms, jerky breaths, and misshapen head. My sense of detachment was slipping. I could do one of two things: spend more time with

51

Florio on his business calls, or swear off murder scenes for good. Considering the nature of my job, I doubted I'd seen my last corpse, so it looked as though Florio and I were destined for a closer relationship.

I left Fifth Avenue heading west on 51st and made a stronger effort to push last night's chaos from my mind. With luck, Ira would have pictures of Peters, without a bullet in his head, and of Reid, Bergman, and anyone else associated with him. Peters's name was familiar to me, but I needed to place him visually in my mind. I doubted Ira would have a picture of Matt Harwood, the Chinese takeout guy. I'd have to stop by the police department and go through the mug books for his. I wondered what he'd seen, or heard? Something. Enough to cost him his life.

I crossed Sixth Avenue and headed south for Times Square, turning the corner onto 43rd Street at 10:52 according to the clock above the revolving doors. I was standing in Katz's office moments later.

I hadn't seen Ira in a couple of months. It seemed our relationship went in spurts. Even when I worked for the paper it was that way. I spent more time talking to him on the phone than in person. After I left, we stayed loosely in touch with a beer now and again, sometimes lunch, but mostly as need dictated. It was definitely a two-way street, however, and a comfortable association. I had often wondered how a black man from Five Points, North Carolina, ended up with a moniker like Ira Katz and a job with a conservative Northern paper. I asked him about it once, and he shuffled some papers around his desk and then told me a story. It was a folksy tale about being down on Delancey Street one time and seeing a sign above a hardware store that read Steinberg & Callahan. He was so impressed, he said, that he went inside and introduced himself to a man behind the counter who was wearing a full beard and a *yarmulkah*. Katz said he told the guy how pleased he was to see such an example of Judeo-Irish relations and the guy said to him "Well, I've got another surprise for you, I'm Callahan." That was all he'd ever said about his background.

52

One thing definite about Ira was his handshake. His hands were enormous, soft, and they engulfed mine. He had the build of an athlete and I imagine he did more at Auburn as an undergrad than go to class.

"Good to see you, Ira. I appreciate this."

"Don't mention it. In fact, the first thing I want you to do is meet someone." He gripped my arm and led me through the maze of desks and computer terminals that constituted the newsroom. The twists and turns brought us to a small office with no windows, next to the reference books. "Her name is Harriet Folkes, but everyone here calls her Josey, don't ask why because I don't know. She's supposed to be retired, but she still comes in twice a week or so to make sure we're doing OK. For about forty-seven years she's been handling the society columns and people notes and it occurred to me she might know something." Josey's small office suddenly became extremely tight quarters as Ira and I stood in front of her desk. "Josey, this is David Hamilton. He has a few questions you might be able to help him with." Turning to leave, he asked, "You want anything, Ham? Coffee?"

"No, I'm fine, thanks." With that he was gone and I took a quick glance around Ms. Folkes's office. Books, books, books. No mess. No clutter. Just books and more books. The lady was much like her office: neat, ordered, and, I hoped, packed with information. Her hair was gray and pulled into a bun with a long ebony needle pushed through its center. Her dress had style without being flashy, and she wore a large silk scarf over her shoulders. She still had her own teeth.

"I'm doing some background work on Lane Peters, who was killed—murdered—last night in the apartment of my employer's best friend. Ira seemed to think you could help."

"Certainly, I hope so. For whom do you work, Mr. Hamilton?"

"Arthur Roseman."

"Yes, I see. A very wonderful man, and if I may add personally, an honorable one as well." She removed her half-

53

glasses and folded her hands in front of her. "I had some notice of your coming so I spoke with one of the researchers to find that this production of *Macbeth* is, excuse me, was Mr. Peters' third major off-Broadway show. All of them, it seems, of increasing quality. There were plans to take this show to one of the smaller Broadway houses; I would imagine those plans have now changed."

"Had he done anything prior to the New York theater?"

"Yes. In California he'd made one feature film for Universal in which he played a second lead. It was not a commercial success. There were also a couple of made-for-TV movies. Then he came here and began working for the New Reach Theater on Second Avenue and Thirteenth Street. Shelton Sharp is the producer, I believe."

"It takes quite a bit of money to bring a show up to Broadway, doesn't it?"

"Yes, quite a bit. Even single-set, small-cast productions can easily run in the $500,000 range. Musicals, of course, are much more."

"Was this a musical?"

"Of *Macbeth*?" She recoiled.

"I've sat through more unusual productions," I said, and asked, "Where was the money coming from, do you know?"

"Some from backers," she said, sending a hand to check the ebony needle, "but the bulk of support came from Samantha Reyes, initially, via her husband, Leonard Craig; then later from Banks Reid."

"Yeah, I just found out about him."

"It's interesting to note that his involvement with the play has only been since she filed the divorce papers. Evidently her husband's actions didn't sit well with her."

"Evidently," I mumbled. "Leonard didn't indicate it had gone as far as divorce."

"Well, it had."

Oh Christ, I thought, this is getting worse by the second. A less optimistic man might have been depressed. I reminded myself that if I had any brains I might not be quite so optimistic.

"So do you go along with the idea that the relationship between Samantha and Banks Reid was based solely on his agreeing to replace Leonard Craig as the major financial support for the play?"

"Yes, at least on her part. However, Banks Reid was deeply in love with Samantha and had been, in fact, since before her marriage to Leonard."

"Reid was a contender?"

"A finalist," she said, as though it was an accomplishment. "At one point they were engaged."

"Reid is much more her contemporary," I commented. "I'm surprised she didn't stick with him."

"You shouldn't be."

"Money, huh?"

"Precisely, and a good deal more of it."

"So when Leonard stopped the cash flow, she just mooed and gooed Reid back into active duty?"

"So it appears, and she was preparing to moo and goo her way back into his life."

"Maybe not," I proposed. Josey raised a questioning eyebrow. "The divorce papers might have been required. You know, a show of commitment in order to get Reid's wallet open."

"Ah yes."

"But I wouldn't think she'd actually go through with it. Samantha doesn't strike me as the sort of woman who is interested in taking a step down the ladder of wealth."

"Precisely."

"I mean, she's doing all this for Peters in the first place, right?" I said, trying to explain matters to myself. "I don't think Reid would be as open-minded about the sleeping arrangements as Leonard."

"You've lost me, sorry."

"Never mind, I'm rambling. What's Reid's background?"

"He comes from Boston manufacturing money; relatively new money at that. Computer software," she said, giving it some thought. "He moved to the city only recently and handles the family investments through a Wall Street firm. He also fulfills the company's New York obligations for his father—gladhanding, galas and such. He is attractive in an unremarkable, slightly overweight sort of way, and, as you have pointed out, seems favorably disposed toward four-hundred-year-old English drama when properly enticed."

"Do you also happen to know a man named Randall Bergman?"

"Yes, I do. A fawning, insidious little man, to my mind," she said evenly. "Very old New York banking money. The family institution was bought out quite some time ago, so there's little left to divide among the great-grandchildren, of which he is one. He's well educated, but he hasn't done anything since graduation except spend his share of the inheritance. I don't think he even pretends to have a job, though to believe the gossip, he needs one to help support his favorite . . . pastime? Or should I call it a habit?"

"He seems to have been closely associated with Samantha: regular dinner guest, escort, that sort of thing. Do you know any specifics?"

"Nothing other than to observe that people as abrasive and manipulative as Mrs. Craig often have few companions from whom to choose. In this instance, however, I believe Bergman was more aligned with Banks Reid than Samantha."

"In what capacity?"

"Randall moves comfortably in the social circles just entered by Reid. He knows all the right people; he just doesn't have the money to associate with them anymore. So, essentially, Bergman became a sort of walking, talking social directory."

"Mutual necessity."

"Exactly."

"Do you know how long Samantha has been seeing Reid this time around?"

"Well, the play's been running about three months, another two for rehearsals. I'd say four or five months."

"You've been a great help. Could I possibly have your home phone number in case I need to reach you again?"

"Certainly," she said, jotting it on a notepad. "Ira tells me you see a good deal of Marilyn Chabor. A lovely girl, I know her mother well."

"She and I seem to spend more time going round and round than going out," I said candidly.

"I hope you can work things out to everyone's satisfaction," she said rising, no doubt squelching a desire for more intimate detail. We shook hands and I walked back across the newsroom to the photo morgue and prepared to immerse myself in the files of wire shots and staff pictures.

Once again, Ira was ahead of me. He had already requested available photos on Peters, Samantha Craig, Banks Reid, and Randall Bergman, and they were arranged in neat, separate piles on a corner table. I slid the pictures of Lane Peters across the table and fanned them out in front of me. There were seven of them showing a young man wearing varying shades of tights, gesturing and looking very dramatic. Undeniably, he was once very attractive. So much so that it was hard for me to imagine why he ever left Hollywood to come to New York. I don't claim to be a casting director, but to me he looked like he was on the right coast to start with.

There were only two pictures of Banks Reid, both at award functions in Boston. In one he was accepting a plaque for encouraging economic development in his sovereign state by expanding his factories in the good old U.S. of A. instead of Taiwan. The other photo had him saying a word or two about the importance of homes for orphans and why he was so pleased to give $100,000 toward that end. The man looked as nervous giving away money as he did accepting accolades: dark hair plastered straight back, smile askew, and the personality, seemingly, of a bloated carcass. I told myself that this was an unfair judgment since anybody can look stupid in a tuxedo, and he'd probably just eaten a bad roast beef dinner, which would account for the awkward smile. I decided to wait until we met before signing him off as a jerk. In my way, I can be very magnanimous.

The photos of Samantha were radiant even in black and white. The woman was beautiful and she jumped out at you from the picture. Standing next to her, Leonard Craig looked like a fifty-pound bag of feed grain, and he was at her side in every shot: parties, openings, benefits. Very nice, indeed. She was even more attractive than I remembered. The afterglow of conquest, I guessed.

There were more pictures of Randall Bergman than I would have expected, though in each he was never more than a face among others, no stand alones. This minor celebrity had to rely on the grease pencil's circle to set him apart from the crowd. He was handsome in an angular, small-featured way, and I noticed that all the photos were taken at glitterball late-night spots à la Studio 54. Everybody with a drink, a laugh, a cigarette, and that see-me-first look in their eyes.

I pulled the pictures of Leonard and Samantha back into view, comparing the people in them to those with Bergman and his lot. Day and night. The power holders and the power seekers. Eventually, the lesser would become the greater, it was only a matter of time and inheritance. Except for Bergman, who had already spent his. He'd be interesting to meet. More slippery than slimy, I figured, taking one more look at his blazing smile. Christ, he could be drunk for all I knew, or coked out his ears. That'd give me the same kind of glimmering sheen.

I slid one of Reid's pictures into line next to Bergman and Samantha. The comparison was jarring: Reid, stiff and ill at ease; Bergman, all plastic; Samantha, comfortably monied; and Leonard, just happy to be at the party. Looking at these people all together, it was easy to see where Reid would need somebody's help in going from his photograph to Samantha's.

I pushed the pictures away from me and stood up, blinking twice under the fluorescent lighting to clear my vision. Some cast, I thought, feeling the first ripples of a headache start to finger my temples. Some cast, indeed.

58

Leaving the photos on the table, I stopped by Ira's desk on the way out.

"Are you sure the ape who tried to gun you down last night was driving a dark blue Buick?" he asked, grinning hard.

"I can't swear it was blue," I said, "but it was a dark color and it was a Buick. Not a new one either. I filed a statement with Florio."

"Yeah, I know," he said, delighted, "we got a copy of it, but that's not important. I just ran a check through Motor Vehicles in Albany: Randall Bergman owns a Buick."

"Holy shit!"

"And he keeps it garaged at Seventy-ninth and Third. Convenient or what?"

"Yeah, very convenient," I answered. "You going to run that?"

"Why not," he exclaimed with obvious surprise. "Wouldn't you? DMV information isn't privileged."

"I know, but without positive ID—and I didn't see the license plate—it's just circumstantial, you're guessing."

"It's good journalism and judicious use of the freedom of information act," he answered. "I can't help it if Florio didn't think to do it himself."

"Well, you're right there, but goddamn, it's going to piss him off."

"Tough shit."

"Listen," I said, turning to leave. "If you get anything else as background on Bergman, I'd appreciate a call. He's the one I know the least about."

"Will do, Ham."

"Thanks again for your help, Ira."

"Right. My turn to buy next time."

Maybe Ira would turn up something to help me understand what a dirt ball like Bergman could find to hang on a guy like Leonard Craig. At the moment, I didn't have a clue and could use some help.

Once outside, I dropped into the subway, took the shuttle to

Grand Central, and caught the local uptown to Lexington and 77th Street. Coming out at the south end of the platform, I was across the street from Lenox Hill Hospital's emergency entrance. Without making a conscious decision to do so, I crossed the street and walked into the waiting room. For midafternoon, they were doing a good, one might say healthy, business. There were fifteen or twenty people seated in the multicolored plastic chairs that ringed the outer wall of the room. There were chairs in the center of the room as well, but only one or two of those were occupied. As I glanced over the vacant faces of the people near me, it was difficult to identify immediately their maladies; one black man—he looked about fifty—held onto a pair of crutches, and another fellow, a few chairs down, wore a cast on his right leg, but otherwise they just sat, keeping their illnesses wrapped in their overcoats, and waited.

As the events of the night before began to rush back with pain and clarity, I bent down to speak through the hole in the Plexiglas window separating me from the reception desk.

"Hi," I said awkwardly, trying to adjust to the three-inch opening. "Would you ask Dr. Carlson if she has a minute to see me, please?"

"Dr. Carlson isn't on duty this afternoon, sir," the nurse said, looking up at me. "Could someone else help you?"

"No, I wanted to see Rachel . . . Dr. Carlson."

"We don't take appointments in the emergency room, sir."

"Oh no, I'm not sick," I started to explain, feeling ridiculous at having to focus everything into the tiny opening and speak at what, I thought, seemed like full volume. "I'm a friend and just wanted to say hello."

The nurse eyed me pretty hard, considering my physical qualifications no doubt, and then decided to stick with her story. "Dr. Carlson isn't scheduled for this afternoon, I'll be glad to take a message."

"No thanks," I said, straightening up and fighting back the urge to stick my face into that stupid little hole and scream that if she'd given me her goddamn phone number when I asked for it, I wouldn't be standing here making a spectacle out of myself in front of a group of people whose collective fevers probably exceeded the surface temperature of the sun. What the hell was the matter with me? I hadn't behaved like this in years. Shades of high school. Shades of early college romance. Shades of . . . and then I knew what it was. Rather, I knew who it was; who this Carlson, Rachel F., M.D., reminded me of and why I had been so instantly drawn to her. It wasn't a pleasant memory.

In my defense, I was young and wanted out of a situation that I didn't know how to end gracefully, so I just ended it; called her from a friend's house one afternoon and told her it was over. No preamble. No explanation. It was the most callous thing I had ever done and for no particular reason, either. She was a pretty girl, intelligent, socially graceful with an air of confidence and capability that I responded to, liked, appreciated. The very same qualities I sensed in Carlson, Rachel F., M.D.

". . . just slip out the back, Jack. Make a new plan, Stan. No need to be coy, Roy. Just get yourself free." Well, I caught the metaphorical bus, but what Mr. Simon failed to explain in his song is how you deal with the sense of guilt, for me at least, that follows after you hack off the offending personage. Goddamn, I just wasn't ready, that's all. Now I'm older. A big boy, more mature. I can handle emotions like an adult. So, have a gin and take Marilyn out to dinner. If Marilyn's not available, call someone else. After all, it's the type, not the individual, right? Isn't that what you've opted for ever since? The attractive? The light? The fanciful and not too substantial? Isn't that the point?

Jesus, Ham, You've reduced the human experience to a weight watchers' special. And, to be fair, there's more to Marilyn then her glib-manner-shallow-intellect allows you to see. Oh, yeah? Yeah. I'm just waiting for her to grow up into the woman I left. Christ! That's it. Bonus points. And with Carlson, Rachel F., M.D., there would be no wait. That's why you're behaving like an unlaid adolescent. You're afraid to admit just how long you've been waiting for someone of her . . . what? caliber? to come along. Maybe you've got a chance to correct a past mistake and it scares the shit out of you.

"Excuse me, sir," said a firm voice beside me. "Did you want to see a doctor?"

"Huh? No, I mean, yes . . . but she's not here."

"I beg your pardon?" she said, studying my face, trying to decide whether I was lost or in need of the resident psychiatrist.

Glancing at her nametag, I saw she was the triage nurse—responsible for assessing injuries and the priority of treatment of anyone coming into the ER. If she sounded no-nonsense, it was her job.

"Sorry, I was just thinking about something, someone," I said, realizing I must have been standing there for some time soaring through mental merryland. "I'll get out of your way. I stopped by to see Rachel Carlson, but she's not here."

"I'll tell her you came by."

"Thanks," I said, feeling my face redden and heading toward the door. Outside, I sucked cold air into my lungs and walked west to Park Avenue. It took me about ten minutes to reach the lobby of Samantha Craig's apartment house. I gave my name to the doorman and he called upstairs to announce me. There seemed to be some hesitation on Samantha's part so I said I had information about her husband. She was at least interested enough to see me.

As I reached for the elevator button, the doors opened and a sharp-nosed man in his early thirties came out. We stepped around each other with a polite "excuse me," and I backed into the elevator thinking that his face was familiar. It wasn't until I rocked gently to a halt at the penthouse level that I realized who the guy was: Randall Bergman—I'd been looking at his face all afternoon.

The lovely Mrs. Craig was standing in the doorway when the elevator opened. One hand held a cigarette and the other about three inches of what might have been Listerine without ice, but wasn't. If she was concerned about where her husband was, it didn't show. She must have put on a better act for Florio.

"You know something about Leonard?" she said with no introduction.

"Yes, I do, and if I can use your phone a minute, I'll know more."

She thought about that one for a second or two and then stepped back to let me in. I went straight to the telephone and saw the surprise register in her face that I was so familiar with the apartment.

"I was here last night," I said, dialing Roseman's number. She dropped into an armchair and nursed her drink while cigarette ash dropped onto that same beautiful rug. Kripp answered and said Arthur had gone back upstairs to the office; our guest was asleep. I held the line while Kripp transferred the call. I tapped my foot in mock impatience.

"I ran into your pal downstairs," I said just to be chatty. "He stopped by to offer condolences?"

"No," she said absently. "Actually he was looking for something. He thought he'd left it here."

"Last night?"

"Hardly," she scoffed.

The tone of her response wasn't what I'd expected.

"I figured you two for good friends," I said. "You know, the theater and all." Samantha's laugh was dry and staccato.

"That greasy little creep? He wouldn't help his mother out of a burning building."

"Sorry I brought it up. I don't imagine he found what he was looking for, though."

"How do you know that?"

"Little secrets," I told her and was about to add something else about notes in small envelopes when the phone clicked.

"Arthur Roseman."

"Hi, it's me. What's new?"

"Oh yes, David, fine. Good to hear from you. Everything went splendidly. Very well indeed. Captain Florio has only just left. He was rather abrupt in his manner, but quite efficient and not without tact. He was immediately aware of Leonard's poor condition and, in his way, your Captain was almost gentle with his questions; the medical mumbo-jinxs weren't necessary. And you? What have you learned?"

"I can't really talk," I told him, watching my hostess ease off her two-inch heels and slowly rub her left instep up the side of her long, long, lovely right leg. "Sorry, Arthur, I lost my thought there for a moment. I'm calling from Leonard's. His wife was concerned . . ." Roseman made a gutteral sound that astounded me and Samantha blew smoke out of her nose trying to keep a straight face. "I was mostly interested in knowing what Florio had decided to do?"

"In the end, only to leave—for which I am grateful. He did bring along a young man who took Leonard's fingerprints, but it was a simple procedure and passed smoothly. Leonard is in no condition for even the slightest ordeal. He's asleep now with the help of a sedative. You'll be here for dinner?"

"Yes."

"I'll see you then."

Samantha looked up as the conversation ended. "Your husband has been at Arthur Roseman's since late last night. He is not well but currently asleep, by way of a sedative," I said, "and though a prime suspect in the death of your lover—you don't mind if I call a spade a shovel do you?—not yet in police custody."

The lady's lethargy evaporated immediately. Her feet came up under her chair searching for shoes, the cigarette got mauled into the ashtray, and the slight little thing gulped down her Listerine and slammed the glass onto the mahogany sidetable. Coming to her feet, she looked at me hard and spit out, "You have the makings of a real sonofabitch."

"I'm flattered. Really." She started to respond but checked herself and stormed to the bar for another drink. I couldn't take my eyes off her legs. She was light on her feet and put lots of motion in her hips.

"I think you'd better leave," she said, looking up from her bottle.

"Let's not fight, Samantha. You're tired, upset, worried about who to turn to. Besides, when you pout it makes your mouth go soft and your chin sag." The crystal highball glass sailed past me wide to the left, caught the curtain and dropped onto the carpet unbroken.

"Nice toss," I said, "but I don't plan to leave."

"Well, you're too big to push, so suit yourself," she snapped, picking up another glass. "I don't plan to talk."

"I'm sorry," I said, using my best Jimmy Stewart stammer. "I've had a long, excruciating morning under the thumb of Captain Florio. My boss happens to be your husband's best friend, and he's all over my ass to keep Leonard out of jail. I've been up most of the night, watched two men die, got shot myself, and I'm really tired. I don't mean to be a jerk. I just can't help myself." I moved to the bar, lifted a bottle of Bombay, and added, "One quick gin and I'll be out of here."

"The well-dressed Captain Florio was swaggering around here earlier, so I know how subtle he can be. Here," she said, handing me her fresh glass, "make mine a scotch." She took her drink and headed back to the couch. Her shoes came off by the telephone stand. She didn't offer conversation and I didn't try to make any. I finished my drink in silence and watched her smoke one cigarette and light a second.

"Were you serious about the divorce?" I finally asked.

She kept her gaze out the window, pushed blue-white smoke through her lips, and said, "No." It was a comfortable answer, followed by a comfortable silence. I fixed another scotch, for her, added a splash of water, spun the ice cubes with my finger, and took a seat across from her, leaving the drink within reach on the table.

"Thanks," she said. It wasn't a word that came out of her mouth easily. I went back to the bar for another gin. When she spoke, it was to my back. "After Leonard quit supplying money for the play, I wanted to do something to hurt him, scare him, anything to get the money back. It didn't work," she said with a sigh. "Not immediately anyway."

65

"So you picked up Banks Reid again for financial insurance."

"You seem well informed and a little unforgiving, but yes, I picked him back up. He's had nothing to complain about."

"He loves you."

"So do a lot of men." She was simply stating a fact.

"Didn't that liaison rub Peters the wrong way?" I asked, regretting the way my question came out, "or was he broad-minded enough to see it as a means to an end?"

"I appreciate a sense of humor, Mr. Hamilton, but not at my expense. To be frank, I don't know what Lane thought. I did once, or believed I did. In any event"—she took a long pull on her drink—"Leonard was on the verge of folding. I'd have had the money back. He happens to love me, too."

"I'm sure he does," I said and stared into my gin. "What did Reid think about your relationship with Lane?" She looked startled. "Leonard told me he made the announcement at dinner last night."

"Banks didn't believe him."

"You sure about that?" I said. Her eyes turned to slits and her jaw set. "Sorry, I forgot. He loves you. What did the two of you do after the Carlyle?"

"Saw the first act of *Macbeth*. Then we went to SoHo for a gallery opening. I didn't know about the shooting until I got home around six this morning."

"Where had you been?"

"With Banks, of course."

"And where was that?"

"He has an apartment in town."

"That's your alibi?"

"And I'm sticking to it."

I let the subject drop and took a sip of my drink.

"Do you find Banks interesting?"

"Depends on what you mean by interesting."

"Well, I've never met him so I'm working from a disadvantage, but he doesn't seem, you know . . ."

"To be my kind of guy?"

I nodded. "He's active in the church, looks after orphans, belongs to Rotary. Not exactly your speed. Probably doesn't even drink."

"He doesn't. He believes it's poison."

"The body being the house of the Lord and all." She nodded. "So if he doesn't drink, what did you guys do until six in the morning?"

She smiled warmly and set down her drink.

"We lay in each other's arms," she said lightly.

Dressed or undressed was going to be my next question, but there didn't seem any point in ruining a fine conversation.

"Dinner, the play, SoHo, and Xanadu, huh?"

She laughed and picked up her drink again. I drained mine and took the empty to the bar.

"So you didn't speak to Lane last night. You only saw him on stage."

"That's right. He looks very good in tights."

"I agree. Did you and Leonard fight often?"

"Constantly."

"In public?"

"As infrequently as possible."

"What kind of things did you fight about?"

"Oh, you know, the usual thirty-year-old wife, seventy-year-old husband things; he was too old to fuck and I didn't like to sit at home and read."

I didn't exactly know how to respond to that statement, so I didn't.

"Are you fond of Chinese food?" I asked.

"Can't stand it," she said with an emphatic wave of her cigarette. "But Lane loved . . ." She caught herself in midsentence and stopped abruptly. "Why would you ask me a question like that?" Her confusion was genuine.

"It wasn't a trick question. The police found a couple of take-out orders on the kitchen counter. I thought they might have been yours."

She nodded and took a drink.

"A fellow named Matthew Harwood made the delivery last night. I think he saw whoever was here with Lane and could have identified him."

"The murderer?"

"Yes, most likely."

"Then he would know what happened. He could . . . I mean, have you spoken to him? Have the police . . ."

"He's dead."

"Oh." She seemed greatly distressed.

"Haven't you seen a morning paper?"

"No, I haven't. It's still on the table. I'll be sure to look at it after you go."

"Which has to be right now," I said finishing my drink. "I'd like to meet your boyfriend sometime. Maybe you'd introduce us."

She stood up, moving with me toward the door.

"I'd be glad to," she offered, sliding her hand under my elbow. "We're having dinner at Maribella's on First Avenue tonight. Stop by and have a drink or two. I can't speak for Banks, but it would be nice to see you again so soon."

My breathing was starting to get shallow and I could hear my heart beginning to go pitty-pat. "Have you ever read any poems by Robert Service?" I asked trying to stick to business.

"You are incredible! What could you possibly be thinking about to come up with a question like that?"

"Among other things, the fact that he wrote a ballad about Dan McGrew. In one part it goes, 'I ducked my head, the lights went out and two guns blazed in the dark. A woman screamed . . .' And I was wondering if you were that woman?" Wow, talk about having too much gin on an empty stomach.

She slowly withdrew her hand, and the friendly attitude cooled quickly. "Good afternoon," she said, her voice distant, firm.

"Yes, well, thanks for the conversation and the gin. I'll see you tonight." She didn't move. She seemed barely to breathe. I left my glass on the bar and walked out.

CHAPTER FIVE

Downstairs I stepped into a cab just as it was vacated by a middle-aged couple with two off-white Chows that probably ate better than I did. As the Chevy pulled out into traffic, I settled back amid the faint odor of disinfectant tinged with the house perfume of Madame LaBark's Pooch Caboose. Jesus, people and their pets. Whatever happened to Rusty and Rin Tin Tin? Sergeant Preston and King? A man and his dog for Christ sakes?

I went straight back to Roseman's and nearly knocked Leonard Craig down as I walked in the door. He still hadn't changed his clothes from the evening before, and I wondered if anyone had thought of sending over to his place for a couple of suits. Maybe he was on his way to collect them himself when I arrived.

"Hi, Leonard, you feeling better?" I asked, thinking he didn't look it if he did.

"Yes, I am. Kripp has been feeding me constantly."

"He's like that. You have to be careful or else not mind having your pants let out."

"How are you . . . coming along," he said, stumbling to get the words out. "I mean, the police, do you think . . ."

I put my hands on his shoulders, pressed toward the middle, and he quit talking, blinked several times, and rumbled some phlegm around down in his throat.

"Leonard, your friend Arthur is the best there is," I told him. "He also hires quality help, that's me. You're not supposed to do anything but rest and get your strength back. OK?"

"I know," he said, weakly, "but I'm worried about Samantha. I should be at home with her."

"Save yourself the angst, Leonard. Has anyone sent for your clothes?"

"Yes, they're here. I just haven't had the energy to change."

"Why don't you do that. Take a shower, get into some different clothes, and join us for dinner. You'll feel better." He didn't answer; instead he shuffled away down the hall, his shoulders stooped, head bowed. What would be important enough to make an old man like Leonard pay blackmail? I should just ask him, but then it would be out and he might tell Roseman, in which case I'd have to produce the note and we'd all go to jail. Shit. Forget it. I stood and watched him disappear into his room, then headed for the kitchen.

Kripp was nowhere to be seen. I called the office upstairs and Sandra said Roseman was on the phone to somebody in Bermuda about extradition papers being filed in Nevada on a twice-convicted child molester who skipped bail. It was already a forty-minute call so I decided not to hold. I hung up and the phone rang almost immediately. "Well, I called to see if you were going to live or should I send your mother some flowers?"

"I'm OK, Jordan. It oozes a little now and then, but I'm healing."

"Fine. I was worried. You might have called. Do you have my gun?"

Nobody could make me laugh like Jordan. Gin or no gin, he was one of the quirkiest little men I'd ever known, and once on track, he was not to be deterred. "No, I didn't need your gun. I had a safe, uneventful trip home. It was as if the Lord were with me."

"Not that He would do you any good. If God lived in New York they'd break out His windows. You've got some messages here," he said, and I heard papers shuffle. "Marilyn called just after lunch, said she'd already tried the office and would call again later. Making some improvement there, huh?" he commented snidely. "Then we have Ira Katz who said he had information you might want . . . left his number. You know *bubee*, you shouldn't associate with so many Jews, it'll keep you out of the best clubs."

"Shocking."

"True."

"Not that I would ever want to join, but, you're right, one does like to be asked."

"Don't be a stranger," he said, and hung up.

Roseman came through the door before I could catch my breath, opened the fridge, poured himself a glass of milk, drank half of it, took the stool next to me, and came to rest with his elbows planted on the tabletop. "Good afternoon, David," he said, the thin white trace of milk above his lip disappearing with a wipe of his tongue.

"Good afternoon. I ran into Leonard just as I was coming in a few minutes ago. I think he had travel on his mind."

"That would not be advisable. I'll speak to him. How did he seem to you, physically I mean?"

"Oh, putting up a good front. It was actually a little depressing having to talk to him. Is he going home any time soon?"

"Samantha called to say he wasn't welcome," he said, swirling the last of the milk around the bottom of his glass. "She has essentially locked him out of his own house. I'm not surprised in the least. In fact, I rather expected it."

"Can she do that, legally I mean?"

"For the time being I think it is just as well that we let her. Leonard is not progressing as quickly as I had hoped he

71

might. How was your day?" he continued, pushing that subject aside.

"Very fruitful."

"Really? Good."

"Yes, I had my first chat with Leonard's adoring wife, I saw, but I didn't speak to, Randall Bergman, and I'm having drinks later with Banks Reid."

"Excellent. How did Samantha strike you?"

"Almost physically."

"Oh, dear," he said, mildly disapproving some unrevealed lack of social grace on my part that must have provoked such a response. Then he continued. "Have you spoken with the producer, Shelton Sharp? Do you know what he's like?"

"No, I haven't and don't, but I plan to drop in on him tonight after my drink with Reid. You want some more milk?" I asked, getting up for a soda.

"No, thank you. Perhaps you will also plan to change your approach, beginning tonight. More flies are caught with honey, as I am sure you are aware, and I would hate for Captain Florio to discover your beaten body in some dreary back alleyway."

He was kidding, but he was also serious. I made a mental note of his comment.

"Do you know what we're having for dinner?" he asked.

Not until then did I notice how still the kitchen was. No simmering pots, no aromas wafting out from the oven, no vegetable ends scattered over the center table used for salad assembly. I was about to comment on Kripp's absence when he burst through the door carrying two brown bags showing grease stains in several places. The smells were unmistakable.

"Sorry, Mr. Roseman," Kripp gushed, setting dinner down on the table. "The gas is out for about a three-block radius and Con Ed said it'll be noon tomorrow before they get the service back. I hope you don't mind, but I went out for Chinese." He began pulling out containers and setting them in front of us. "Hot and sour soup, chicken with snow peas, tofu in garlic, and sesame noodles."

72

Kripp started for the plates and bowls while I opened the cartons. Then we all sat down, turned on the color set attached to the wall above the pastry table, and watched the evening news.

I was making quick work of the tofu in garlic and half listening to Roseman debate Kripp on the relative merits of TV anchormen, specifically those for ABC and CBS, while they flipped back and forth between networks; I popped another can of soda and was starting to actually pay attention to their argument when the phone rang. I said I'd get it and, taking my soda with me, headed for the extension in the living room.

"Arthur Roseman's."

"You go see Samantha Craig this afternoon?" Florio asked with a voice that had smoked too many cigarettes.

"Yeah, we had a chat. How come?"

"We've got her boyfriend, Banks Reid, down here and he's pretty pissed about it. She let you inside? Everything kosher about that?"

"Sure."

"OK, just checking. Have to be careful with these self-important types, especially the ones with money."

"How long you going to keep him, Marc?"

"Couple of hours maybe. He's being a real asshole, so I might let him sit longer. Why?"

"I had an invitation from Samantha to join them for drinks later, but considering, I may let it slide."

"Good thinking," he said and laughed. "Save yourself some trouble."

"Thanks, I will," I said, feeling a slight sense of disappointment about not seeing Samantha Craig again. "Marc, since you've got him down there, maybe I could come by for a couple of questions myself?"

"Ah, that would be tough, you being private and all. Of course, you could come by, say hello to Marston, have some coffee, and be out front when he hit the street."

"Great, what time?"

"It's ten after six, so let's say eight o'clock or so."

"See you then," I said, and I hung up, thinking I still had time for a drink at The Burlington.

CHAPTER SIX

What I like best about Jordan's place is the view you get coming through the door. A solid mahogany bar runs down the wall on your right backed by a full mirror. The light from the room ricochets off the glassware into the mirror and back out onto the bar area giving a soft, hazy yellow glow to the front of the room. Tables here are sparse, and unnecessary, as most people prefer to maneuver for a bar stool. About halfway down the room a freestanding chair rail sets off the first sitting area where wooden tables, stained dark and marred with use, are arranged loosely. It's a casual dining area that blends in with the bar, creating a tavern atmosphere. Just past these tables is another partition, slightly less than head high, with swinging saloon doors. Here, white cotton tablecloths are dressed with candles and small flower arrangements. There's an upscale atmosphere and expanded menu but the same general air of comfort and ease. It's a great bar. A good tavern. A fine restaurant. And all three had Jordan, whom, incidentally, I didn't happen to see at the moment. Martin swept through from the kitchen just then with three plates and a pitcher of iced tea. I caught his eye.

"Where's Jordan?" I mouthed with upturned palms. Martin disappeared through the saloon doors and reappeared seconds later wiping his hands on a white bar towel.

"Jordan's finishing dinner with a friend of yours," he said, giving me a wink.

"Oh yeah? He or she?"

"She. I'll bring you a drink to the table."

"Fine, but make it a diet soda, OK?"

"Hmm" was Martin's disapproving response to that one, and I felt the need to say something in defense of my near alcoholism.

"I'm working. And besides, I barely made it through the afternoon," I said, heading for the saloon doors. Martin whirled, and I caught the last of his ". . . I've always liked working men myself."

"Martin!" I said over my shoulder, "stop that . . ." but he had swept out of sight.

Jordan and Rachel sat facing each other at the table like two riverboat gamblers who were about to accuse each other of cheating. The fact that they weren't having a good time was inconceivable to me, because Jordan could entertain the dead. What could be his problem with a beautiful, intelligent woman? I couldn't figure it.

"Hi guys," I said, pulling out a chair. "Just give me the general topic of your conversation and I'll jump right in."

"Self-awareness," Jordan said in a low voice with no humor. Rachel smiled and said hello, so it must have gone over her head, too.

"I stopped in to see you this afternoon," I said to her, trying to ignore Jordan's attitude. "I was in the neighborhood."

"Sorry, I wasn't there," she said, brushing back her hair with fingers tipped by brilliant red nails. "I work four nights on, five off, and I'm not due this evening till seven-thirty. I was just leaving, in fact."

"I wish I'd known you were here," I gushed, surprising myself. "I'd have joined you two for dinner."

"Tut, tut," Jordan said with obvious sarcasm that still,

seemingly, escaped Rachel. "You might not have been invited. Besides, we've had a lovely time without you. Emergency medicine is fascinating, and did you know she graduated from Stanford only twenty-four years after I did? She's virtually a child."

I glared at him, but he hardly noticed. "Insufferable occasionally describes you very well, Jordan," I said in my hard-ass voice. He laughed, damn him.

"Isn't emergency medicine an unusual choice for a . . ." I stopped myself, realizing how badly the question was coming out. The cross tensions at the table had me confused and a little flustered. "Let me rephrase that; why did you . . ." I reined in my tongue again, put both hands on the table, took a breath, and said. "How come a nice girl like you works in a place like that?"

"It's perfectly simple," she said, with a crisp professionalism that seemed to clash with the soft lights and silver place settings. "I decided, even before I went to medical school, that I didn't want to be dragged out of bed at all hours delivering babies. I'm a person of habit and schedule. When I work, I like to work. When I'm not working, I have better things to do than dispense prescriptions for marginal illnesses."

Whoa Mamma, somebody stop this truck, I thought.

"So, when I was approached by two of my colleagues about forming a partnership and contracting the emergency care at Lenox Hill, it seemed the thing to do."

"Wouldn't there be more profit in private practice?" I asked.

"Perhaps, but not a lot. Besides, I have my own money and, medically speaking, I know I wouldn't see the variety of problems I do in ER. The big plus to me, of course, is the schedule; set hours, known responsibilities."

"That's remarkable," I told her, stunned. I wondered if she actually ever made the connection between what she considered problems and the person who had them. "Really remarkable," I heard myself say. This couldn't possibly be the same woman I met earlier. She must have had a brain transplant or something.

"I didn't know doctors did that sort of thing. I thought you all had office hours and took referrals."

"It's practical is what it is," she stated categorically, then perhaps hearing her own strident tone, qualified herself. "At least to me."

I decided to give her the benefit of the doubt; she was too beautiful not to. I renewed my enthusiasm. "Well, for one so practical, it seems you would have called me instead of sitting through dinner with this guy." I jerked my head in Jordan's direction.

"I didn't expect to have dinner myself," she said, nodding across the table. "I stopped in to see this place in the light of day so I'd know if I could come back." Then smiling, she added, "With or without an invitation."

Something in the way she said "this place" made me resent the hell out of her last statement. It was like she was sizing up the joint to see if it met her criteria for acceptable places to be seen congregating. Jordan passed me a knowing look and I felt a sinking in my stomach.

"She had just settled into a cup of coffee," he explained, "when I introduced myself. After some persistent, and calcu-lated, probing, out popped your name."

"Well . . . good," I said, trying to mean it. I still wasn't ready to call it quits so I regrouped once more. "It occurred to me that I might have come off a little jerky this morning, but I did want to see you again." She didn't answer. Instead, she just looked at me with those enormous hazel eyes. "I mean, I understand your hesitation."

"I am cautious, you're right about that, but you didn't worry me," she said, confidently running a spoon through her coffee. "I have excellent instincts when it comes to people, and I rely on that a lot. My mother says those instincts will get me in trouble one day; I don't think so." She took a sip and narrowed her eyes at Jordan.

"Mothers often know best," I said.

"Rachel and I were talking about a logistical problem she has with her mother right before you came in," Jordan said.

I turned to Rachel. "Does she live in the city?"

"Yes, we live in Brooklyn Heights."

"Together?"

"Not yet. I'm trying to get her to move in."

"Ohh," I said slowly. "How old is she?"

"Seventy-one and very active. In fact," and here she showed the first glimmer of the person she'd been eighteen hours before, "that's the main reason I want her to come live with me. I worry she's going to lift something too heavy or fall off a step stool or any one of a thousand different things I think up every day."

"Is this strictly a matter of concern for her safety?" I asked, catching a sense of something else. Her immediate reflex was to laugh and fidget with her coffee cup.

"No, it's not, you're right. I think she gets very lonely, especially since Daddy died. And being in that house by herself, she's so isolated."

"Does she live far from you? Would it be a big move for her?"

"Next door."

"I'm not following this very well," I said, truly puzzled. "If your mother lives in the apartment next door to you, why would you want her to move in the first place?"

Martin came by with my soda and refilled Rachel's coffee. Jordan passed on the coffee but gave no indication that he was leaving any time soon. "Oh, it's not an apartment," she said, not wanting me to misunderstand, "it's the building next door." She shook some sweetener into her coffee. I shook myself. "Before my father died, he owned a number of apartment buildings in Brooklyn, two of which were town houses. They back onto the promenade, overlooking the harbor. I live in one and Ruthie, that's my mother, lives in the other."

"Those are wonderful views," Jordan said to me.

"Yes, spectacular," she agreed. "My sister and I were raised in the town house where Ruthie still lives and Dad rented the other one along with the larger apartment houses. Then I went to medical school, my sister married a lawyer from Poughkeepsie, and not long after that, Dad died." Her eyes went dark and she got quiet.

"That must have been a great loss," I said.

"It was." She sipped more coffee. "Anyway, when I finished my residency I came back here to work. I needed a place to stay, so I moved into the second town house."

"Right. And how did you get the other tenants out?" I asked derisively. "Bomb threats? There are still people living in the Plaza Hotel from World War Two under rent control, you know."

"The Plaza Hotel is not an owner-occupied residence with less than four tenants," she said pointedly. It was my turn to fall silent. "It took a while, but as the leases came up for renewal, I was able to make the rents unaccommodating enough that everyone finally left." Her dad would have been proud, I thought.

"Listen," I offered, "if you really want Ruthie as a roommate, ignore her for a couple of weeks. That'll get her attention."

"Oh, I couldn't do that," she said, shocked by the prospect. "I would miss her too much. We talk all the time. Why, when I come home from work, I go straight there for tea; I can hardly pass a day without seeing her. And there are so many things I do for her. No, two weeks is out of the question."

"Believe me," Jordan piped in, "Ruthie knows that."

"Maybe you should move in with her," I suggested.

"I want to live in my own house, thank you."

"So," Jordan said, "she lives here, her mother lives there, and it looks like that's the way it's going to stay."

"Why not knock a passageway through to her place from the second floor? You could always wall it back up if you wanted to sell or rent it in the future."

"What a wonderful idea!" she exclaimed. "I can't believe I didn't think of it myself."

"I'm sure you would have," Jordan assured her.

"You might not want to mention it," I added. "Just have the contractor show up one morning while you take her out for the day."

"Thank you for your suggestion," she said. "I'll call someone about it tomorrow." She glanced at her watch, finished her coffee, and said she needed to go. We all moved out toward the bar where Martin materialized with her overcoat. "Thank you for dinner, Jordan," she said, and they exchanged a firm handshake. Turning to me she added, "Good to see you again. Next time I will call first."

I started to tell her to save the quarter but said "Goodnight" instead. She turned and was gone.

"Some ego, huh?" I said after the door shut behind her.

"The kind that makes emperors. Disappointed?"

"Yeah, she wasn't even remotely like the same person."

"A lot of that veneer is her job," Jordan said. "I've known a lot of women just like her; not all of them doctors, but made of the same fiber." He gave my arm a wise pat. "In order to get her attention, you either need to encounter her from a stretcher, which you did, or resemble a two-hundred-milliliter beaker, which you don't, and that's just to get her attention. I don't know that you can expect to hold it under any circumstances."

"Well, she came down here, didn't she? She's looking for something. I'm assuming it was me. Maybe there's hope. She might warm up, come around."

Jordan laughed. "White man think with prick, not head."

"I've never thought Jay Silverheels was one of your better impersonations," I said, trying to hurt his feelings, "and why wouldn't she loosen up with the right encouragement?"

"Because of who she is."

I raised my eyebrows and ventured a guess, "Daddy's little girl?"

"You can bet she didn't get her driving ambition from playing intercollegiate field hockey."

"So?"

"So, she's spent her life becoming the son her father never

81

had. She's the head of the family. That sister in Poughkeepsie probably isn't even in the will. Rachel's so tied to that town house next door you'll never get her away from it."

"Why would I want to?"

"Because if you think breaking through her cool marble exterior is going to be tough, wait until Ruthie calls muster." I looked at him blankly. "You're not even Jewish, Ham! Even your name is against you." He sighed and decided to stop lobbying. "Besides, you're too tall for her."

"Naw, it'll be all right. She's too arrogant to know she's short."

"You've got a point there," he agreed. "Listen, don't let me talk you out of anything. Give it another try if you want."

"We'll see."

At that moment, the front door opened admitting an attractive, slight, short-nosed blond with her hair cut to suit a fifteen-year-old English schoolboy: long and floppy on top but trimmed short and close above the ears. She was wrapped in an array of colorful scarves that fell down the front of her coal-black, waist-length fur. In any situation Marilyn remained unmistakable in her expensive, ever-so-casual appearance. Jordan went out to take her hand and spun her onto the nearest bar stool. I stepped over and kissed her lightly.

"Herman," I said to the bartender, "may I have a gin martini, extra dry, straight up with a twist, and a vodka tonic please." Jordan disappeared among his customers.

"Thanks for the music," she said, easing out of her coat and shaking an armful of bracelets down off her wrist. Thin elegant fingers drew a cigarette out of a black clutch bag and I struck a match. "It was thoughtful of you. Feeling sheepish again? Cheers." She raised her glass.

I took the martini in a single gulp and pushed the empty across the bar where Herman deftly snatched it up for refilling. I looked at the woman next to me and wondered what it was I saw in this expertly customized female. Certainly not depth or substance. Wealth? Not really. Roseman paid me well, enough

82

for my needs and caprices. Plus I'd seen too many dead heirs and fallen magnates who chose to suck on a gun muzzle rather than face the perceived ignominy of reduced economics to be impressed by money, or the people who had it.

Love perhaps? I'd known Marilyn a long time. We'd been in and out of sorts, bed, and touch almost since day one. Always separating, reconciling. Christ, she was fun, engaging, effervescent, and ready to pick up and go at a moment's notice. I liked her. Loved her? I liked her. She was certainly a friend; an early morning drunken confidante. I'd never been in need of anything she hadn't tried to supply, with the noted exception of consistency.

We shared a lot of history, Marilyn and I. Maybe that was the basis of our relationship; shared experiences piled up over time. Not having to explain or affirm your existence for the benefit of someone new. The comfort in silence that comes from familiarity mingled with affection. Was that love or habit? She had shied as often as I had, and both of us with reason. Goddamn, I didn't have any answers. I drained my second martini.

"No, I wasn't feeling sheepish," I said, hailing Herman again. "I missed you, that's all. And I felt bad about fighting. So, failing to reach you by phone, I sent a messenger. You do remember hanging up on me don't you?"

"It was late."

"I've called later. What was wrong, you have somebody in bed with you? Embarrassed to talk?"

"I came here to complete a reconciliation, not start another china-smashing brawl."

Her voice was edgy and I noticed she'd avoided my last question. It hurt. Why did that surprise me? I decided to strike back.

"Kripp said he saw you in front of Altman's yesterday in the company of a very attractive young man. Was he on sale in the Men's Department? No? So you just took him home as a loaner to see if he clashed with the bedroom wallpaper. Is that it?"

"Stop, damn you! Stop!" She banged her empty glass on the

bar. She stared straight ahead, silent, momentarily angry, possibly even slightly hurt, while Herman made a fresh drink. Looking at her profile, I saw the color rising to her cheeks; those soft, slightly rouged cheeks.

"I'm sorry," I mumbled.

"The hell you are."

"I don't know why I let it get to me. Sometimes we're so happy and then at the least provocation you run off to spend ungodly amounts of money and drag home the first stiff dick you find. I mean, it's like a goddamn light switch; off and on, off and on."

The fight had been drained out of me. I gave up and slid my glass in Herman's direction. Marilyn took half her drink in the first gulp and set it down quietly, purposefully, in front of her.

"I'm glad you think it's worth saving," she said, crushing out her cigarette and reached for another. "I always am."

"Always am what?"

"Glad you call. Glad you send flowers. Glad"—I lit her Salem—"we make up. I don't know. Maybe it should be permanent."

"We've tried that," I reminded her, "not once, or twice, but three times. Four, if you count San Diego."

"Perhaps we didn't try hard enough. Perhaps we should try it five times, six, seven, whatever it takes until we get it right."

I ran a finger down her slender forearm, feeling its warmth, noting its softness. Maybe she was right. With a sudden motion, she came off the bar stool and took up her fur.

"I shouldn't have come because I can't stay and I need to."

I looked at her blankly.

"I mean, I want to stay and talk, but I have a date for the opera. I'm late already."

"That's unfortunate."

"I'm sorry." She was embarrassed.

"I've been a busy bee. Want to hear a tidy little tale of murder, intrigue, and derring-do?"

"I've been reading about it in the paper," she said, watching

84

the smoke curl off the end of her cigarette. "It sounds horrible."

"Which opera?"

"*Aida* at the Met."

"Who's your date?"

"No one you know. Harold Asher. I'll be home by twelve. Will you come by?" Her eyes were clear, unblinking, and as blue as the broken china that had littered her kitchen. Her voice was level, honest. It was like the 700th performance of a Broadway melodrama, familiar and well acted.

"I'd like that," I said quietly and on cue.

"Me, too." And she kissed my cheek. "To be honest, you're the only man who has never clashed with my wallpaper; no matter how often I change it."

I took her compliment like dirty money, walked her to the door, and got her a taxi. Suddenly, standing there on the sidewalk, watching the cab's taillights turn uptown, I felt exhausted.

"Enough is enough already, huh?" Jordan said from behind me.

"Yes, it is. I don't know which takes more out of me, my work or my personal life."

"Which is more rewarding?"

"I don't know the answer to that either, Jordan. Listen, I'm out of here."

"No time for another drink?"

"Can't. I have to meet Florio uptown in twenty minutes."

"Later then," he said with a wave and went back inside.

I reached the corner of Eighth Avenue and stood waiting for a taxi. There wasn't much traffic and I could see that finding a cab was going to be neither easy nor immediate.

I'd made the decision to walk a few more blocks when I noticed a late model Ford parked across the avenue. The rear, left-side door opened, allowing the streetlight directly above the car to reflect dully off a rifle barrel that was pointed toward me. I started moving left in the direction of the only cover available— a panel truck parked about fifteen feet away—when I saw the muzzle flash. I flinched, but nothing happened. I couldn't believe he'd missed. Not at this distance. I looked down to check myself and saw the prettiest feathered dart sticking through my breast pocket.

It was red and yellow and just the tiniest thing you ever saw. It reminded me of one of those free gifts you find in the bottom of a cereal box. I was amazed. My chin came to rest on my chest as I stared more and more intensely at the dart. Jungle Jim! Johnny Weissmuller! Tarzan and the apes! I couldn't even raise my hand to pull it out. As I focused on the multicolored feathers, I sank to my knees, confounded, confused, vaguely aware of running feet and hands reaching under my arms.

CHAPTER SEVEN

I came to feeling pretty uncomfortable.

A rope was tied around my ankles and twisted up behind me to my wrists, pulling my shoulders back so far they ached. It hurt, but I wasn't in agony.

I also didn't have any feeling in my left leg and my sight was a little blurred . . . like when you wake up after a blind drunk and realize you forgot to take out your contacts.

I didn't seem to be bleeding anywhere though, and that was a relief. All things considered, I was OK. Not great, but OK. On the minus side, I couldn't remember ever having been in a worse set of circumstances and I didn't have a clue as to how I was going to improve them. But I was OK, I kept telling myself, I was OK.

Curled up against the wall as I was, I figured the numbness in my leg was due to sitting on it for hours. The rope around my ankles had cut off the circulation to my feet and they, along with my hands, felt like water-filled balloons. It was getting to the point I couldn't make a fist any more. I figured it wouldn't be long before my arms joined my left leg in the land of no feeling.

The rope was tight, well tied, and felt like half-inch raw hemp. It took only a few tugs for me to realize that I wasn't going to get loose, and that I was definitely going to be here a while. I didn't have much struggle in me anyway. My stomach needed an Alka-Seltzer and the thought of lifting my head was more than I could deal with. Consequently, I threw up on myself.

The room was empty and three-quarters dark. The only light crept in from under the door, giving the walls an orange tint. Thinking about the light, I decided it came from a sixty-watt soft-glow bulb in a table lamp with an off-white shade. Failing that, my second bet was a naked hundred-watter stuck in an exposed ceiling fixture.

"Well done, Holmes!"

"Thank you, Watson, it was nothing really. Just a mental exercise to keep me alert."

The floor was hardwood and dusty. I could see footprints near the door disappearing into darkness as they approached me. The walls were Sheetrock and unpainted. There were no pictures, no windows, and only two electrical outlets, maybe three—I couldn't see part of the opposite wall. The room itself was about fifteen by twenty. A storeroom of some sort, I guessed. Well, what next? My accumulated observations and one of the Hardy Boys would get me out of this.

Christ! If I carried in my pockets all the stuff that the Hardy Boys did, I could get out of a federal prison in a wheelchair.

"Blow torch, Frank?"

"No thanks, Joe. I've got one right here in my pocket. Always be prepared is what Dad says, remember?"

The most disconcerting aspect of my captivity was the Chinaman. Actually, it was his gun. And I'm only guessing that he was Chinese. He was, without doubt, Oriental. Korean? Vietnamese? He might have been Malaysian. I couldn't see him well enough to guess. Not that he wasn't close by. He was hunkered down on a pair of straw sandals right next to me with the barrel of a gun propping up the left side of my cheek.

Nice gun. It looked like a .38-caliber long-barrel. He held it steady and slightly pressed into my skin. I guess he didn't want to miss if he had to shoot. He never blinked, and his dark eyes were set deep in an exceptionally thin face. He wore a faded red T-shirt and a pair of shorts I would have liked to see on a couple of women I knew. At least he was quiet and I had my thoughts to myself.

This was just too ridiculous. Hog-tied, doped, locked in a dark room with Charlie Chan's brother playing a silent part in *Apocalypse Now*. I rolled my head a little to the right and vomited again. The Chinaman inched forward, his sandals scraping lightly over the dusty floor, and nudged the gun barrel back into my cheek. I passed out.

CHAPTER EIGHT

Coming to for the second time, I found myself lying face down on the floor. The room was completely dark, suspending time. I could have been here a year for all I knew. Without moving, I took inventory and realized that I was no longer tied. The numbness in my legs had dissipated and my hands, though tingling and stiff, were free. I pushed up into a sitting position and almost gagged at the smell of myself. With some difficulty, I worked out of my suitcoat. It was stiff with dried vomit and beyond salvaging. I tossed it away from me. Taking a few deep breaths, I felt better; clear-headed, alert. I tried standing, slowly inching up the wall with my hands behind me for support. A couple more deep breaths and I was beginning to get optimistic about my prospects. There wasn't time to enjoy the relief, because the light in the outside room came on again. I couldn't hear any voices, but sensed movement outside the door.

I crouched against the wall directly opposite the door and waited. It swung open spilling light—blinding, dazzling light— into the room. I screamed at the top of my voice and lunged forward landing my forehead squarely in the middle of my little friend's chest. Momentum carried us back through the doorway and over the arm of an upholstered chair. We came to rest on the floor, our legs splayed out in a tangled web that kept both of us from getting up. A blue porcelain lamp crashed across my back and I pushed over a table to get more room. I came to my knees with a handful of red T-shirt and put my fist into the center of his face as hard as I could. He went limp. I lowered his body back to the floor and turned him loose. His head rolled to one side and a trickle of blood ran from the corner of his mouth.

I started looking for the .38. With the lamp gone, I had to rely on light from the hall and I couldn't see much. I was on my stomach by a couch when someone turned on the overhead light. Shit! Not enough time. At least now I could see the pistol—it was about halfway under the couch and pointed away from me. I rolled onto my back and looked toward the door.

"My, my, my, Randall Bergman. How unexpected. I wish I'd known. I'd have gotten my suit pressed, all this vomit." He didn't laugh. "You were on my list of things to do tomorrow. Couldn't wait, huh? It must be important."

"I want that note."

"Note," I said half aloud, thinking that in a Polo shirt and blue jeans he looked younger and very current. The gun really seemed to clash with his ensemble, though. "How did you know I had the note?"

"Samantha."

"Ah yes, little secrets. My mistake. You must be better friends than she let on."

"Samantha doesn't allow herself to have friends," he said, looking down at the Chinaman and back at me.

"Well, what do you suppose she does at Christmas?" I asked with a laugh and inched my hand closer to the gun.

"Cut the crap," he snapped. "And tell me where the note is." I stayed quiet. "Goddamn it, I didn't kill Peters and I can prove it. I admit to blackmailing Craig, but I'm not going to prison for it because some limp-dick detective like you stumbles onto something." He took a quick glance down the hall and then looked back at me expectantly.

92

For all his effort to emulate the great American hard-ass, Bergman couldn't keep the worry out of his face. He may have been greasy, like Samantha said, but I believed him when he denied killing Peters. And I also believed—even as he tried to keep his gun leveled at me—that he had never shot anyone. Unless I missed my guess, face to face with the lights on, he was going to hesitate. I was counting on it. Again he cut his eyes down the hall as though he was looking for someone, and wagged his pistol in agitation.

Suddenly I heard a door open. Bergman stepped back and made a half-turn, shouting, "It's about fucking time!" This was the best chance I was going to get, and I made a move for the gun. If the .38 had been a snubnose, it would have cleared the couch with no problem and I might have dropped Bergman where he stood. But the long barrel caught the frame with a loud thud that made him jump. He turned, saw the gun in my hand, brought his arm straight up, and fired twice.

The first bullet splintered one of the couch legs, sending wood fragments in all directions. The second one I felt tear into my lower rib cage as I rolled right and fired toward the doorway. Bergman ducked out of sight. I hadn't even been close.

I got to my feet, looking for cover. There wasn't any.

"Damn!"

Then three things happened at once: Bergman stepped back into the doorway, the Chinaman stood up, and I shot out the overhead light. Bergman fired into the half-lit room, hitting the Asian in the small of his back. He fired again, but I was lost in the shadows just inside the door to my former cell. The Asian crashed to the floor, lifeless. Bergman froze for a second, undecided on his next move. I shot twice without aiming and hit him in the head. He dropped to his knees, then slumped forward onto the hardwood floor. My ears rang in the silence, my side hurt, and I was wheezing like an old man at a porno flick, but I was still standing. Me and Elton, still standing. I was also bleeding badly and realized I didn't have long to find out where I was and get help.

A telephone. I needed a telephone. I didn't know what path the bullet had taken. I was rolling when Bergman hit me; I didn't know if it had traveled down through my intestines or up, across my stomach. I knew it hurt to breathe and I knew I needed to hurry; I was already getting light-headed. I wasn't frightened, yet, just gearing up to some serious apprehension.

I stepped over Bergman's body into the hallway. Christ, what a mess, I thought looking down at his bloodied head. I didn't want to think about what my stomach was like. The pain that I felt told me it wasn't good, and that was enough.

The hallway had a concrete floor and ran about thirty feet directly to a fire exit. There was a short flight of steps just inside the door, leading up to the right. The exit was glass paneled and opened onto an alley that seemed gray and cold in the late afternoon light. It was filled with boxes, cans, and garbage dumpsters. The street was at least another two hundred feet away. I'd never make it, so I decided to climb the stairs, slowly.

After six or seven steps, I pushed open a door and entered semidarkness. When my vision adjusted, I recognized the interior of a nightclub. There were tables, chairs, a stage, curtained windows, and a bar. There would be a telephone somewhere near the cash register. The ten feet over to the polished oak flattop took forever and I wasn't steady on my feet. I reached for the bar, missed, and did a half turn on my way to the floor. I ended up flat on my back with a restricted view of the painted tin ceiling; an interesting design, those old things. You can buy them now, reproductions of the original tin plate. The stench of stale beer and accumulated grime was overwhelming. I saw the telephone just above me and a little farther down the bar. A Princess phone. How cute. Pink, too. I slid down the floor, pushing with my feet, and reached for the receiver. The numbers lit up like a pinball machine in my hand and I punched the buttons wondering if it was as difficult to get a replay from AT&T as it was from Bally.

"Marc Florio," I said as soon as the phone clicked. I tried to relax.

"Homicide, Sergeant Davis." The voice was strong, eager.

"Sergeant, is Florio there?"

"No sir, he's not back from dinner. May I help you?"

"Yes, I've been shot, badly I think, and two other men are dead. I need help quickly."

I could hear the sergeant clearing his desk for a place to write. "Your name." His tone had changed completely; still crisp and clear, but now professionally concerned.

"David Hamilton."

"Where are you, Mr. Hamilton?"

"I don't know." The pause bespoke his confusion. "Scout's honor," I said, and I held up my three-fingers salute in the dark. "I just came up from the basement. It's a bar or nightclub of some sort. It's closed and I don't know where it is." I was already tired of talking. The explanation was going to kill me.

"John!" Davis shouted on his end. "Lieutenant, come over here . . ." his hand covered the mouthpiece and I heard bits and pieces of a garbled exchange.

"David, this is Marston," said a now-familiar voice. "What the hell do you mean you don't know where you are?"

"I don't John." I had to stop for a breath. "I've been drugged and tied up, and locked in a room . . ."

"Ham!" he shouted, "you're fading. Speak up!"

"I just got out and had to shoot Randall Bergman to do it. There's also another guy . . . wow, John, I'm not doing so good."

Marston told Davis to bring up Bergman's file on the computer, check his business addresses, and then get the phone company on another line. He came back to me. "David, what's the phone number. Read it off the receiver."

"There isn't one. I've looked," I said, the ridiculousness of the situation getting to me. "It's a silly-assed little pink Princess phone that doesn't even have a slot for a phone number."

"OK, just stay calm," he urged. "Now look around. How about a sign on the wall, some matches, another telephone?"

"I'm flat on my back behind the bar, John. I don't think I can

95

get up." With my left hand, I searched the shelves near me, pulling down ashtrays, towels, two packs of condoms, swizzle sticks of a useless generic variety, and finally a carton of matches. "The Velvet Mace, Ninth Street and West Side Highway, open ten P.M. until, and then there's a place for my phone number."

"Shut up!" he said, changing gears and reading the address to Davis. "How badly are you hurt?"

"A bullet across the stomach from the right side," I said. "No exit. I'm dizzy, bleeding heavily, and I have trouble concentrating. This pissant phone is even getting heavy."

"OK, don't hang up whatever happens. The ambulance is on its way and St. Vincent's is close. Just stay with us."

"They can't get in, John."

"Bullshit! The fire department will take care of the door."

"I can hear them already," I told him as the first sounds of the sirens reached me. "How long have I been here?"

"Jesus, Ham, nobody's seen you since Wednesday."

"Wednesday? . . ."

"Today's Friday! Jordan's a wreck. Marilyn and Roseman aren't far behind. Listen, don't talk anymore. I'm going to leave Davis on this end and I'll meet you at St. Vincent's. We'll go over everything there. Hang on a sec." He laid down the phone and I turned my attention to the approaching sirens. They were very close now. I took another deep breath wishing them Godspeed. But if it took an hour, I wasn't going to lose consciousness. Not this time. I wasn't going to take any more shit. This time around I was going to be bigger than the Duke. I was going to be Robert Ryan and William Holden rolled together.

A car screeched to a halt outside. Doors slammed, more sirens arrived, and suddenly a window shattered, setting off a clanging, ear-splitting alarm. Light spilled in, wiping out the muted atmosphere that cloaked the Velvet Mace. What a dump, as Bette said. Good lighting in a place like this is definitely a fashion don't; cracked walls, and soot and tobacco stains covered everything. Even the neon beer signs showed a yellow tint in the unfiltered headlights.

Finally they were beside me. Cold, proficient hands cut away my shirt, inserted an IV, and fired penlights into the back of my eyes. I made a concerted effort to relax, not to stiffen or yell as they lifted me from behind the bar onto a stretcher. Someone finally shut off the alarm and I made it outside with only two winces and one "Jesus Christ." As I was loaded into the ambulance, I apologized to the attendants about the way I smelled. The black paramedic beside me waved it off.

"You're OK man," he said. "Believe me, you ain't nothing compared to some of the shit we pick up off the street."

I took him at his word and tried to enjoy the ride.

CHAPTER NINE

I spent the next two hours in surgery—not that I remember any of it, but after I came to I had a chat with a doctor who told me exactly how the bullet had traveled through my stomach, stopping an inch shy of making an exit; he'd left and I was still mulling over his verbal diagram when my first visitor arrived. Florio came through the door of my hospital room like a fat kid on a skateboard, banging into the door frame and then slamming into the medicine cart before coming to rest at the foot of the bed. He paced a little trying to get a hold on his temper. Marston was about ten seconds behind him and came straight to the bedside, reaching for his pen.

"Hey, Ham," Marston said, his voice friendly. "How do you feel?"

"Remarkably well, thanks," I said, "considering I have one tube in my arm and another up my nose. What's wrong with our friend?" Marston rolled his eyes.

"You shot one of my goddamn suspects," Florio steamed. "That's what's wrong. Jesus! Did you have to kill him? Was it absolutely necessary to blow his head off?"

"I didn't have time to think about it, Marc," I said. "We

weren't filming a Randolph Scott western. He wasn't just going to shoot me in the left arm and leave me there to be found by the posse. I fired without aiming, and strictly out of desperation." I didn't sound too convincing, even to myself, but what I wanted to say was that taking a man's life didn't come easy.

The door eased open and Roseman poked in his head. "Join you?" he asked civilly. Roseman walked to the bed and shook my hand. The relief in his face was unmistakable.

"Shit, forget it," Florio said, ending our exchange and sitting down on the end of the bed. He lit a cigarette. "Tell me about it. Everything you remember." And I did. Marston took notes.

I took the opportunity to get Bergman's blackmail story out in the open. I fit in everything I knew short of naming Peters; that fact was still too damning. As long as Leonard was still in imminent danger of going to jail, Peters could play only one part: a corpse.

I also didn't mention the note. With both Peters and Bergman dead, its importance had been diminished. Not totally, because Leonard could have killed Lane to save some dark secret. But I didn't think so. As far as I was concerned, the note, and my lifting it, had become superfluous. I'd been wrong before, would be again. I just had a feeling.

"So the only time you spoke to Bergman was right before you shot him," Florio stated.

"That's right. I literally ran into him earlier that day outside Samantha's, but we didn't do anything other than exchange excuse-me's. And if I hadn't just spent the morning poring over his photograph, I wouldn't even have recognized him. Is there anything to the Buick I saw being the one Bergman owned?" I asked.

"Didn't pan out," Marston said. "No tag number and the garage attendant said it had been out for several days."

"So we can forget about blue Buicks," Florio rumbled. "Got any ideas on why he nabbed you?"

"Maybe he doesn't like my religious affiliations."

"That's funny," Florio commented.

100

"OK, how about to keep me off the blackmail angle?"

"Why would Bergman have thought you knew anything about the blackmail?" Florio asked, getting testy.

"A miscalculation on his part."

"Bullshit!" Florio snapped.

"Bergman must have figured Leonard told us everything," I persisted. "It was in the papers that he was staying with Arthur and what good friends they are. Bergman just assumed too much."

"Like Banks Reid assumed you forced your way into Samantha's place?" Marston suggested.

"She might have told him I did."

"We asked her," Florio said, "she didn't."

"You believe her?" I asked. Florio shrugged. "My feeling is that Reid's worried I'm going to incriminate his sweetheart, that's all."

"He's worried about more than that," Florio said. "We didn't have him in the office five minutes before he admitted to being at the apartment the night of the murder. Said Peters was dead when he and Samantha got there. So it's the same alibi, only different."

"Well what else did he say?" I asked, getting excited.

"Nothing," Marston chipped in.

"Nothing?" I echoed.

"He suddenly lost his voice," Florio said, adding, "He seemed torn between telling us his life's story and keeping his mouth shut till his lawyer got there."

"Maybe he doesn't lie very well," I suggested.

"Yeah, maybe," Florio scoffed.

"Did Samantha back him up?" I asked him.

"Faced with Reid's admission," Marston answered, "she couldn't do much else."

"She hemmed and hawed a little," Florio said, "but finally admitted they arrived at the apartment around eleven-thirty, found the body, and being uncertain what to do, left again almost immediately."

101

"And that's it?"

"Yep," Florio answered, clapping his hands, "two little birdies, frightened but very innocent."

"Any guesses on what else Reid might have said if his nerves hadn't failed him?" I asked.

"Perhaps he's involved with the blackmail," Roseman offered.

"I doubt it," Florio said curtly. "The nervous types don't usually go in for that." Arthur, who I knew was trying to help as much as his position would allow, looked abashed by Florio's blunt manner, and Florio softened his tone. "Listen, I'm sorry your friend was getting a double squeeze from his wife and Bergman, but blackmail's not homicide and right now we can't prove any of it. We'll work that angle as part of the overall investigation," he said, "but it's not priority."

"I understand completely, Captain. Thank you."

I couldn't have wished for more. This way, Bergman and his blackmail became one more facet in an already confusing case; something to be followed up in due course. No priority meant more time for me. Maybe just a day, but it might be enough to keep Florio from jerking Craig out of Roseman's and tossing him behind bars. My immediate objective was not to prove Leonard innocent but rather to generate enough motive on the part of everybody else so that when Florio did find out that Peters was in on the blackmail—and I was sure he would eventually—his first thought wouldn't be Leonard Craig.

"Captain," Roseman began, "on the basis of what you have just heard, have you changed your view of my client's alleged involvement in the death of Lane Peters?"

Florio dropped his cigarette into my water glass. It hissed, sank, and bobbed back to the surface. "Yes, I have to admit I have," he said. "I'm not sure where it leaves us, but it does change things."

Marston glanced up from his notebook and I asked him, "You ever get down to see Shelton Sharp?"

"Yeah, I did. He's a strange bird. Seemed genuinely upset

about Peters' death, which, among the crowd we're dealing with, is surprising."

"I wonder if he's more concerned about the death of a friend or the disappearance of his financial backing," I said. "No Petey, no money, no trippy to the big Broadway."

"Too late now, anyway," Florio said, getting to his feet. "They closed last night. Come on, let's go. Ham, I'm glad you're back. You had a lot of people worried. See you tomorrow." Marston followed him out pausing just long enough to give me a thumbs-up.

Roseman pulled a chair alongside the bed and sat down. It took him a moment to get settled. "I feel comfortable that Leonard may no longer be the Captain's leading suspect." He whispered as though he thought the room might be bugged. "But I'm not confident enough to suggest we drop our end of the inquiry. Agreed?"

"Sure. Have we talked about a raise recently?"

"No, but I'm sure we shall," he said with a faint smile.

"The only trouble I see with proceeding is where do we go from here?" I told him. "Which of the dynamic duo do you think is going to talk? Samantha's hard as nails and Reid gets too much legal advice—no offense, sir." He nodded and I added in exasperation, "Anybody who might have had an inclination to talk is dead."

"Bergman's death may indeed have changed the chemistry of things," Roseman said. "A second chat with both of them is in order as soon as you've seen this Sharp fellow." He looked at me plaintively. "When will you be well enough to leave here?"

"I don't know," I said. "When I spoke to the doctor, he didn't mention a time frame. If I could stand up, I'd leave now. But speaking of medical opinions," I added, seeing Rachel at the door, "let's ask this doctor."

"I don't know whether to hug you or slap your face," she said seriously, pressing her palm flat against my forehead as though I was twelve and needed to be checked for a fever. "I don't think I want to know you any better than I already do." Her statement

103

was frank, but her hand was warm and soft; so were her eyes. Maybe Jordan was right—I'd do well with this woman as long as I was in the hospital. This was the role she played best. She was in charge, relaxed, comfortable in her expertise: the healer, the absolute authority. Looking into her face, I saw concern, worry, and a few other peripheral emotions I couldn't catch right off. I was still hopeful. She might have a rough edge or two left on the social development side of her personality, but this was the second gesture on her part: first the Burlington, now here. The reach was tentative, the intent was clear. I wasn't about to slap her hand.

"Excuse me, Arthur. I don't believe you two have met." And I introduced Rachel to Roseman, explaining that she usually patrolled the halls up on 77th Street. They exchanged hellos and then she turned back to me.

"How are you?" she asked.

"We were hoping you could tell us," Roseman said. "With indications, of course, as to his possible length of stay."

"What?" she said, as if surprised by the question. Then her color started to rise. "Oh, I see. Have you seen the X rays?" Neither Roseman nor I spoke and she didn't slow down. "You can't possibly leave this bed for ten days. That bullet caught the last two ribs on your right side and was deflected horizonally across your stomach, barely missing the large intestines. As it is, the hole in your stomach won't heal for a month and if the bullet had been anything larger than a .32, you'd be dead! Do you understand that! Dead!"

Having effectively put the two of us in our places, she continued. "I'm sure they'll have you moving some soon, maybe tomorrow or the next day, but nothing too strenuous that might tear the stitches. You just stay put for a while." She glared at us.

"Maybe I could transfer to Lenox Hill so you wouldn't have so far to travel during visiting hours," I suggested lightly. She didn't laugh.

"You stay put," she said, bending down to look me straight in the eye. "I'll make the trip."

104

I picked up her hand from the sheet beside me and she offered no resistance as I wrapped my fingers around hers.

"Any luck with your mom?" I asked casually.

"Oh yes." She lit up like a movie marquee. "I took your advice and had the contractor come and do the work. I think Ruthie was very pleased."

"But of course she didn't show it."

"Not a smile, not a word," she said. "It'll take a year to get rid of the plaster dust, though, and the construction workers—what slobs. They tracked in a ton of dirt, and everything they touched got smudge marks—the walls, the lamps, nothing was spared."

"Terrific," I said laughing. "You'll have to invite me over sometime so I can pass beneath the arch."

"I was thinking I might do that very thing."

"Something reckless and totally out of character?"

"Right," she said, and she laughed with honesty.

Roseman, who basically had been ignored during this exchange, cleared his throat.

"Excuse me," he said. "I thought I was about to be embarrassed."

"Relax, Arthur. Propriety prevails." He seemed to take comfort in my assurance.

"I have to go," Rachel announced, and looking at me she added, "I just stopped in to make my own observations."

"Any conclusions?"

"Yes, you'll be fine." From the tone of her voice I wasn't sure whether she was pronouncing a medical opinion or sizing me up for an audience with Ruthie. Encouraging, very encouraging.

The door breezed open as a stainless-steel tray followed by a tin-heart nurse came in. Pill time, shots optional. Roseman and Rachel began gathering their coats to leave.

"I wish you guys would stay."

"Can't," they said in unison, Roseman rising. "Dr. Carlson, may I offer you a ride home?"

"Thanks, I'd appreciate that."

"Kripp's here?" I asked, taking a white pill cup from the nurse; a prim, well-scrubbed, unobtrusive woman in her early twenties.

"Yes, but I'm afraid he's double-parked," Roseman explained. "I've promised him tomorrow morning off. He'll be here then."

"Thanks for coming," I said. "Both of you."

"I'll stop in again, when I can," Rachel said, bending over to kiss me lightly on the forehead.

"Don't move," I said, grabbing her wrist. "I'm trying to look down your blouse."

She stepped back, smiled that beautiful smile, and said, "See you." She turned and walked out into the hall.

Roseman held back a little and in a whispered aside said, "You realize, of course, that ten days in this institution is completely out of the question. It is imperative you be on your feet at the first possible moment."

"Yes," I said, and I swallowed a blue-coated tablet as the nurse swabbed a spot on my upper arm with alcohol and reached for her needle.

"I'll call," he said and was about to let the door go when the phone rang.

"Wait, it might be for you," I said, answering. The needle went home with a sting as I said, "Hi, Marilyn. Sorry I missed you the other night, but have I got a story to tell." Roseman waved, the nurse sighed, and I started at the top.

CHAPTER TEN

My first full day in St. Vincent's started when Jordan arrived along with my breakfast tray at 6:40 A.M. He knew one of the male nurses on my floor and thus was exempt from the limitations of regular visiting hours. Jordan attached himself to the foot of my bed and proceeded to preach, prance, and tell me funny stories. Then he left, promising to return. Marilyn called back to remind me that she couldn't stand hospitals and would visit when I got home. Ira called, torn between friendship and journalistic duty. Kripp stopped by as promised. Marston checked in, too. Florio called not long after his lieutenant to ask why the phone was so goddamn busy all the time and to see if I needed anything. He also wanted to know if I'd sign a typed statement if he had it brought by. I reminded him I'd been shot in the stomach, not the left hand, and would be happy to sign anything he thought important. He said he'd send it over.

Martin sent flowers as did Sandra and the office staff. Roseman checked in. My mother called from Virginia to see if she needed to come up or send my father. I said I was fine, travel wouldn't be necessary, and I'd write later.

Ira called again, just after lunch, to confirm information

about Bergman's death that was going into the next day's edition. I refused to be quoted, which made him mad, but I always refuse to be quoted. He knows that. I hate being in the papers. I'm very happy with a low profile. So we fought the same old battle once more and toward the end of our discussion I had the bad taste to imply that the press was coming down pretty hard on Florio and the department.

"As far as the *Times* is concerned," he said curtly, "this story is great metropolitan news, and I think we've played it pretty straight. But I have to admit the tabloids are kicking the shit out of your pals, and why the hell not? It was four days ago that Peters was killed and nothing has happened. No arrests, no warrants, nothing.

"Goddamn, Ham," he said starting to hit his stride, "monied Manhattan is shocked, adulterers everywhere are terrified, and Florio's troops are doing a bad imitation of the Marx Brothers. What can I tell you, it's been an easy week for headlines."

"Florio's a good man, Ira."

"He's an Italian prima donna in a five-hundred-dollar suit and he's not up to speed on this one."

"It's an unusual case," I tried to explain. "Things aren't progressing normally."

"If you mean people are dying at breakneck speed, you're not saying it."

"Goddamn, Ira, ease off! And when, now that I think of it, did I become your primary source?"

"Bullshit!" he said, his temper rising. "Ham, you've been front-page Metro for three days now. So don't give me any more of this low profile crap. The only reason your mug isn't right next to Florio's is because you and Roseman don't have a Public Affairs Department and aren't required to issue periodic statements to the press."

"Well, thank God for private enterprise," I shouted into the phone.

That shut him up and for a moment the two of us breathed heavily at each other.

108

"Why won't you confirm these facts?" he asked, backing off, but adding, "You did, after all, kill the man."

"Fuck you!"

"Come on, I've covered your ass often enough. You owe me this."

"And I've given you enough inside dope to get my license permanently revoked and my friendship with Florio thrown out the window."

"You're right," he said. "OK, forget it."

"Thanks," I said, calming down. "I'll stay in touch."

"You do that," he said. "Oh, before I forget, you might want to talk to a kid named Paul Hemp."

"Who's he?"

"A part-time assistant on that production of *Macbeth*. He wasn't one of the original crew, but came in later, after the murder. He's a real talker—gossip mostly—but he may give you something useful if you wade through enough of the shit. He seemed to know a lot about everyone at the theater, anyway."

"Thanks, I'll call him."

"He's in the book or try the Cherry Lane Theatre on Commerce Street."

After Ira hung up, I had a weak moment when I felt bad that I hadn't told him about Bergman's blackmail, and maybe if we hadn't argued I would have. Let it pass, I told myself. He'll get it from Florio later.

By the time Jordan arrived, around four o'clock, I was worn out. We talked briefly, I spoke to Roseman twice, and a little past eight I told the switchboard to disconnect the phone. Jordan tucked me in, and by eight-thirty I was asleep.

He came back the next afternoon, got a nurse to unhook my gastro/nasal tube from the pump, stuffed the loose end inside the breast pocket of my nightgown, and took me for a slow, shuffling walk down the hall. With one hand I gripped the metal stanchion that rolled along holding my IV bag. My other hand rested on Jordan's shoulder. We made the first fifty feet in comfortable silence, turned around, and started back to the room. By the time he helped me back onto the edge of the bed, I felt I had gone ten rounds with Sonny Liston. I rolled back and slowly stretched out. Jordan jerked the covers up under my chin and reconnected the NG tube to the bedside pump. He was about to say something when a knock at the door preceded its opening. The nurse came in with a stunning arrangement of fresh cut flowers and I knew immediately where they had come from.

"They are absolutely gorgeous," Jordan said, pulling out the card and handing it to me. "Marilyn certainly knows how to get her money's worth." The comment stung and he knew it. His voice didn't carry the same edge when he added, "I'll put them over here with the others she sent."

"Jordan, I . . ."

"I'm sorry, David. I should apologize to you; that was uncalled for." He set the flowers down and picked up his coat. "The doctor said you'll be able to have some liquids by mouth soon. I'll try to slip in with something from the kitchen. Between Kripp and me, we'll get you out of here in record time."

"I can hardly wait," I mumbled.

"You can hardly keep your eyes open. A nap would do you good." He crossed to the bed and took my hand.

"Thanks for coming," I said, drawing strength from his grip.

"Don't mention it."

I fell asleep.

CHAPTER ELEVEN

They buried Lane Peters the next morning following a private ceremony at St. Bart's. The funeral had been delayed by the autopsy and his family's inability to get to New York right away. They decided to bury him here instead of taking the body back to Kansas, which I guess was a gesture of some sort on their part.

I tried several times to reach Florio to see if he had attended the services, but he was out—working on some drug-related double murder, according to the sergeant on duty, hardly an excuse. Marston also wasn't available. Then I tried to get in touch with the Hemp kid Ira had told me about. No luck there, either. I spoke to his answering machine twice and to three different people at the theater, but never got him.

Jordan came by just after lunch and we took another stroll down the hall. Afterward, I slept off and on, read what there was about Peters's funeral in the afternoon papers, and tried to work the crossword puzzle. In addition to the Peters obit, there were a couple of stories about Bergman's death and how he had gone down in a blazing gun battle with me. A ten-inch sidebar about my association with Roseman made me sound like someone out of a Mickey Spillane novel, and the picture they used must have come out of my high school annual.

The Chinaman who died along with Bergman was identified as Eddie Chang, a legalized American citizen with a Mott Street address. We'd never even spoken and now he was dead. And that face, God it was thin. I tossed the papers and rang the nurse for another pill.

The next day Jordan's schedule prevented him from coming by, and with Kripp unable to break away, the high-water mark of my day remained the removal of the stomach tube. It wasn't pleasant having three feet of polyvinyl tubing extracted from my nasal cavity, but I felt human again, almost. I was ready for some diversion when Florio dropped in unannounced. He was by himself and arrived to find me propped up with my dinner still stretched across my lap. The meal was another of those prefab culinary delights that I'd been unable to come to terms with; I was especially deterred by the film that arrived on top of the mashed pears.

Florio offered to move the tray and I gladly accepted. He made a few light comments about hospital food and wandered around the room poking at the flowers. His heart wasn't in his humor and he looked tired. Finally, he settled at the foot of the bed, threw one leg up on the covers and propped the other in a chair. I clicked off the television and gave him my full attention.

"Cigarette?" he offered, lighting one himself.

"No thanks. They took that tube out of my nose this afternoon and it feels like I've got strep throat; real scratchy and raw, so I'll pass."

"You don't mind if I . . ." And he raised his cigarette.

"Help yourself." I got the feeling this visit was more personal than professional so I let the time pass. Whatever it was, I could see him going over it in his head. Sometimes a guy just needs a place to sit. After a minute or two I tried a question.

"Kids still raising hell at home?"

"Huh?" He was somewhere else entirely. "Oh, no. I mean, yeah; they've taken up bobsledding."

112

"You're kidding. In September?"

"Not that kind. They take their sleeping bags—those nylon jobbers—and they get inside these things up at the top of the stairs, shove off, and pile into each other at the bottom. . . . I keep expecting them to go right through the Sheetrock." He lit another cigarette and chuckled to himself. "I gave them a big speech last night about going down one at a time. You'd've thought I asked them to walk on broken glass."

"Meaniac."

"Right." He laughed. "They just go so fast, Jeez."

He smoked in silence for a minute and then completed his thought. "I love those kids, Ham. They drive me crazy at times, but I love them."

"Of course you do." He was quiet again. "So what else is on your mind?" He looked from me to his cigarette. "You keep drifting off to somewhere. What's up? The Peters case?"

"More or less."

"Which one?"

"More."

"Want to talk about it?"

"Not especially. I've talked to my detectives. I've talked to my boss. I've talked to the commissioner. I'm pretty talked out."

"Have you also been talked to?"

Turn key, push button for ignition. Florio came to life like a Wood Brothers' Ford on race day.

"Goddamnit," he shouted, coming off the bed and losing his cigarette in a wild hand motion. "I don't need some asshole administrator telling me I'm not upholding the image of the department."

"That's right out of the Bureaucrats Handbook of Clichés, Marc. I can't believe someone actually said that to you."

"The Chief. This afternoon. I almost quit on the spot. I couldn't believe it. I've been a cop for twenty years and I've known the son-of-a-bitching Eddie Harter since day one. I don't need him telling me that kind of shit. And what does he expect

113

me to do? Answer that for me. All of the suspects in the case are standing pat with alibis to back them."

Florio stopped talking, stooped, snatched his cigarette off the floor and gave it a couple of tentative puffs to make sure it was still lit. Then he sucked the smoke deep into his lungs.

"You know it was politics," I said. "The Chief caught hell because the Commissioner caught hell because—"

"That's not the point!" he said still pissed. "I'm not some rookie right out of the academy. I know my job and I damn well know my responsibilities."

"Did you tell him that?"

Florio dropped the butt of his cigarette onto the floor and ground it under the toe of his shoe.

"No, I didn't," he said quietly. "It wasn't the time. The commissioner and the mayor were both there, and you're right, it was only politics. But the next time I see him down at Central Booking or in the squad room, I'm going to crawl all over his bony little ass. I deserved his fucking support. Not that it's worth much, but he could have made an effort."

The storm was over. Florio sat back down on the bed and lit a fresh cigarette. He felt much better; it was evident in the way he struck the match. He didn't say anything for a bit and when he did speak, the subject caught me off guard.

"How come you work for Roseman? And don't give me the blah, blah, bullshit about he pays well. You could be independent, set up your own office, make some real cash."

"But think of all the photographs I'd have to take of cheating husbands, may God save me." Florio laughed in appreciation. "At least this way I'm assured of being able to retire with a good heart, move to Miami, and run the security team for some dog track."

"Ha! I like that," he boomed. "You can be such a jerk sometimes, but I like that."

"I'm more serious than you think, Marc. I'm not money-motivated like some people. I think I realized that when I went to work for Tim Ellerton at the medical examiner's office. That

114

was a great job. The people down there were terrific and by that I mean they were committed, interested, and interesting. Something was going on all the time. If the job at the *Times* hadn't come along, I'd still be there."

"But it did come along."

"And when I took it, I stepped a little deeper into the sewer." Florio tossed off the comment with a shrug of his shoulders. I hadn't meant to step on his toes. "Downtown," I explained, "I only saw the aftermath of violence; the bodies, the bullet holes, the knife wounds. I saw them in a sterile environment under perfect lighting that masked where they'd come from, and I seldom thought, other than abstractly, why they were there in the first place.

"As a cop reporter, I got to see the whole sordid mess; everything from blood-drenched car trunks to charred bone fragments in apartment house furnaces. It made my guts roll over, but it also made me appreciate what you do virtually every day of your life. And you're a young man, Marc. It's a long way to retirement. How could you help but love your kids? If you're honest with yourself, you'll admit they have more to do with keeping you sane than driving you crazy." He didn't respond.

"Well, I knew I wasn't going to last longer than a couple of years with the paper, and I couldn't go back to Thirtieth Street—I mean, having one job ruined the other." Florio nodded understanding. "So when I heard Roseman was looking for a gofer, I applied. I wasn't sure about the work, but I was certain about the man. I'd watched Roseman in court, seen the way he tried cases. He was intelligent and dedicated. Do you know where Kripp came from?" I asked rhetorically. "Special probation program for first offenders. Roseman's always doing something like that. Most of those lawyers down there are hustling their asses off to make the next payment on their BMW, but Roseman's got that Mother Teresa, they're-at-your-feet, bend-down-and-do-something attitude. That's what motivates me. That's why I work for him; I feel like I'm doing something worthwhile, making a difference. I have to put up with a little blood and guts, but that I can do." I stopped

115

for a breath. "I might well ask you the same question about why you haven't gone private," I said.

He took a pull on his cigarette and smiled. "Because you and I are looking at the same dog track in Miami." We both laughed.

"Good answer, good answer. You want to watch 'Star Trek'?" I asked. Florio squinted at me through the cigarette smoke. "I'm serious. It's the episode where Spock goes on trial for treason. You'll enjoy it."

"You've seen it, then?"

"Of course I've seen it," I said, turning the TV back on. "I've seen them all about four times each. There's a soda machine in the stairwell by the nurse's station." He stood up, crushed out his smoke, and reached in his pocket for change.

"You want one?"

"No, thanks, I'll stick with my juice." Good, I thought to myself as he headed out the door. With luck I can get him to stay for the Knicks game at eight. I turned up the volume.

CHAPTER TWELVE

To Rachel's consternation, the nursing staff's amazement, and Roseman's relief, I left St. Vincent's Hospital the day after Florio's visit. I rode down to the lobby in a wheelchair armed with pain pills and copious instructions, and frightened by the threat of a colostomy bag from an irate resident specializing in internal medicine. I even needed Kripp's help to get into the car, but I knew that in twenty minutes I would be home.

On the ride uptown, I reflected on my time abed and decided it did more to worsen my condition than to improve it. Norman Cousins was right, a hospital is no place to get well.

No matter how bad I felt, I took courage from the sight of Leonard Craig. He was seated in Roseman's living room when Kripp and I arrived. He looked up as we came in. Roseman had said he'd been drinking heavily, and I noticed a glass already in his hand and it was barely the P.M.

"Leonard," I called to him, "how are you?" His head turned slowly in response to my voice. There was no sign of recognition. Aha, not his first drink, I deduced, feeling relieved that my hospital stay hadn't dulled my razor-sharp sense of Holmesian observation. Leonard blinked slowly like a leopard in the sun.

117

"Good to see you're doing better, as well," I answered for him. Kripp laughed and went to hang up our coats. I shuffled into Roseman's office and took the red-leather chair by the window overlooking Fifth Avenue.

"Do you feel as though you're pushing yourself, David?" Roseman asked, pouring himself a coffee.

"Yes, I do a little," I answered. "It's not being stiff or sore as much as the memory of that arrogant asshole waving an intestinal bypass at me as I got into the elevator to leave." Roseman looked away and bounced the eraser end of a pencil off his palm several times. Damn! Why couldn't I be Gary Cooper? Brave it out? Win the fight? Keep the girl? The park below was beautiful. "Leonard sure doesn't look good."

"I'm afraid not. I doubt he will ever fully recover emotionally. Even the news of Captain Florio's semidecreased interest in him as a suspect had no impact. His attitude is beginning to get under my skin."

Roseman was a vital, robust, and mentally alert man who was aging well, unlike many of his friends and contemporaries. He had watched most of them wither, stumble, forget, and often finally give up. He was fast running out of bridge partners and seldom dared plan an evening for more than two tables. I had no intention of commenting, however respectfully, on the deterioration of one of the remaining few, so I changed the subject.

"If you can spare Kripp and the car, I'll make a trip down to the New Reach Theatre."

"Fine, I have no use for either at present," he said, setting down his cup. "Just be careful. Don't overdo and come straight back."

I nodded and asked as an afterthought, "Do you think Leonard could have shot Peters? Honestly?"

"That would be a wonderfully simple solution," he said, moving over to the windows, "but he didn't. Honestly."

"Peters, Samantha Craig, Banks Reid, Randall Bergman, Leonard Craig, and the take-out guy," I said, counting each one on my fingers. "They could have had a bar mitzvah in that

118

apartment before the lights went out. Of course, we might solve this one by attrition." Roseman looked at me with mild exasperation. "We'll finally end up with just one little Indian and he'll be our man."

"May Dame Agatha forgive you," he quipped. "That scenario wouldn't showcase our talents very well, would it? Keep digging, keep asking questions, keep pushing the point, and somewhere the chain will break. When it does, we shall have arrived."

"Arrived?" I asked. "Arrived where? That's what I'd like to know."

"Indeed. Be careful, David." I left him gazing out over the park.

Kripp drove as selectively as he could down Second Avenue, but even his best wasn't good enough. Every bump made my body scream. By the time we got to 34th Street I was beginning to think I'd made a serious mistake. The Rolls would have been more comfortable, but I'd suggested taking the Chevy wagon. The shocks were giving me hell, but I hated going out on business and dragging all that glitz along. People see a $70,000 car and immediately think you're an asshole. The Chevy, with a couple of dents, a cracked windshield, and a big way-back to throw all kinds of shit in, looked like something a messenger service would use, which kept things in perspective.

The New Reach Theatre was a diamond in the rough. Five years ago, Shelton Sharp took an old movie house, renovated it into a legitimate theater, and built one of the premier off-Broadway centers in the city. Though Sharp worked with a small core group of actors, the New Reach wasn't a repertory company, and the members had changed regularly with the exception of Peters. He had been the focal point.

Kripp double-parked and stayed with the car. I took my time getting to the sidewalk. The outer doors were open, but nobody was visible in the lobby. I pulled back a heavy dark curtain under a sign marked Orchestra Right, took a couple of steps inside, and waited for my eyes to adjust. The stage was set for the bedroom of a castle, no doubt in Scotland, with the centerpiece a huge

119

four-poster that struck me as being a little out of place. I assumed that the aged oak door just past the bed was the sticking place where one screwed his ever-slipping courage. I eased on down the aisle with the intention of checking for life backstage but got stopped short.

"May I help you?"

The voice made me jump. "Yes," I said, trying to locate the speaker, "I'm looking for Shelton Sharp."

"Who wants him?" The voice came from near the bed, but I couldn't place anyone.

"My name is David Hamilton," I said, still moving toward the stage. I stopped at row BB. "And I'm looking into the death of Lane Peters."

"The untimely, sudden, inexplicable, and devastating death of Lane Peters?" the voice asked, and then there he was in a chair by the tapestry. The gray of his oversized sweater blended in well with the upholstery. His hair matched his surroundings enough to make him virtually invisible.

"Are you Shelton Sharp?"

"I am, and I can't say I'm glad to see you. I've laid my professional entrails out before several public officials already. I'm not inclined to do it again for an unofficial type such as yourself."

"Maybe I'm not unofficial."

"Ah, but you see, I've read all about you in the papers," he said shaking a finger at me.

"Well, how about your personal entrails then?" I asked, thinking of my own, which throbbed appropriately.

"I'm afraid I don't follow your question, Mr. Hamilton, or may I call you David?"

"Please do. My question is simple enough. Was Peters' death a personal loss to you . . ." I paused, "more so than a professional one?"

"Ah, a probing question indeed. I'm not quite sure how to parry it."

"I've found a straightforward answer is usually best," I

120

recommended, taking the steps from the orchestra up to the stage slowly and trying not to visibly grind my teeth. "Simple answers don't wrap around your feet and cause you to trip later; believe me, I know what I'm talking about." Sharp hadn't moved. I saw now that he was drinking—right from the bottle, I guessed, since I saw no glass. He was a handsome man with a manufactured theatrical look: longish hair casually thrown out of place and held there with styling mousse; expensive suede shoes; loose socks jumbled down around his ankles; the enormous sweater and baggy pants. All style, no form. Lots of expression but no statement. His ears would work against him in later years, they were really big, but the hair helped hide their size. His complexion was ruddy, perhaps from the alcohol, and he had a marvelous way of speaking fashioned after James Earl Jones delivering the voiceover for a tire commercial.

"Peters was unquestionably a major part of your professional life," I said, crossing the stage to him.

"And what, sir," his voice dripping with sarcasm, "do you know about my professional life, or, for that matter, the theater in general? Have you ever even read *Macbeth*, Mr. Hamilton?"

I looked at him a moment, wondering if he was worth the effort. What the hell, I needed his cooperation.

"*Macbeth* is the shortest of Shakespeare's plays," I began. "Written in 1606, it is a tragedy often referred to as a study in fear. Some scholars find a strong probability that it was written as a tribute to King James I. You see,"—I had Sharp's unwavering attention at this point—"James was a great believer in the supernatural and Macbeth is finely interwoven with things 'other worldly.' James was also of the Stuart line and Shakespeare paints an attractive picture of the early Stuarts in the play, showing he knew how to flatter as well as write. I hope I'm not boring you."

"Oh no, not in the least. Please continue."

"The play is somewhat factual and its basis can be found in Holinshed's *Chronicles* of 1577. It seems there was a real Macbeth who died around 1058 and he allegedly killed one of Scotland's kings, named Duncan, by the way, to gain the throne.

He held power for seventeen years until Duncan's son, Malcolm, came back to overthrow him. It is arguable, but the most famous of Shakespeare's scenes would seem to be Lady Macbeth's sleepwalking in the fifth act, when, overcome by her actions, she tries to wash the bloodstains from her hands." I gave a stiff bow and Sharp applauded approvingly.

"You should teach," he said, at once more relaxed and friendly.

"Doesn't pay enough," I said, equally as warm.

"Pity. It's a loss." He closed his eyes briefly. "You were asking about Lane?"

"Well, according to one critic," I said, quoting, "'the recent success of Shelton Sharp's New Reach Theatre can be directly attributed to the increasing popularity of Lane Peters as a performer among New York's theatergoing public.' I was just wondering if you were close friends as well as artistic collaborators?" He didn't answer immediately, so I sat down in a chair facing him. It felt good to get off my feet.

"We were close," he said, stringing the words out.

"Had you known him in California?"

"No." He didn't elaborate. "Care for a drink, David? I do have glassware."

"No." I didn't elaborate either. "How did you two meet?"

"Ah ha!" he said, coming to life. "We met while he was in a horrible little production of *Edward II*." Suddenly, Sharp was on his feet and fully animated. "He played the young lover of the king and looked spectacular on stage. Stage! God, it was a postage stamp. They were in a loft over on West Thirty-ninth Street. You sat in folding chairs on risers. It was hilarious. One of those shows where there were more people in the cast than in the audience; helmets, spears, shields, swords clanging up and down the aisles. It was a riot. And there he was among the rabble and confusion; controlled, prepared, and very sincere."

Sharp took a sizable pull from his bottle and set it down. "Anyway," he began again, continuing to use his arms in windmill action and thrusting imaginary swords through imaginary ene-

122

mies of the king, "a friend of mine knew the director. We went intending to leave after the first act, if not sooner, but once we saw Lane, neither of us wanted to go. Afterward, we went backstage and were introduced. He had left Los Angeles only a short time before. His first New York performance. God, it was rich!"

"Did he ever give a reason for leaving California?" I asked. "I'd have thought with all the television and film production out there . . ."

"That was the beauty of it," Sharp said, cutting me off. "He tried that circus and hated it. He wanted to be on the stage. Live! In front of an audience with something of substance to convey. There's the excitement. That's the turn-on. And he was great. All he needed was direction."

"And that's where you came in?"

"Yes," he said, crossing back up to his chair. "I was just getting my hands on this place." He turned, spreading his arms wide to indicate the theater. "Hard work, small-cast productions, and the right person in audience development. That's all it took."

"Was Peters always in your shows?"

"Yes, when it was feasible. We did a one-woman production of Emily Dickenson's life that would have been difficult, but he did make an excellent stage manager."

"How well did you know Randall Bergman?" I asked, changing the subject abruptly.

"Oh, my, Randall . . . I knew him well enough to be grateful for his past support and to regret his passing. I understand he almost took you with him when he went."

"It was nip and tuck, let's just leave it at that. Can I assume that at some point Bergman was putting up money for you?"

"Yes," he said, readjusting himself in the chair, "and I really don't mean to be vague or mysterious. Randall and I have known . . . excuse me, knew each other for years. He used to have quite a lot of money, you know." I said I knew. "And he was very free with it."

"Love of theater?"

"Exactly. We had bills, he helped pay them. Then one day, unfortunately, he ran dry."

"What did he get in return for his investment besides tax loss carry forwards?"

"An association with the arts and the opportunity to help guide this theater's growth by serving on our board of directors."

"Love of theater, again?"

"There often isn't much else."

"I can think of one or two people who didn't like him."

"Only someone who didn't know how generous he could be when involved with something he cared about."

"Was he still involved with this theater?"

"Not directly, but he came to see the shows and I often invited him to other functions."

"Backer parties?"

"Yes, Randall was very knowledgeable about theater and the financing that makes it work. I don't know what your point is in all of this, but you'll not get me to say anything against him. Especially now that he's dead."

"Did you arrange for him to meet Banks Reid?"

"Well, aren't we the mathematician, adding things up."

"Seems natural you would want someone close to you to be close to Reid . . . new source of income and all that."

"The first time Samantha brought Banks down here—we were having a small gathering, drinks and so on—he confided to me that he felt uncomfortable . . . uh, out of place was the phrase he used I think . . . not knowing anybody. . . ."

"And Bergman knew a lot of people, right?"

"Everyone. They were the perfect match, and as you've guessed Randall was also able to keep a finger on our new friend's financial disposition."

"Well, that was nice and tidy. Tell me," I said, straightening my back, "what was the deal you and Lane had with Samantha?"

"What do you mean?" he said, sitting up.

"When did you two realize you could go into the fund-raising business with nothing more than a stiff dick?"

124

"I have no interest at all in discussing that wretched woman."

"But if you felt that way about her," I said, "why did you guys play up to her? Was the money that necessary? There must have been other backers available."

He stared blankly at me for a moment, as one would at any novice, and said, "There hasn't been a successful Broadway production of *Macbeth* since the Dark Ages. Of any Shakespeare for that matter. It's not a musical. There are no fancy lights and magical tricks to capture the imagination of the masses. Backers don't come out of the woodwork begging you to take their money for three-hour, large-cast productions that require the audience to pay attention." He leaned back in his chair, the bottle in his lap.

"Samantha met Lane at a cocktail party given by one of our board members," he said softly. "She kept telling me how 'enthralled' she was with him. 'Enchanted, Shelton, I'm just enchanted with him.' God!"

"But she was wealthy," I prompted, "or at least she had access to money."

"Yes. The idea really occurred to both of us at the same time, and she is remarkably attractive. If the little woman was interested in supporting live theater for ulterior motives, that was fine with us—and with our accountants as well, I might add."

"So Peters just responded to her advances and nature took its course?"

"Essentially. Lane said he could play the part of a selfless lover if necessary, and I believe it really didn't matter to him. In fact, they hardly ever slept together. She got off on sporting him around in public and goading her pathetically impotent husband with him in private."

"How much did you get out of him?"

"Ninety-seven thousand dollars," he said without a blink. I gave a low whistle. "Yes, it was a lot of money and there was more to come until that senile old husband of her's got jealous."

"Even then she showed some pretty fancy footwork. You

125

have to admit that the switch from Leonard Craig to Banks Reid was smoothly handled."

Sharp took another drink. "We never missed a payroll," he acknowledged grudgingly.

"It's right to give credit where it's due."

"I don't give that bitch an ounce of credit for anything," Sharp said aggressively. "On one hand she's got a senile old goat who thinks he's in love with Snow White, and on the other she's got a befuddled industrialist who thinks his dick is the largest in a four-state area. She would mate with sheep if the thought struck her."

I laughed and he joined me; but on this, his second outburst, it occurred to me that the subject of Samantha always struck a sore spot. Maybe Sharp was another of her cast-offs? Maybe he was the first batter in the box, with Lane stepping up later to take his place? Maybe? Maybe.

"I know you've been over this with the police already, but could you tell me about the night Lane was shot?"

Sharp dropped the laugh and let his gaze fall back to his bottle. He was quiet for a while, chewing on a thought. It occurred to me then that Sharp might not be as drunk as he would like me to believe: illusion and reality, life in the theater, that sort of thing.

"I feel largely responsible for Lane's death," he said soulfully.

"In what way?"

He threw his head back and looked up into the darkness of the theater behind me. "Because I should have recognized a crisis situation sooner." He dropped his gaze to me. I looked attentive. "After Samantha's husband found out about the affair, Lane wanted to call it quits—drop the pretense—but I said no, not yet. In time, yes, but we still needed her support. If not with her husband, then with Banks Reid."

"Until the play got uptown?"

"Yes," he said heavily. "I didn't see the old goat as much of a threat, and I was right. It was Samantha—Samantha was the

126

dangerous one. I never imagined she would take the news so badly. She became violent, frighteningly violent."

"What news was this?"

"That Lane was going to leave her."

"So he did tell her he wanted to end the relationship?"

"Even though I tried to stop him."

"When did this take place?" I asked.

"The day before his death."

"And what was her response?"

"She wanted a meeting, a chance to talk things out, and Lane said no, but I talked him into agreeing. They were to meet the following night after the show."

"At her apartment?"

"Yes. Lane was hesitant. He said I didn't know how violent she could be. According to Lane, the best thing to do was batten down the hatches till the storm passed."

"But you couldn't give up the cash?"

"It cost my friend his life." He stopped and drank a little, then continued. "I remember it took a long time to convince him to go. I told him what it would mean to the theater, his future."

"Yours."

Sharp quickly turned on me, but there was no force behind his stare. He went back to his bottle with a mumbled, "You're right, I told him that, too."

"Did you go up there with him? Make sure he arrived?"

"Lane insisted. He was terribly frightened. If I hadn't agreed to be close by, I never would have convinced him to go."

Sharp went silent again.

"But, " he began again. "I got tied up here. Not for long, an hour maybe. Lane went on ahead by himself and I came up later . . ."

"I guess instead of meeting Samantha, Lane must have run into Leonard. They argued, fought, and the old man shot him. Is that how you see it?"

"Oh no, not at all," Sharp said without hesitation. "Samantha killed Lane."

He rocked me back with that one, and it took a second to come around.

"Maybe I could have that drink now," I said, needing time to think.

"Certainly, I'll get you a glass." He walked quietly off into the wings. A remarkable accusation and a complete change of direction. Florio was going to break into song when I told him about this. As to why Sharp was putting the finger on Samantha, I didn't have a clue, but obviously he wanted me to be the messenger.

Sharp came back with a water glass into which he splashed about two inches of scotch. I took the drink, thanked him, and moistened my lips while he returned to his chair.

"Shelton," I said as soon as he was seated, "Samantha has admitted to being in the apartment the night Lane died."

"I didn't know that."

"She has. Not that she wanted to, but after Reid coughed up the information to Florio, she didn't have much choice. They both swear Lane was already on the floor when they got there, so if you're implying that she's still not telling the whole truth, you'll have to be specific."

"I can't be too specific," he said, peeking out at me from his red, swollen eyes.

"You've just accused someone of murder and you can't be specific? Come on, talk to me."

"It was actually over when I got there."

"What was over? The shooting? The fight? What?"

"Everybody was still . . ."

"Who is everybody?" I broke in, getting exasperated. "Name them."

"Samantha, Reid, Randall Bergman, and then, there was Lane, of course, on the floor."

"You didn't see Leonard Craig then?" I asked him.

"No, not at first."

"What did you see?"

He leaned forward, his elbows on his knees, looking straight at me.

"Samantha had a gun in her hand when I came in. She was holding it down by her side and she was standing right next to Lane. I was so shocked, so surprised. I started to cry out but I couldn't speak. And then she looked at me and let the gun drop to the floor. They were all just standing around her."

"Why haven't you told this to the police?"

"I just didn't . . . think . . ." the words stumbled coming out, as he fought to hold himself together. "The sight of his body and the blood . . . it was horrible. I didn't know what to do. I needed time to think. I realize now that I've got to speak out. I wish I could have sooner."

"OK, calm down," I said and crossed over to him. I picked up the bottle from his lap and squatted next to his chair. Sharp began to get a grip on his emotions and I continued with the quietly sympathetic bit. He steadied himself and looked at me.

"I just can't come to terms with his being dead," he said softly.

I didn't know what to say that wouldn't sound trite, so I patted his knee and asked another question. "Did you ask what happened?" He nodded yes. "What did they tell you?"

"Nobody knew."

"What do you mean, nobody knew? Samantha holding a gun over a dead body with two men at her side and nobody knows what happened?"

He shrugged and repeated, "Nobody knew. Reid said Lane was lying there when they arrived. Bergman backed him up and Samantha wasn't talking."

If that was true, then by the time Leonard arrived it was way after the fact and the scene with the lights and gunshots was staged. The point being, he was likely to get pinned with first-degree murder. Convenient but complicated. It must have taken time to pull the plan together, they must have talked. Bargained, more like it. A hard-ass crowd. I walked back to the bed to get my coat, taking the bottle with me.

"And you told none of this to the police?"

"That's right," he said, rubbing color into his face with both hands. "All I told them was that I stayed here at the theater after the show and then went home. It was unsubstantiated but perfectly reasonable."

"And why did you choose to lie about being at the apartment?"

"Why? I was frightened; afraid I might be implicated, too. Mostly, like I said, I needed time to think everything through."

It sounded pretty thin and I figured he was only telling me what was necessary to get things moving toward Samantha's arrest.

"By the way. Did you ever check to make sure Peters was dead?" I asked, feeling my face flush red.

"No," he answered and seemed defensive about it. "I didn't know how. I was frightened, confused; he wasn't moving, or breathing. I mean, I was in shock. They all said he was dead; I just took their word for it."

"Your friend, who you pressed into this meeting, is stretched out on the floor, shot in the head, and you don't bother to check his pulse?" It was too incredible for me. "He wasn't dead, you know," I fired at him. "He lived another thirty, forty minutes. He might have been saved." I failed to add that had he lived he would certainly have been a vegetable, but I didn't want to be kind.

"When I read that in the paper," Sharp said quietly, "about Lane not dying until later, I couldn't believe it. I couldn't believe it."

The whole idea of setting Craig up had me reeling. Their collective, callous disregard was simply incomprehensible. Now, Sharp had decided to break from the pack and finger Samantha. I was dying to know why.

"Why didn't you say something?" I asked him. "The obvious implication was that Samantha killed Lane and you let it ride?" He didn't answer. He actually turned his face away. The only answer had to be the unthinkable. So I said it out loud just to

130

hear how it sounded. "You stood there over his body and struck a deal with, what did you call him? a befuddled industrialist? to save Samantha's ass for money, didn't you? Is that right? You didn't see Samantha. You didn't see a gun. You didn't see anything. Was the deal straight cash or did they promise to build you a shiny new theater, too?"

Sharp looked at me and I wanted to spit on him. I think it was his eyes that bothered me most; that please punish me look that made me want to puke. Taking the half empty scotch bottle in my left hand I threw it at him hard enough to make my side hurt. He sat watching the bottle sail toward him, making no effort to move or protect himself. It struck flat against his chest, splashing some of the distilled contents into his face before falling across his legs and rolling onto the stage.

"Get down on your knees and suck that up, Sharp. You'll need it to get through the rest of your life." I started for the steps. I'd gotten to the aisle before he spoke.

"I thought he was dead."

I kept on going.

Kripp saw me exit the theater and hopped out to help me into the Chevy. As he pulled into traffic, I asked him to find a deli. I was starved and wanted a roast beef on rye with mustard but was going to have to settle for an extra light coffee with two sugars.

"You must have a bad taste in your mouth, Ham," he said, glancing both ways for a place to stop, "'cause you got an awful bad look on your face."

"Goddamn right I do," I said harshly. "If it wouldn't hurt so bad, I'd throw up."

"Right," was all he said; he turned his attention to driving. We caught a deli on the corner of St. Mark's Place. Kripp left the motor running and went in. He brought back the coffee and had already peeled a hole in the white plastic top to keep down the spillage going uptown. Made me feel like a real shit for shouting at him.

"Sorry I bit your head off, Kripp."

131

"No problem. It's your job. Dealing with all that human trash, you forget about us normal folk."

We both laughed. I drank some of the coffee and felt better. On the way up Bowery to Third Avenue I rolled Sharp's story over in my head. It was hard to believe that a group of people could be so cold-blooded. One person, two maybe, but four? You'd think there'd have been some compassion among them somewhere. The big question, though, was why Sharp had decided to cut from the pack. If this really was a "gang of four" they weren't going to take his defection too well.

"Pull over to that payphone please, Kripp," I said, coming out of my stupor and scribbling down a phone number while I held the coffee in my teeth. "Here, give Florio a call and ask him to meet us at home for a drink. Tell him it's important and he needs the entertainment. Then you better call Roseman and let him know we're on our way."

"Right," he answered, and he pulled to the curb. As he started to get out I handed him a second phone number, Paul Hemp's.

"Call this guy, too. If he answers, I'll talk to him."

"Sure."

"Have you got enough change?"

"Yeah."

"Thanks."

He got back into the car moments later to say that Florio was on his way, Roseman would be ready, and he'd left a message on Hemp's machine. That done, we started back uptown.

CHAPTER THIRTEEN

Roseman met us at the door with no coat, rolled shirtsleeves, striped bow tie, and holding a screwdriver. He looked slightly bewildered.

"I've been trying to get into a tin of herring," he explained. "The screwkey broke and I'm having a go with this." He vaguely indicated the yellow-handled screwdriver. "With little success, I might add."

"Here, let me take that," said Kripp, heading in the direction of the kitchen.

"By all means," Roseman said after him, "we'll be in the library."

"Florio's big on cheese," I offered to Kripp, adding, "nothing fancy, crackers, sliced onions, and some spicy mustard. And I'd love another coffee." Turning to Roseman, I steadied myself on his arm and we moved into the library. "Well, Arthur, let me get comfortable and I'll tell you quite a story," I said, settling onto the leather sofa. I kicked off my shoes and eased down until I was stretched out. Roseman offered a pillow, but I shook it off. "This is great," I said with feeling. "I may never move again."

Roseman rearranged the two wingback chairs near the

fireplace, got a third from across the room, and said he was going to the kitchen for ice. I took a rest.

The doorbell rang before Roseman returned and the voices in the hall told me that Florio and Marston had arrived. The bits of conversation that reached me were casual, friendly. Florio's bass rumble overrode the soft Ivy League tones of Marston and Roseman's English sing-song. They came into the library together, Kripp and a tray of food at their heels. Drifting out from the kitchen, the smell of coffee was strong and satisfying. I still wanted a roast beef on rye.

Florio stopped beside the sofa and lit a cigarette. "Look a little pale, Ham," he said, taking a bourbon and water from Roseman. "Your ass ought to be in bed. How's the stomach?"

"It hurts, but I'll live," I told him. Marston said hello and twisted the cap off a cold beer. I watched him tilt the glass and pour, the head rising full, thick, and white to the top. He set the empty bottle down and turned his attention to the thousand tiny beads drifting up through the golden liquid's center. Then he moistened his lips and brought the glass to his mouth. I couldn't remember ever seeing anyone enjoy a beer more. When Kripp showed with my coffeed milk, Marston was twisting his second cap.

Florio plopped into the large red leather chair next to the food tray. It seemed made for him and was diminished by his bulk. Marston took the chair opposite and Roseman remained standing, as was his preference, placing his scotch on the fireplace mantel.

"What did Shelton Sharp tell you about his movements on the night Peters was killed?" I asked Marston.

"Not a lot," he said, running a napkin over his upper lip. "Something about resetting props and general clean-up because the stage manager was sick."

"Did you check that out?" I asked.

Florio feigned insult. "Yes," he said, his mouth full as he pushed in yet another onion—it baffled me how a man with his marked taste in clothes could have such abominable eating habits. "The guy—Marston, what was his name?"

"Brock Leland."

"He had a viral infection," he continued, "fever, the shits. He checked out."

"Well, guess what?" I handed my cup to Kripp for a refill. "We've been jacked around, intentionally."

It took me almost forty minutes to relay the finer points of my visit to the New Reach Theatre and I was tired when I stopped talking. By then, Florio had finished the food and there were two more empties in front of Marston's chair.

"So the lousy son of a bitch lied," Florio fumed as soon as I stopped talking.

"That shouldn't surprise you," Roseman said, mildly amused. "Everyone else has."

"It doesn't surprise me, it pisses me off," he responded gruffly. "Marston!"

"Yes, sir."

"Make an appointment to see Sharp tomorrow! Not at the theater, uptown in the office. And make it early."

"Done," he replied twisting another bottle cap.

"This is great," Florio continued to me. "It's the break we've needed. It's great. Absolutely fucking great!"

"If the story holds up," I said, "then you were right about Reid having a lot more on his mind than just being at the scene of the crime." Florio's smile widened.

"Assuming Samantha shot Lane Peters in a fit of jealous pique," Roseman said, pointing to Florio with his highball glass, "what reason do we have for the others, who arrived soon thereafter, not to turn her in? You mentioned continued financial support for the theater as Sharp's possible motive. Do we have devoted love and affection on behalf of her remaining lover, Banks Reid?"

"If he really cares for her, it would make sense," Marston said. "But it's hard for me to believe that four people could agree to implicate a fifth, innocent party, in murder."

"I agree with that," I said, "but you've got to look at who we're dealing with. We've got two theatrical types, slash, business partners—Lane who prostitutes himself and Sharp who prods him—and they use this deceit and sexual trickery to defraud an old man out of money via his unloving sexually frustrated wife; then there's the infatuated industrialist, Banks Reid; Randall Bergman, the tag along blackmailer; and finally, the woman pulling all the strings, Ms. Amoral of the year, Samantha Craig. These are not, by any stretch of the imagination, nice people."

Florio brushed crumbs off his tie. "He's right," he said. "Leonard Craig as the murderer of Lane Peters suits everyone's purposes."

"Did you ever speak with Leonard about why he was paying off Bergman?" I asked. Roseman glanced at me.

"No," he answered quietly. "I tell myself I haven't pressed the issue due to his poor physical state, but in truth, I suppose I just don't want to hear the grotty little details."

"It needs to be done," Florio said, starting to come out of his chair. "I could do it officially if you want me to."

"Please, Captain," Roseman said, placing a hand on Florio's shoulder to keep him in place. "I'll attend to it in good time, thank you."

The mood in the room had reached an alcoholic euphoria. I slurped my coffee, smacked my lips, and generally felt at home enjoying the company.

Roseman went to the bar and adjusted his drink from regular to high test, cleared his throat, and addressed the group. "Are we really so willing," he asked, drawing everyone's attention, "to believe Sharp's view that Samantha killed her lover after realizing he was going to terminate their relationship?"

"Nobody's believing anything until after we have a second chat with Sharp," Florio said forcefully. "But Forensics says the only fingerprints on the murder weapon are hers."

"You may well believe I've heard that one before," Roseman

136

countered. "Laboratory analysis can only tell you what is there, not what was wiped away."

Florio agreed and dribbled more bourbon into his glass from the decanter.

Roseman continued. "If Banks Reid was prepared to lie to keep Samantha untainted, he certainly won't stand for Sharp's sniveling little melodrama about her holding the proverbial smoking gun."

"You think Reid is going to do something?" Florio asked.

"Perhaps, but not him necessarily," Roseman said, "it's simply that I feel an unqualified apprehension."

"You're not the only one," Florio said, coming to his feet. "Thanks for the drinks." He seemed to have a second thought and walked over to Roseman at the mantel. "Do you want to go ask Craig what it was Bergman had on him?"

"Yes, of course," Roseman replied, setting down his drink. "I suppose it's unavoidable." But as he turned to leave, Leonard stepped into the living room. Florio and Marston froze. I stared at the ceiling and held my breath. Once the moment had passed, all attention turned to Roseman's friend. He seemed unsteady, his face pale and the neck behind his collar thin and wrinkled. There was no telling how long he had been standing there. The slippers on his sockless feet explained his muffled approach.

Roseman started to speak, but Leonard raised a wavering hand that cut him off. When he spoke, his voice was uneven, his tone slightly off pitch.

"Please don't be embarrassed on my account, especially you, Arthur," he said as Roseman stepped to his side. "I know I've been a fool. One worthy of not just your laughter, but also your contempt."

"Leonard please," Roseman started, "don't misunderstand. We were just—"

"I know what you were doing, Arthur. You were having a frank assessment of the circumstances surrounding a violent murder. You have been trying to help and I haven't been very cooperative . . . or truthful." Leonard's lips kept moving for

137

several beats after he quit talking. Then he turned to Florio and seemed to square his shoulders.

"Captain, I was playing blackmail to Randall Bergman and I am not proud of having done it, but I did . . . for a while at least."

"You mean you stopped paying?"

"Yes, it was only a couple of days before the murder, but I told Randall—wrote him a note, actually, and said I was through; there would not be another payment."

"Did you have any contact with him after he received the note?"

"No, I didn't."

Florio started another question, but he, too, got cut off by the wavering hand.

"There's more, Captain . . . that I need to tell you." Roseman tensed and Marston set down his beer. I hoped for deliverance. "Randall Bergman was not alone in his . . . plan, scheme, he had a partner."

"Who!" Florio barked, making Roseman jump.

"Lane Peters."

"Fuck!" he said between clenched teeth, and for a moment I thought he was going to hit the ceiling. Florio shifted his weight, slipped both hands into his trouser pockets, and said roughly, "Ten days ago that piece of information would have put your ass in jail."

"But we didn't know it ten days ago," Roseman said, stepping forward to defend his friend, who was really starting to look unhealthy, "and during that interval, we have uncovered multiple motives from a variety of sources; something that might not have happened if we'd been apprised of it initially. I don't deny it blackens the case against Leonard, but it only makes him equally suspect with others."

"Maybe," Florio said, completely sober. "But only maybe. What were they using against you, Craig?" Florio demanded unkindly. "It couldn't have been your wife's infidelity because

138

everybody knew about that. Hell, everybody seems to have had a piece."

"Goddamnit, Marc!" I shouted, and Marston stepped over to Florio's side placing a calming hand on his boss's arm. Leonard stared at Florio for a second, stunned by the brutal frankness of his statement. He worked his jaw soundlessly and then, to everyone's surprise, his eyes rolled back and he started for the floor. He would have landed hard had Roseman not gotten his arms under him before he hit. With Kripp's help, Roseman laid his friend on his back, supporting his head with a cushion.

"Call an ambulance," Roseman said and Kripp dashed for the kitchen.

Florio didn't give an inch. He looked from me to Roseman and back to Leonard. "If your friend thinks that passing out is going to keep me off his ass, he's wrong. I plan to be there when he wakes up."

"I'm sure you'll do what you think best, Captain," Roseman said crisply, trying to make Leonard as comfortable as possible. His attentions had little effect, however, as his friend's breathing was becoming more labored with each faltering heave of the frail, aged chest. In less than ten minutes the room was full of medical personnel and it was déjà vu all over again. As they wheeled Leonard out the door, I asked Florio what his immediate plans were.

"I was planning another visit to Samantha," he said. "But I want to follow this up at the hospital and that could take time. So, it looks like it's off for now."

"I could do it first thing in the morning while you guys are pinning Sharp to the wall again." Florio thought it over.

"OK," the big man said, "but when you go, John's going with you." He looked at Marston. "Got it?"

"Got it," I said. Marston nodded.

"Fine," Florio said, "I'll be in touch," and he marched out the door.

Not good I thought. Not good at all.

With the room empty, my get-up-and-go went. Like water spiraling clockwise down a sink trap, it disappeared with a slurp, gurgle, and belch. I had done too much in this my first day out of the hospital. The dull ache in my lower torso told me I had been a bad boy. What I needed was to get up, if I could, go downstairs to my bed, and sleep for fourteen hours. But at the moment, I wasn't up to moving. Kripp came and went several times carrying glasses and plates to the kitchen. I faded in and out, too tired to hold on, wanting to sleep.

"Ham." It was Kripp's voice close to my ear. "Ham, you need to take a couple of these pills. Sit up a little."

"I need to get downstairs," I managed to say.

"Fine by me, but first take these."

Saucer-shaped and cream-colored, the tablets he handed me looked like faded M&M's. They went down just as easily.

"Now stay put till I finish in the kitchen," he said, as if I was going to run away. I don't now how long it was before he returned, but by then the pills had kicked in.

I vaguely remember Kripp helping me to my feet. He leaned me against the bookcases in order to get the elevator door open and then helped me inside.

"Holy shit," I said, feeling the dope lift me off the floor. "I don't need an elevator. Silly person, I can float downstairs."

"Man, you are weird," he said tipping me into bed.

"You know, Kripp," I said, trying to focus on his face, "we haven't played Name That Tune recently. Isn't this Black Music Appreciation Week or something? Ha, ha, ha."

"No, we haven't," he said and slipped off my shoes. He did the same with my pants and tossed them over a chair. Then he tucked my feet into the middle of the bed. "Maybe we can play tomorrow."

"Tomorrow," I echoed emphatically. "And tomorrow and tomorrow creeps in this petty pace . . ."

"Good Lord, Ham," Kripp said, rolling his eyes. "I'll leave your shirt on, since I don't want to be sleeping down here with a naked white man, not after what I've been listening to upstairs."

"Staying over, Kripp?"

140

"Yeah, I'll be in the other bedroom. Mr. Roseman thought it would be best. I'll enjoy a good sleep and a morning away from the kids. That is, if you don't rant and rave all night." He pulled the comforter up under my chin and gave it a couple of pats. I was quiet for a few minutes watching the room change colors. I could feel myself starting to slip into slumber land; home to James and his Giant Peach, Marjorie Daw, and Peter Rabbit.

"Goodnight, David."

"Goodnight, Kripp," I called out, "and goodnight for NBC." He laughed all the way down the hall.

CHAPTER FOURTEEN

I woke to a familiar aroma. I couldn't place it at first, coffee? after-shave? I didn't know. Lingering there on the cusp of reality, where bells and whistles slip in and become part of your dreams, I wrestled with the particular responses it created in my mind until, finally, I was fully awake.

Marilyn.

Of course, the most familiar person I knew. She was bright as sunshine and drinking coffee in a chair next to the bed, wonderful posture. Let's see, I thought, putting my imagination in gear, who is she today? Perhaps a character out of *The Jungle Book*. Me Marilyn, friend to Kim, lover of animals. I wasn't far off, she was wearing a black, padded-shoulder sweater with gold tiger markings across the front and slacks that came out of a Banana Republic outlet. For accessories she had ivory earrings and no less than ten matching bracelets that rattled down her arm with every sip of steaming coffee. Seeing that I was awake, she smiled. A lovely smile. A beautiful girl. I don't know why I was being so critical.

"You don't give a guy much chance, do you?" I said over a

tongue as thick as elephant skin. "I haven't even brushed my teeth."

"That doesn't matter," she said sweetly. "I've already kissed you."

"Ah, that's what woke me, a concentrated whiff of my favorite perfume."

"Probably." She beamed. "You looked darling."

"Really? Slack-mouthed and drooling, I bet I was. Anything to make you laugh."

"I wasn't laughing," she said and kissed me again. "Kripp said you needed to be up anyway. Twelve hours is a long time to sleep."

"Twelve hours! What time is it?"

"Ten of eight," she said, checking her wrist. "Places to go? People to see?"

"If I can." I edged my back up against the headboard. "How about some coffee? Then you can go upstairs and visit while I work the kinks out." She gave me a kicked-dog look, but I hung tough. "Just think how you'd feel if you didn't have a chance to primp for your favorite man? Huh?"

"Absolutely horrible," she said, stirring cream and sugar into a second cup. "I wouldn't stand for it. But you, on the other hand, look very handsome with a day's growth of beard and wearing a wrinkled dress shirt."

"Do I?"

"Oh yes!"

"Movie idol?"

"Of course."

"Which one?"

"Louis Jourdan."

"How flattering. Really?"

"Really."

"Thanks."

"I'm sorry I didn't come to the hospital. I couldn't."

"I know."

"Forgive me? Please!" she said earnestly.

144

"I understand," I said, taking the cup. "I feel the same about illness and hospitals. I do understand. Besides, you called, sent me flowers, a nice card. All that counts. OK?" Who was I trying to convince? "Come on, help me to the bathroom."

With Marilyn's arm to lean on, I got as far as the dresser and stopped for breath. Something had been nagging at me ever since that last bunch of flowers ended up in Jordan's hands at the hospital. I figured now was as good a time as any to get it off my chest. I put my right arm on top of the dresser for support.

"OK," I said. "I lied." And her china blue eyes focused intently on my face. "It did bother me that you never came to the hospital. Intellectually, I have a perfect understanding of why you didn't, but I needed you. You! Not your voice over a telephone line. I wanted to see you, have you there. It didn't seem like a lot to ask. I guess I thought in a crisis situation you might suffer a little inconvenience, rise to the occasion. Isn't that a part of loving someone?"

"How can you speak to me like that?" she said, not at all pleased with my rebuke. "This past week my life has been turmoil . . ."

"Your life! Jesus Christ woman, I almost lost mine. No, wait, I see. No date for the opera, was that it? And did you have to rearrange your dinner schedule at the last minute? Were you desperate to find a replacement, frantic calls all over Manhattan?"

"You bastard!" And she meant it. "It's easy enough to ridicule me. I may even have some of it coming, but by God I've never heard you complain about fresh linen sheets, or having to eat two nights running at Lutèce. And just when in the hell did you get religion, buster?"

"Well great!" and if it hadn't hurt so much I would have yelled louder. "That's just great, but maybe I've changed. Maybe I would like something more than clean sheets, good food, and athletic sex. Maybe I'd like a piece of your heart. You. I'd like that."

"Let me tell you something, David Hamilton," she said in a

145

low, trembling voice, grabbing the front of my shirt. "I have spent the last five days worried sick over you; thinking about us, our lives together, our lives apart, and I came here this morning full of feelings I've never had before about anyone or anything. Look at me!" she yelled. "Look at me, goddamnit! It's eight o'clock in the fucking morning and I look like a million dollars. I've been up since four fighting with my insides and trying to get ready to come over here, and you treat me like some sort of office temporary that can't handle the job . . ." and then she came apart into little pieces. The tears exploded from her eyes. Suddenly it was me, David the righteous, the unjustly ignored, the unloved, who felt like a total shit. I turned my back full against the dresser and wrapped her in my arms. Her sobs pounded my heart like a butcher tenderizing meat. I held her tightly, rumpled her hair, and rubbed her back until she calmed down. We stood there for a long time, breathing against each other, holding on.

"I still need to go to the bathroom," I said softly.

"I bet you do." She buried her face into my shirt to wipe her tears. "I could use a tissue for my nose, too."

The walk to the john was a killer. The trip back was better but bordered on masochism. We sat on the bed for another cup of coffee. Neither of us said much. We just sat there, holding hands, drinking. Then Marilyn ran upstairs to tell Kripp I was hungry. Lumberjack hungry. As soon as she was gone, I worked my way back to the dresser and pulled Leonard's note to Bergman out of the top drawer. I tore it and the envelope into fourths, then eighths, sixteenths, and dropped the pieces into the toilet. One flush and they were away. Gone. I'll never do that again, I thought, watching the water level return to normal in the bowl. Never say never, David. Never.

Kripp phoned down to say forget the Northwest menu. I could have warm oatmeal run through the Cuisinart and some yogurt. Period. Did I have a favorite fruit flavor? Oatmeal and yogurt. Jesus. A man could die.

Kripp also relayed a couple of messages. Jordan had called

and Rachel had left a death threat, which roughly translated into "What in the hell did I think I was doing wandering around town in my condition."

"She said she'd come by this morning," Kripp warned, sotto voce.

"Christ! What time? Did she say? Did she leave a number? No, forget all that. The best thing will be to play dumb and hope she doesn't catch me sneaking out the door." There was no way I could hurry Marilyn out either, not after what we'd just been through. I considered my situation silently for a moment. "Any word on Leonard?"

Kripp drew a deep breath. "The good news is he's alive. The bad news is he's weak and still only semiconscious. He's in intensive care at Lenox Hill. Mr. Roseman didn't come in until about seven this morning and he went straight to his office . . . I sent breakfast there."

"OK, thanks, Kripp. I'll be up in a minute."

Goddamn! What am I doing? I said to myself, hanging up. What in the hell am I doing? Juggling women like a ten-cent Casanova. I splashed cold water into my face, then adjusted the hot tap and stuck my head under the steaming cascade. I'd feel better after a general clean-up, I told myself, looking in the mirror. Well, I'd look better anyway. "Just concentrate on work," I mumbled, back under the water. "Just take care of business."

I was toweling off my head when the phone buzzed.

"Hi, Florio's on two," Kripp said and rang off.

"Morning Marc, how's things?"

"Pretty fair," he said. "You feeling all right?"

"Yes, better, thanks. Were you at the hospital long last night?"

"Long enough." In his brief answer there was a hint of embarrassment, and I figured he was feeling responsibility, if not outright guilt, for his verbal abuse of Leonard the night before. "Marston will be by to pick you up in thirty minutes, around ten."

"Fine. Would you tell him I'll be at Madison and Sixty-First, northwest corner. No sense him coming by here."

"Will do," he said, and he was gone.

I buzzed the kitchen. "Kripp, let me speak to Marilyn." I didn't wait long. "Hi, again. Would you bring my bowl of porridge down here, please? Florio called and I need to hurry. Thanks." I hung up and pulled a navy blazer, charcoal slacks, and a blue oxford shirt out of the closet. All I needed now was a school tie. Right, me and Holden Caulfield.

I looked back into the full-length mirror attached to the back of my closet door. No pretense here. Not today at least. Generally, I was content to brush fingers over the few emerging gray hairs at my temple and mutter, tut, tut. Today it was different; facing the world in my BVDs I saw a man feeling every single day of two steps past thirty. I poked a thumb into my side and was pleased to see it didn't disappear too far. I was never one for weights, but I did manage to get in a regular swim and enough sit-ups to keep my stomach behind my belt. That wouldn't be a problem for a while, I decided, tracing the stitches across my stomach. Still, at just over six feet, I carried 187 pounds easily and had good legs and lots of brown hair, which reminded me I needed to stop by the drugstore and pick up some Tenax and toothpaste.

As I looked for a tie, I half-considered the school ensemble, then chose instead a bright orange and blue striped bow tie. I was stepping into a pair of loafers when Marilyn arrived with breakfast. Kripp had sprinkled enough brown sugar over the pureed oatmeal to make it palatable. The warmth of its bulk felt good in my stomach.

"Will you be gone all day?" she asked, as I scraped the bowl clean and set it on the dresser.

"Shouldn't be. Why? Have you got plans?"

"Marsha invited me out to the Island for the weekend. I was going to take her up on it if you thought you might come."

"When would you leave?" I asked, paying attention to getting the bow right in my tie.

148

"Tomorrow morning. The earlier the better really. I hate trying to drive out in all that traffic." She looked at me in the mirror. "How about it? We could sit in the sun, have some nonathletic sex, and talk to each other."

"Thanks," I said, and jerked the knot tight, "I'd like that. But I can't leave until something breaks here." I turned around to face her and pushed a wisp of hair off her forehead. It was too short to stay and fell back. We kissed gently and I hugged her.

"Stop that, or I'll start to cry again. OK?"

"I'll tell you what. Let's meet at Jordan's around one or one-thirty for lunch. I'll know more about the status of the case and we can decide something then. If nothing else, maybe I could take the train out later."

"You could use the rest," she said, perky as hell all of a sudden. "The salt air is bound to be good for you. One o'clock then?"

"One o'clock," I said, lifting an automatic off the bureau and dropping it into my coat pocket. I took her arm and we headed downstairs. Once outside, I breathed easier for not having encountered Rachel, and we shuffled over to Madison together. I started to hail her a cab, but she said she'd like a walk. Marston pulled up before the light changed and I said good-bye on the corner with a squeeze of her hand. Most of the passionate sidewalk tongues-in-mouths are simply sideshows for the benefit of the eight or nine hundred people streaming by you at that particular moment. I hate public displays of affection.

Marston was well scrubbed and tidy, in direct contrast to the interior of his unmarked patrol car. Papers, envelopes, and file folders were jammed between the dash and the grime-streaked windshield, making it difficult to see. The glove compartment door fell open with every bump, banging my knees until I gave up and just let it stay down. The car reeked of stale cigarettes. The ashtray was overflowing and there were seven or eight holes burned in the vinyl upholstery. In general it looked like one of the backrooms at Harry's, a well-known after-hours gambling oasis up on Riverside Drive.

"Jesus, John, where'd you get this car?"

"Real piece of shit, isn't it? Motor pool said it was the only thing they had. They use it for undercover work in the Bronx. Now you know why I always ride with Florio. He gets the community service parolees to keep his car clean." Marston made a quick move to the left, barely avoiding a city bus as it barreled out into traffic, leaving behind a screen of diesel smoke. The lurch dumped everything onto our laps: the papers, the pens, even the boxes crammed behind the sunvisors. There was nothing else to do but laugh, and we couldn't stop ourselves until we were past Seventy-second Street.

Samantha Craig met us at the door wearing a loose silk blouse and a pleated skirt. She had her shoes on this time and a pair of sheer stockings that glinted in the morning sunlight as it flooded through her living room windows.

"Come in, Lieutenant," she said in a strictly business voice. She exchanged glances with me. We followed her across the living room. The rug had been taken out, leaving the naked oak floor to show off its shine.

"After you called," she said, turning to Marston, "I spoke with my lawyer. He advised me to say nothing without him present, but depending on the questions I may decide that won't be necessary."

"Would you like to hear an update on your husband's condition?" Marston asked.

"Not particularly. I've spoken to Leonard's doctor this morning."

Marston nodded and pulled out a cigarette and his gold lighter, offered her one, then lit them both. "We have some new information that changes the perspective of our investigation," he said curtly. "I see no reason not to tell you that Captain Florio is, at this moment, with Banks Reid discussing the same matter." There was an air to Marston's manner starting this interview that made me feel he was fed up with all the highbrow low-living surrounding this case. As for Samantha, her face went from corporate congeniality to concentrated concern. She dropped her cigarette into an immaculately clean ashtray, spun on her heels for the telephone, but stopped short of dialing. Marston shifted his weight and continued to smoke quietly with his right hand resting in the side pocket of his coat. His general air was that of a yacht owner on holiday. Tense, but on holiday. Samantha sent him a look that would have erased most men.

"This has to do with my alibi, doesn't it?" she asked.

"Yes, it does," Marston said without inflection.

Samantha walked back to stand directly in front of Marston. She retrieved her cigarette and the two stood smoking at each other like wooden drugstore Indians in a still-life advertisement for the American Cancer Society. A blue-gray haze gathered above their heads, thickened into a cloud, and drifted off toward some unseen return air vent. I stifled a cough and moved upwind.

"What did Shelton tell you?"

"That when he finished at the theater on the night of the murder he didn't go home as he originally told us," Marston said, "but came here instead." He paused for effect, watching her closely. "And saw you."

"Banks and I have already told you we lied about that—"

"He also said you were holding a gun in your hand," Marston interrupted. There was no immediate response.

"Well, I was," she said matter-of-factly. "Are you going to arrest me for that?"

"Perhaps," he said and rubbed out his butt in the ashtray. "It depends on what you have to say this time. Maybe now you should consider calling your attorney."

"No, that won't be necessary," she said definitively. "What I have to say may be a little embarrassing, but it's not criminal. It was a foolish idea to begin with," she said harshly. "I told them that." She looked around the room, her hands clinching at waist level. "Could I have another cigarette, Lieutenant? I seem to have misplaced mine."

I watched the polite exchange with interest. Samantha Craig was more than a little rough around the edges; oversexed, hard-driving, money-hungry, and, unless she was about to come across with an incredibly empathetic story about lost love and momentary insanity, cold and heartless as well. As she reached out with steady fingers to accept Marston's cigarette and calmly bent to his lighter, I had a sense of awesome power poised just below the surface. She was like a big cat crouching for a drink of water, thirsty but ever watchful.

"To make this simple," she said, stepping back from him, "everything I told you earlier was true." Marston nodded vaguely. "I went to dinner with Banks and Randall, Leonard showed up and we had a row, after which Randall and Reid and I went to the theater, then on to the gallery, then they dropped me off here, alone." She paused, watching Marston scribble in his notebook. With emphasis, she added, "I thought he was already dead!" Marston smiled faintly. "I don't care if you don't believe me, it's true!" she said, letting her voice rise slightly. "We all did."

"Fine," he said blankly, "That's fine. Now, let's move on to the parts you neglected to tell us about."

"That's not so easy," she said, pulling hard on her cigarette.

"Force yourself," Marston said, and his tone implied that he was going to hold her feet to the fire. "Think of it as an opportunity for self-improvement."

"Don't get cute, Lieutenant," she said, her voice hard.

"Don't get your back up," was his response. "Just get on with it."

They each held their ground and it seemed the logjam wasn't going to break, so I decided to try diplomacy.

"Samantha," I began. Her gaze shifted toward me. "You're in a tight spot. The way Shelton tells the story, you are the obvious choice for guilty party number one. If the four of you cut a deal that night, tell us about it. Forget the posturing. Nobody wants to be a hard-ass, but if you don't talk we'll all end up in a small room downtown where the furniture's not so nice and the light gets in your eyes. So both of you back off a little bit. Shake hands or something. Just stop trying to stare each other to death. OK?"

"You're right," Marston said to me, then he turned to Samantha. "I apologize." Samantha nodded agreement and the atmosphere almost visibly lightened. Samantha turned and headed for her armchair by the window. When she left her shoes along the way, I knew we were making progress.

"Naturally, I was surprised, shocked." She stopped as though listening to herself and deciding it was too glib. When she spoke again, her voice was lower and held more conviction. "I couldn't believe there was a body on the floor. I thought it was a joke or something. Then I saw it was Lane and I . . ." she let it drop. "I knelt by him. Touched his face and it was cool, not cold, but there was no warmth. I thought he was dead."

Marston was busy writing.

"Did you pick up the gun then?" I asked her.

"No. I didn't do anything. I just stayed there, on the floor. I don't know how long. I'd never seen a dead person before," she said, looking across to Marston. "I just stared at him."

"What was the next thing that happened?" I asked.

"The door opened and Banks came in," she said.

"Did he offer any explanation as to why he'd come back?"

"No, other than to say he felt something was wrong, but . . ."

"But what?" I asked.

"Well, I felt—no, I knew he'd followed me upstairs because of what Leonard had said at dinner that night."

"About you seeing Lane."

"Yes. Banks said he hadn't believed a word Leonard said, but I could tell he had. He was here because he was checking up on me."

"Was he alone?" Marston asked.

"No, Randall was with him," she said. "Randall was always with him."

The cigarette in her hand had burned down to the filter and gone out. She held it without noticing.

"Starting from when Reid and Bergman arrived, what do you recall of the conversation?" I asked.

"Banks rushed over to me and started talking," she said. "I don't really remember what he said, it was a jumble. He gave me something to drink, brandy, scotch, something. He wanted to know what had happened." She paused, then continued. "He wanted to know if I'd shot Lane or if he'd shot himself. I told him the body was there when I came in and that I didn't know anything else."

"Where was Bergman during all this?" Marston asked.

"He was on the other side of Lane's body, kneeling down. He was the reason I picked up the gun."

Marston gave a quick glance of interest. "Could you explain that?" he asked.

"We were all there by the body and he, Randall, said, 'Poor Laney, can't say that I'm surprised,' and then he laughed. I wanted to strangle him, scratch his eyes out. Then I saw the gun. I grabbed it—I don't know what I would have done—and we both jumped up. That's when we noticed Shelton standing in the doorway. The bastard!"

"Who?" I asked.

"Oh, all of them. Randall. Sharp. Lane. Bastards."

The next question seemed obvious enough, so I asked it. "Who suggested that Leonard get pinned with Lane's death?"

"No one at first," Samantha answered. "Everybody just stood and jabbered at each other. What happened? Who did this? My God! Oh, shit! Everyone seemed to come apart all at once. Then we heard the elevator going back down to the lobby."

Marston walked over to her chair and in honest confusion asked, "What were you planning to do? Hide in the closets?"

"We didn't have a plan, Lieutenant," she said forlornly. "Maybe we thought whoever it was would go away." She looked at Marston and said with wonder in her voice, "We hid behind the furniture like children."

"But it turned out to be Leonard and he walked right in," I said.

"Yes."

"Will you clear this up for me?" Marston asked. "Were there a lot of lights on in the apartment? I see three, four, five lamps and no overhead fixtures. Were they all on?"

"No, only the two Chinese porcelains, plus the light in the foyer. They're all controlled by this single panel," she said indicating a row of switches behind her. "Banks was the one who turned them all off."

"Why?" I asked her.

"The pistol. When Leonard came in, he stood there for a moment, called out and then headed straight for the hall closet. He keeps a gun there," she explained. "I whispered to Reid about the gun, he turned the lights out, and Leonard fired a shot." The three of us strolled over to gaze down at the splintered oak flooring where Forensics had dug out the slug from Leonard's gun. "It scared me so badly I jumped, and since I still had the gun in my hand I must have pulled the trigger."

"With all that lead flying around, it's remarkable there was only one body on the floor," I said.

"You're right," Samantha said. "I could easily have hit Leonard."

"That might have been a little more sympathetic than letting him suffer through a jury trial and then possibly spend the rest of his life in jail for murder." There was no forgiveness in Marston's voice and Samantha clearly liked neither the comment nor his tone. For a moment I thought the logjam was back in place, but it passed.

"You don't understand," she said. "Nothing was 'worked out.' We didn't decide to point the finger at Leonard. We didn't do anything. We all scattered. . . . Leonard got knocked down, that's all. There was no discussion about who to blame."

"But on your ride down in the elevator you sort of informally put a limit on what you would say." She looked at me and I plowed ahead. "You never actually said, 'Let's have Leonard take the fall,' but you did agree to a basic outline, didn't you? A simple, 'When I got there he was already dead, Lieutenant,' and

155

if everybody held the line, the only person available would have been Leonard. Process of elimination. It must have seemed brilliant in retrospect."

"It did," she said, finally noticing her cigarette butt and dropping it into a brass trash can under the writing desk.

I looked at Marston and he shrugged slightly. Turning back to Samantha, I asked, "Did either Randall or Banks ever leave you for any length of time that night? From the time you left the theater on?"

She thought for a moment. Not like she was trying to recall something, but as if she were deciding whether to answer at all.

"If you don't tell us now," I counseled, "it'll come out later, somehow, through someone, just like it happened this time."

"Yes. The answer is yes," she said with exasperation. "Not long after we left the theater, Banks said he forgot something— his wallet, a scarf, I don't remember. But he had to go back to the Carlyle. So Randall and I went on to SoHo and Banks took a cab back uptown. Once we were inside the gallery, I lost sight of Randall, too. There were a lot of people there, most of them I knew, so it didn't matter that he wasn't there."

"Was it an extended absence for either man?" Marston asked.

"I couldn't say, really," she answered. "It was a while, but I don't know how long."

The phone rang and Samantha stepped over to pick it up. She turned to Marston, holding out the receiver.

"It's for you."

Marston accepted the receiver and listened, his body motionless.

"Right, we'll be here," he said and hung up. Turning to me he spoke quickly, his face slightly flushed with excitement. "Florio," he said. "Banks Reid is possibly on his way here. Florio was interviewing him, and when he told Reid about Sharp pointing the finger at Mrs. Craig"—he nodded in her direction— "he went . . ."

"Berserk," I offered.

156

"To the bathroom," he finished. "He was gone longer than two shakes." (A Florioism I recognized immediately.) "They went to check and he'd ducked out a bedroom door and down the stairs. There's another reason Florio thinks he may be coming here—he made the mistake of mentioning that we're questioning her." He jerked a thumb in Samantha's direction.

"Oh, Christ," Samantha muttered, rolling her eyes.

"I thought Sharp was at the top of Florio's interview list," I said.

"He was, but the guy skipped, so he doubled back to Reid's."

"Skipped, as in gone?" Samantha asked.

"They couldn't find him in any of the usual places," Marston elaborated. "He'll turn up."

"I hope you realize I'm not going to be much help if Reid roars through that door," I said.

"I don't think it'll come to that. Mrs. Craig," he said, turning to her, "do you know if Banks Reid owns or carries a gun?"

"I know he owns guns," she said, "but I've never undressed him and found one. Does that answer your question?"

"Yes, thank you," Marston said, ignoring the suggestive, challenging tone. "Have you ever seen any kind of gun in his New York apartment? You know, under his bed or in the drawer where he keeps his wallet at night. You do know where he keeps his wallet, right?"

"Come on, John," I said, stepping between them, "take it easy. Samantha, would you please call the doorman and ask him to let us know if Reid comes in?" She hesitated a second. "It would be helpful, OK?"

"Yes, I'll do that." And she started across the room to the intercom panel, but before she could reach it the phone rang again. She stopped, came back, and picked up the receiver. She gave a little flip of her head, throwing her hair out away from her ear as she brought the receiver up, revealing a beautiful green emerald earring set amid a spray of diamonds. It glistened as the light hit it, and I wondered who had given her those. Without speaking, she shoved the phone toward Marston.

"Yeah," he barked into the mouthpiece. After talking briefly, he gave his attention to me and the phone back to Samantha. "Florio wants to see me back at the station," he said. "Could you stay here in case Reid shows up? Florio's worried that he might pick up a gun on his way over here. Wait," he said, cutting my protest short, "a couple of officers are on their way. They'll be downstairs any minute. All I'm asking is that you stay until they arrive. Thanks, Ham."

Marston was already on his way out, and it seemed too late to refuse. Besides, the lady was attractive. I only wished I trusted her more. The door slammed behind him, leaving us in silence.

"Don't look so forlorn, Mr. Hamilton," she said. "I promise not to get violent."

"I think it's Reid we're concerned about," I told her. "I'd be glad to wait downstairs, if you mind my being here."

"Not at all, and I don't think you should be too concerned about Banks; he's not the violent type." She glanced at her watch. "At least you won't have to be here long. It's only ten blocks."

"You don't know too much about New York's finest, do you? Unless Florio is sitting on their ass, those officers might not rush right over. This is Manhattan, not River City, and there are a lot of distractions between here and there."

She laughed and for the first time seemed relaxed. Without the cover of her "don't try to fuck me" attitude, the woman that had turned Leonard Craig and Banks Reid into silly putty began to surface. Her face might not launch a thousand ships, but she could sure fill the harbor with sampans.

"Surely they'd respond to an emergency," she said, amused.

"Picture this," I said and moved over to the couch in front of her. "It's two o'clock Sunday morning and you're in a squad car at Lenox Avenue and 116th Street drinking coffee. Your partner's clipping his nails. The dispatcher comes across with a fight, shots fired, ambulance needed, and requesting closest units respond to the Backdoor Lounge at 127th and Broadway under the el. What happens?"

158

She looked at me wide-eyed and innocent. "I don't know; I suppose they'd speed off into the night like . . . Kojak."

"Really? You watched that show?"

"Oh yes," she said. "One of my favorites. I still like to catch a rerun now and then." She smiled and for the first time I liked her. This was a woman to meet under other circumstances. Leonard Craig wasn't crazy. He might not even have been lonely. Samantha just swept him off his feet and I was beginning to see how. She was more than a sharp tongue. A lot more.

"Well," I continued, "not being Kojak, these guys just sit there and drink coffee, ten-four the dispatcher, and hit the siren so it sounds like they're speeding through the night, at least over the radio. Then, our guy finishes with his hangnail, folds up his clippers, puts them away, and asks, Ready Sam? They cruise through the night making sure to catch most of the lights on the way and by the time they arrive, the fight's over, the smoke has settled, and the only bodies left are the ones on the floor. It's one thing to be responsible in the performance of your duty and quite another to be a dead zealot. You have to know your situation and be familiar with the circumstances."

"I see, I see," she said, laughing. "Very entertaining vignette. Thank you."

"You're welcome."

"Let's have a drink," she suggested, a little attitude slipping back in, but this time an inviting one.

Remembering the last time I stumbled out of her apartment, and the tentative condition of my stomach, I opted for a diet soda and offered to fix her a scotch.

"Is that because of your injury?"

"Yes."

"I read about it. I hope you're all right."

"Fine, really." I handed her the scotch and sipped the fizz off the top of my soda. "Oh, and I found your cigarettes," I said, holding out the pack of Larks, "between the Beefeaters and the Remy Martin." She immediately lit one and produced a billow of smoke.

159

"Tell me something about Lieutenant Marston and Captain Florio," she said, looking at me straight. "What do they think?"

"About what?"

"Me," she said simply. "What do they think about me, my part in these murders."

"Aside from being a possible A-Number-One suspect, they think you tried to play them for fools, which you did. Had they arrested your husband at the beginning," I continued, "and they most certainly would have if Roseman hadn't stepped in, they'd be looking pretty stupid today, now that your little gang-of-four conspiracy has unraveled."

"You think it was destined to unravel?"

"Without question," I said. "The four of you weren't exactly the best of friends. It was just a matter of time before somebody got in a snit and started to blab." She was quiet for a moment, smoking. "Whoever the killer is, he was pretty quick to come to the same conclusion, and he decided not to take any chances. He didn't wait twenty minutes before killing a defenseless ex-con who could have been bought for less money than the cost of the ammunition it took to blow him away. Naw, your little band of merry men had about as much chance of holding together as an Italian coalition government.

"You shouldn't take any chances either," I warned, and she looked at me quickly. "I only mean to say that if you're not Annie Oakley, you could be in serious danger."

"I hadn't thought of that," she said. I believed her, she hadn't. And if she'd thought about her disappearing associates at all it was in terms of not being able to find an even number for dinner. No doubt, she figured she was loved and envied by all, and safe in their adoration.

"You need a drink don't you?" she said, handing me her empty glass. "Don't make a girl drink by herself." I held off.

"None of you could have counted on Leonard's friendship with Roseman," I said, reaching for fresh ice. "You figured Florio and Marston would be like every cop you've ever seen on TV . . ."

160

"Kojak excluded, of course."

"Of course."

"Will they ever forgive me?" she asked coyly as I handed her a second scotch.

"Oh, they'll forgive you, no problem. They also might arrest you."

"What for? I told them the truth."

"Accessory after the fact, obstructing a police investigation, aiding and abetting, lots of little things like that."

"How about that drink now?" she asked.

"No, I don't believe so."

"Is it also because of ethics?"

"Partially," I said, starting to feel uncomfortable.

"Never drink on business. Is that it? You did the other day," she said, crossing to me. "I thought we got along very well. Didn't you?" She placed her hand against my chest, lightly drumming her fingers underneath my bow tie. She smelled wonderful. "Randall must have disliked you very much."

"Never knew the man."

"Well, what could he have had against you, then?"

"I was under the impression you'd supplied him with that information."

She cocked her head and the fingers stopped moving.

"Whatever are you talking about?" she asked with honest curiosity. We spent the next moment searching for truth in each other's eyes; I decided that my uneasiness was not going to dissipate regardless of what I thought I saw in those green liquid pools.

"I had something Randall wanted."

"Oh, my," she said softly, backing up a step. "He called me again, later that same day. He said he had lost a valuable piece of paper; a bearer bond, I believe he called it . . . not that I believed him." She gave me a wide-eyed look, slowly putting things together. "I told him what you said about not finding anything. Little secrets, remember?"

I said I did.

"I had no idea."

"I'm sure you didn't. I should have kept my mouth shut."

"If it means anything, I'm sorry."

"That's OK," I said lightly, and I dropped my gaze to the floor. "You have beautiful feet," I said, surprising myself.

"That's probably the nicest thing anyone's ever said to me," she said, and she stretched one out for a better inspection, flexing and pointing a couple of times; slim ankle, fine skin.

"I didn't mean that as a come-on," I said, feeling ridiculous. "It was only an observation. They look great in heels, too."

"Thank you," she beamed. "Let's have that drink."

It would have been easy to say yes. I wanted to but I couldn't relax. I couldn't let go. I couldn't forget. "I think I'd better wait downstairs." And without looking at her I walked out the door. She didn't try to stop me.

When I got downstairs, there was no sign of Florio's men, so I bummed a cigarette from the doorman and was about halfway through it when a cab screeched to a halt out front. The passenger door flew open and Banks Reid in the flesh, looking soft and padded at about two hundred pounds, pulled himself gracelessly out of the back seat. His face was flushed and he was dead set on rescue, moving straight for the lobby. My immediate impression was how does a guy like that ever rouse himself to murder, but I knew better than to dismiss him as harmless simply based on appearance. Still, first impressions count.

"Hey!" the cabbie screamed, leaning across the front seat. "You owe me!"

Banks turned, dug awkwardly into his pocket, and threw some bills through the cab window before brushing past the doorman into the building.

"Thanks . . . asshole" was the muttered reply, but Banks was beyond hearing.

I stepped inside, picked up the phone, and called 67th Street. Florio was out so I left a message with the sergeant. My guess was Reid would be right up there in Samantha's lap when

162

they finally arrived. So, judging my duties complete, I hailed a cab and went home. I needed rest.

The front rooms of Roseman's apartment were empty when I arrived. In the kitchen, some vegetables were simmering on the stove in what looked like chicken broth—it was a semiclear liquid with yellow grease floating on top—and the *Times* lay on the table opened to the crossword puzzle. I gave it a quick glance; seventeen down, small college in North Carolina, that would be Elon, and I penciled it in for Kripp. Nothing stirring here.

I passed through the library and took the elevator downstairs to my place. Kripp had left a note on the table: "10:20 A.M. Rachel came by. Disposition good. Will call back. Roseman wants to see you. Have gone to Federal Building. Return soon. Kripp." I buzzed Roseman's office and Sandra picked up.

"Hey there," she said, recognizing my voice.

"Arthur wants to see me?"

"Yes, but he's with someone. Are you downstairs?"

"I am, but I have a lunch date at Jordan's."

"That's OK, I think he just wanted to talk about your visit to Mrs. Craig's and his visit to the hospital." Sandra had without question the sunniest voice of anyone I'd ever known, and it matched her disposition exactly. Her tone went confidential. "He said it wasn't important or anything."

"How's Leonard?"

"Not very well, I'm afraid, but he's still hanging on. Say hello to Jordan for me."

I said I would and hung up. I went into the bathroom, pulled my pain prescription from the medicine cabinet, and swallowed a palmful of orange-and-blue-coated tablets. Give me a few gins and I wouldn't need these, I thought, heading for the door. The phone rang as I passed it. I picked up on the first ring.

"Hi, it's Marilyn, glad I caught you. Would it be all right if I canceled lunch?"

"Well," I said, hesitating, "no, I mean, is everything OK?"

"I'm a little tired is all. I've been rushing around like a crazy

163

person trying to get ready to leave and I'm simply exhausted and totally unorganized. I thought maybe we could exchange lunch for dinner. I'll even throw in a movie. In fact, there's a William Holden double feature at the St. Mark's. You love his movies don't you?"

"Yes, but I thought you hated that place because the seats are mushy and your feet stick to the floor."

"I know, but they make their own popcorn."

"OK, it's a deal."

"Great! What do you think about coming out tomorrow?"

"It's still a matter of what happens here," I said. "We'll just have to wait and see."

"Sure. I'll see you about seven then, at Jordan's."

"Fine."

"Love you."

"Love you, too," I said, and wondered if I did. I also wondered if she really loved me or just felt I was being drawn away from her. The natural response to that was an emotional clutch. I didn't know. We'd have to talk it out. At the moment, though, I had a free afternoon and I intended to use it to find Shelton Sharp before the police did.

CHAPTER FIFTEEN

Two and a half hours later, I was traveling west on 17th Street in a cab that had seen action as Rommel's staff car in North Africa. What little piss and vinegar I had left when I'd stepped aboard at Astor Place was knocked out of me by the time I paid off the driver and walked the last block to the Burlington. On my way up the street, I wondered where I ever got the idea I could grow up to be a private detective; a shortstop for the Chicago White Sox maybe, but investigative work was proving to be over my head. Not only had I failed to find Sharp, but I had also been berated by the super in his building when I only offered him twenty bucks to let me into Sharp's apartment. On top of that, I couldn't even locate the two contacts I have in the theater who might have been able to tell me something about Sharp's habits or whereabouts. The kicker was when I asked the young cop on duty at Sharp's theater for permission to look around inside and he told me to go fuck myself. I could have fed the kid's ass to Florio, but by that time I was starting to fade and it didn't seem worth the effort. I needed a drink, not a hassle, thus the cab. I pushed through the door at Jordan's with the clock showing twenty past two. It was good to be home again.

Mid-afternoon is my favorite time in a bar. A dead zone—lunch is over and the evening has yet to start. Customers are few and, generally, the staff relax and negotiate airtime for their favorite music on the sound system while they prep for dinner. Phil Collins and the Talking Heads replace Old Blue Eyes pretty quickly once the last lunch check clears the register. No one is rushed, and if you don't mind the occasional rattle of cutlery and plates it's a great time to lie back and collect yourself over a few drinks.

As I came in, there were four customers still lingering. A slender young woman in blue jeans, new Reeboks, and a heavy sweatshirt pulled over a teal blue shirt that matched her socks sat at the bar reading a Stephen King paperback. At the table immediately on my left, a sandy-haired man in a business suit was browsing through the *Wall Street Journal*, dragging pages across the remains of his long-finished lunch, till a waiter I didn't recognize collected his plate; then a steaming cup of coffee hit the tabletop in front of him just behind the swipe of a damp bar towel. And near the partition at the back, a couple—of undetermined age but obvious intent—whispered to each other and snuck kisses over cappuccino.

Jordan, also seated at the bar, looked up from his paperwork as I approached. He laid down his bifocals, closed the checkbook, and caressed the bridge of his nose with two fingers. Martin was stacking highball glasses, and the two had a brief exchange that I couldn't catch. I walked over, took Jordan's hand, gave it a squeeze, and settled on the stool next to him.

"Buy a wounded man a drink?" I asked him.

"Wounded?" he asked, looking at me hard. "You should live to be a hundred and twenty and ten days."

Martin set a bottle of brandy and two glasses in front of us. "Thanks, Martin," I said, and we exchanged winks. Turning to Jordan I asked, "A hundred and twenty and ten days? What the hell are you talking about? Ten days."

"I wouldn't want you to die suddenly," he said, jerking the

166

cork from the bottle. "This should put some color back in your cheeks."

We touched glasses and drank. It ain't gin, I thought to myself, pouring another, but it does the trick.

"I realized only this morning, Jordan," I said, refilling his glass also, "that if I don't get down here at least every other day, I start to lose continuity in my life. You have created"—I gave a panoramic sweep of my hand across the room—"a real *haimisher mensh* here. Can I say that about a place instead of a person?" And I rolled down the second brandy. "This is where I feel I can come and kick off my shoes, take a rest, you know?" Jordan blew up like an old tire. I wasn't trying to flatter him. It was true. I loved being there, at all hours, on any day, to eat, to drink, or just to sit.

"That's why I'm here," he said. "So that you, and four or five hundred other people, can express exactly the same sentiments every day." Then he added, for my benefit, "Naturally, those sentiments mean more coming from certain people."

Another reason I liked to rest and recuperate at The Burlington was Jordan's ability to listen. He was the consummate sounding board: noncommittal, attentive, discreet. Chatting with Jordan was sort of like praying out loud. By verbalizing my thoughts, I was better able to separate the substantial from the superfluous. I mean, after you actually hear yourself ask God for cash, a Ferrari, and the girl at the next table, it sounds a little tinny. Plus I was comfortable with Jordan. I talked to Florio because I had to, and in Roseman's case it was often just a matter of recital—he drew his own conclusions; but with Jordan, I simply talked about anything that came into my head. It didn't have to relate to the case at hand either.

Unfortunately, there was a down side to this procedure, because Jordan had the irritating habit of retaining the echoes of your past statements, combining them with your premature conclusions, and then tossing them back at you naked and unveiled. He could do this, I suspected, because he wasn't a heavy drinker, and while you were in your cups spouting off, he was eight drinks behind you taking notes. The end result was having to listen to your own stupid, biased observations made without benefit of proper thought. But it worked, so I didn't argue with the process.

"A couple of people called for you," Jordan said, putting his glasses back on and opening a notebook. As he flipped pages I asked Martin for a bowl of tomato soup, french bread, and a gin with lemon.

"You haven't spoken to Arthur since you left your apartment?" Jordan asked, finding the page he wanted.

"No. Sandra said he wanted to talk to me, but not urgently."

"He called," Jordan said, rolling his eyes and muttering in Yiddish something I didn't understand.

"Also," he continued, "Marilyn called . . . she might be a little late."

"What do you think of her?" I asked him.

"Marilyn is a very nice girl, David," he said, pouring himself another brandy. "Lots of money, not quite as much intellect, and possibly no ambition at all; I mean, she's not a lawyer or a doctor and sometimes she's not even very good at conversation. I like her though, don't get me wrong." He threw up his hands dramatically and added, "It doesn't matter what I think, *bubee*."

I looked into my soup. Jordan continued as though we'd paused to discuss the weather.

"John Marston called—now he's an attractive man," he said, putting down his notepad. "Married?"

"I think he's divorced." Even Martin leaned a little in our direction.

"Well, well, well," Jordan mused, "not exactly my type . . ."

"You mean that he's straight or not a doctor?"

"David, please . . ."

"Attractive none the less, huh?"

"Yes, and he dresses so well. Very attractive indeed. Anyway," Jordan reopened the notepad, "the lieutenant called to say they had not picked up Banks Reid, but thank you very much

168

for the phone call and he said drinks were on him next time—here, of course."

"Your suggestion."

"Naturally," he said, and he tried not to look too pleased with himself.

"This is delicious soup by the way," I said, finishing the last bit and wondering why Reid hadn't stayed at Samantha's. "Can Kripp get the recipe?" Martin dutifully headed for the kitchen. Jordan folded his business papers and we carried our drinks over to a table discreetly distanced both from the earnibbling duo and the *WSJ* reader who was working on his second cup of coffee. We were barely settled when Martin arrived with the recipe.

"That man is remarkably efficient," I said as Martin walked away. "If you continue to show interest in Marston, I think he'll deliver more than fresh drinks on a tray, if you get my meaning."

"I certainly do," Jordan said lightly. "I most certainly do. So what's new? What have you been doing these last two days?"

"Not much that you haven't already read about. Trying to stay healthy."

"That I know; I asked what's new?"

"Isn't that enough?"

"Talk to your Uncle Jordan."

"Ah shit, Jordan," I said, "we're back to square one."

"Meaning?"

I tasted my gin and blew out a deep breath.

"Four people are dead, nobody has been arrested, and all the suspects are sticking to their grimy little alibis; the case is dead in the water. Then, all of a sudden, Shelton Sharp breaks from the pack and points an accusing finger at Samantha Craig."

"Sounds like movement in the right direction."

"In a backward sort of way, perhaps. Everybody has to be questioned again and, no doubt, they'll all bend their stories to fit the prevailing wind. It really is exhausting."

"It's movement where there was none before."

"True, but it's the kind of movement that makes me nervous."

"Why do you keep making these enigmatic statements? Talk to me."

I rolled some gin over my tongue and watched the young woman at the bar as she turned a page of her book.

"Jordan, this case started with a lot of movement; it generated four bodies in an awful hurry. Now we've got movement again."

"You don't think it's over, then? The killing?"

"No, I don't." I finished the gin and picked up the one Martin had left.

"Have you talked to Florio about it?"

"Kind of, but not really. He's aware of it, too. We talk around it a lot."

"From what I've read about the remaining suspects, I don't think it will be much of a loss, regardless."

I looked at Jordan, annoyed with him for one of the few times I could remember. "As an abstract intellectualization of the human condition, that's an acceptable statement, Jordan. But in terms of life, liberty, and the pursuit of happiness, it comes up a little short."

"Now you sound like Carl Sagan."

"Yeah, you're right, forget it."

"Death," Jordan said after a moment. "It shouldn't happen to a dog."

We drank for a while, letting the afternoon disappear. Jordan ordered a bowl of french fries à la Burlington: huge strips of potatoes, skins intact, that are pressed out in the kitchen seconds before they hit the grease. Jordan soaked them in vinegar, added enough salt to bloat a cow, and then poured on the ketchup. God knows how he kept his weight down. His blood pressure had to be doing gymnastics. He pushed the bowl toward me and I helped myself.

"Who do you think it is?" Jordan asked, biting a fry in half.

"I don't know." He frowned at me. "Honestly, I don't know. If I did, it'd be over, right? Arrest made. Case closed."

"What you think, and who Florio arrests, often are two

170

very different things," he said matter-of-factly, finishing off the end of his fry and silently sucking his fingertips before dabbing them on his napkin. "I only asked who you thought it was," he repeated. "It's quite possible you think all three of them have equal motive and opportunity. If you'd rather not talk about it, I could always do the crossword."

Wagging a french fry in his direction, I told him what I thought.

"Any one of them could have killed Peters," I said. "Samantha could have shot him moments after she walked in the door, or she could have found him lying there like she told Florio. It is also possible that Banks Reid left Samantha, came back uptown, found Peters, then shot him in a fit of jealousy, leaving him to be found later."

"And Sharp?"

"Sharp started out with the old standby, I was home alone all evening, but now he's changed his tune and is fingering Samantha as the prime suspect."

"Fingering? How?"

I told Jordan all about my meeting with Sharp.

"That's a story you believe?" Jordan asked when I had finished.

"I don't know," I said hopelessly, and I watched the day's fading light drift across the bottles behind the bar.

"He might be lying," Jordan suggested. "With the stage manager out of the way, there's no one to say what Sharp did after the curtain dropped. You only have his word that he got tied up and ran late. He could have gotten there early, left, come back, left again."

"I realize that."

"A man isn't a thief just because he doesn't have a chance to steal," Jordan said.

"I know, I know. And the stage manager was sent home, he didn't elect to go. The guy said he didn't feel great but he could have stuck it out. Sharp urged him to leave. That's an important distinction."

171

"So Sharp created a situation he could take advantage of."

"You're right," I agreed. "But it sounds kind of weak to me. I've been trying to reach a kid named Paul Hemp." I pulled a scrap of paper out of my pocket, unfolded it on the table, and tried to smooth out the wrinkles so I could read the phone numbers.

"Who is he?" Jordan wanted to know, reaching for another napkin.

"The stage manager who took over for the few days while his colleague was ill," I told him, and he nodded vaguely and shook more ketchup into the bowl. I picked up our glasses and carried them to the bar for refills. There was no bartender in sight so I stepped around the corner to fix them myself. "He would have been the guy to oversee the play's run that night," I said loudly enough to carry back to the table, "lights, sound effects, cues, curtain, everything would have been his responsibility with the stage manager out sick."

"You think he might substantiate Sharp's story?" Jordan said.

"He certainly would know a lot about what went on that night. Problem is, I haven't caught him at home or the theater." The young woman reading Stephen King marked her page and set it aside. She asked for a white wine, which I poured and rang into the register before going back to the table. "Depending on what time Marilyn arrives, I thought we would eat something here and maybe stop by his apartment before the movie."

"Friday afternoon," Jordan said. "I imagine he's at the theater already."

"That's a thought," I said, sipping the tonic off the top of my gin. I went back to the bar, dialed the kid's number, and got a roommate who told me he had left about an hour ago for the Cherry Lane Theater. He gave me the number. I hung up and turned to Jordan.

"There's something else that bothers me, too," I said to him as he looked up from his bowl, "the Chinese food."

"What about it?"

"The fact that it was there at all; that somebody took the time

172

to order it; presumably Lane, since Samantha says she never eats the stuff."

"I see."

"Do you?"

"No, I guess I don't," he said, reconsidering.

"When do you order Chinese takeout, Jordan?"

"When the kitchen is closed."

"Goddamnit, Jordan, be serious for a minute."

"OK. I order Chinese takeout when: I don't feel like fixing anything for myself; it's late and I want a nosh before turning in; or I'm about to get into bed with someone interesting and watch an old Cary Grant movie—sex always makes me ravenous."

"Exactly."

"Exactly what?"

"You're exactly right. The other day Kripp brought home some Chinese and we spread it all over the kitchen, kicked back, and watched the news."

"That's not what I call sex and I still don't follow you."

"Chinese take-out is casual, mobile, relaxed; it's not the sort of thing you'd expect someone to do if he was dreading a confrontation with a rejected lover, is it?"

"So maybe they weren't going to fight," Jordan concluded, joining my train of thought at last. "Maybe they were going to watch . . . an old Cary Grant movie," we said in unison.

"So why did Sharp give you the song and dance routine?" he asked. I ignored him. "I'm listening."

I ignored him again, dialed, and asked for the kid by name. Two clicks later, a young, vibrant voice said, "Paul Hemp here."

"Hi, Paul, my name is David Hamilton and I'm investigating the death of Lane Peters."

"Oh, yeah, I got a couple of messages that you'd called."

"Are you always so prompt in getting back to people?"

"Only if it's my agent; otherwise, it might be someone from the night before and I just can't place the name, you know?"

"Well, not recently," I said and got a laugh.

"What can I do for you, Mr. Hamilton?"

"I understand you work with Brock Leland quite often and, in fact, you were with *Macbeth* at the New Reach before it closed."

"Yeah, we're good friends. But I don't work with him as much as work for him."

"I don't follow."

"Well, usually, Brock's running one show and I'll have my own, like here at the Cherry Lane. If something comes up, you know, he gets sick or wants a night off, then, I'll fill in for him."

"What about the show you're working on in a case like that?"

"If I'm in production, he asks somebody else, but with rehearsals, I can usually cut loose."

"Is that what happened with *Macbeth*?"

"Basically, yeah. The first night Shelton covered the show himself, because Brock went home sick in the middle of the second or third act. I was there the next night and then Brock came back."

"Was everything in order for you the night you worked the show? I mean, did you just walk in, turn on the lights, and raise the curtain?"

"When you've got an understudy replacing your lead, you never just walk in and turn on the lights," he said, laughing. "Brock uses good people and they'd been running for almost ten weeks, so there weren't any real surprises, considering everyone was suffering from the shock of Lane's death."

"Anything at all strike you as unusual?"

"No, not really. Well, maybe. The set was a real mess now that I think about it. Yeah, I remember coming in early the first night and being glad I had because none of the props were set. We even had to rewind the sound tape. It took three of us the better part of an hour to get everything ready and double checked, but once we got it up, the show ran well."

"Did you see Sharp at all the first night?"

"Well, we spoke by phone right after the show came down the night Brock got sick, but I actually didn't see him until late

174

the next day. He was already drunk by then and what he said didn't make much sense."

"Yeah, he was pretty tanked the day I talked to him, too. Is he a big boozer?"

"Not out of line for someone in the theater." I laughed at that. "But when your leading man gets blown away like Lane did, I think a guy deserves a few drinks."

"You're right there."

"And if he also happens to be your lover, then even drunk is understandable."

"Lover?"

"Yeah."

"As in gay?"

"Right."

"Queer?"

"Yes." He laughed this time. "They were lovers."

"Christ," I said slowly. "How long?"

"Since Lane first came to the theater, I think. Certainly as long as I can remember."

"Was that general knowledge?"

"Sure, if you knew them, but Shelton liked to keep it kind of quiet."

"Whatever for?"

"Well, I guess not to offend any of the backers. You know . . ." he chuckled to himself, "a lot of those people like for you to think they're liberal as hell—some of my best friends and all that bullshit. But the truth is if they ever knowingly sat down to dinner with a homosexual they'd gag on their lamb."

"I see your point. Thanks, Paul."

"You're welcome."

"But next time, answer your goddamn messages, I might be casting a show for Hal Prince."

"Yeah, sure."

"Oh, one more thing. Do you know who Sharp was involved with prior to Lane Peters?"

"Randall Bergman."

"For a long time?"

"Years."

"Thanks again."

"You bet." The line went dead.

"I knew it," I mumbled to myself. "Goddamn, it makes sense now." I hung up and turned to Jordan. "I'm so fucking stupid I can't believe it."

"Stupid?" he said, puzzled, and dusted a fry with another layer of salt.

"Yes, stupid. Shelton lied."

"Who hasn't? All have sinned and come short of the glory of God."

"Don't be so deflating and listen." Noticing that I had gained the undivided attention of The Burlington's only four paying customers, I lowered my voice and crossed back to the table. "Sharp lied to Florio about staying around after the show that night. He definitely had time to get to the apartment ahead of anyone else and shoot Lane."

"Why?"

"Because Sharp and Lane were lovers." He looked at me blankly. "They were lovers," I repeated.

"You've said that."

"Lovers quarrel. Lovers fight. Lovers get jealous of partners who enjoy themselves and order Chinese food while they watch old Cary Grant movies in bed with lovely women."

"Agreed, but all you've got now is someone else with opportunity as well as motive."

"Boy, you're no fun today."

The phone rang and it was answered in the kitchen. Seconds later, Herman pushed open the swinging door to the accompaniment of clanging pots and raging faucets to tell me that I had a phone call. I drained the gin and, feeling almost youthful, crossed back to the bar.

"Hamilton," I said expecting Marilyn with more delaying tactics.

176

"You better get up here," Marston said, with no fun in his voice.

"Where are you?"

"Craig's and hurry, the morgue's already on its way." My stomach sank. I didn't ask for details. I just hung up.

"You've lost your color again," Jordan said, slipping on his glasses. "Is it bad news?"

"Another body," I told him. "Another goddamn body."

"Who is it?"

"I didn't ask. I didn't want to know. They're at the Craigs' apartment, so it's natural to assume . . ." I let it drop. "Listen, if I'm not back by the time Marilyn gets here, would you see that she doesn't eat alone?"

"Not to worry, Uncle Jordan will take care of everything."

"I'll call as soon as I know something," I said to him and ran for the door.

CHAPTER SIXTEEN

Samantha Craig hung from a cross beam in the center of her kitchen. A thick purple cord with gold fringe at the ends was knotted at the beam and wrapped once around her neck before dropping to the floor. Her feet—those fine-boned, delicate feet—swung gently in a nonexistent breeze, touching lightly against the stainless steel sink then swinging back in the direction of the pantry closet across the room. She was naked except for a white terry cloth bathrobe that had fallen open, exposing her breasts and trim body. I noticed that her stomach was remarkably flat and firm, then, disgusted with myself, I turned away.

Florio was huddled with two uniformed officers near the telephone on the other side of the couch, so I picked on Marston who was standing just outside the kitchen door lighting a fresh cigarette off the butt of his last one.

"Can't you get her down for Christ sakes!" I shouted at him.

"No, I can't," he snapped back. "It's not a suicide, which makes it murder and Florio doesn't want the body moved until the ME gets here. OK?"

"I can't fuckin' believe this," I said, staring back into the kitchen. "I can't fucking believe it."

Marston looked at me with sadness, guilt, and regret all registered in his face. "I know exactly what you mean," he said and pulled on his smoke.

"What happened? Didn't those officers stay? Wasn't there supposed to be somebody downstairs? What the fuck happened?" I was shouting again; Florio glanced over, then looked away.

"I don't know what the fuck happened," Marston insisted. "We had two men out front and they didn't see anything, but no one was watching the back, so it's conceivable that someone came up through the service entrance."

"Have you ruled out suicide entirely?"

"Come on, Ham," he said, jabbing his cigarette at the body swaying in the kitchen, "women like Samantha don't kill themselves. They want to survive."

"You're right," I admitted. "I can't picture her climbing up on a kitchen counter either."

"I'll bet my next paycheck the medical examiner finds she was dead before she was strung up," Marston continued, and I had to agree with him again.

"Her neck is definitely broken," I said, stepping into the kitchen and looking back up at the body. I had to squint because of the recessed light fixture near her head.

"How can you tell?" Marston asked, following me through the door.

"I'm only guessing from this distance, but for one thing, right at the base of the skull, can you see that large bruise? And then there's the way the head twists as it lays over."

"Jesus Christ, Ham."

"Sorry, John, too many years with the medical examiner."

The tip of Marston's cigarette glowed red hot and smoke billowed downward against his shirt and tie as he exhaled through his nose. "She might have been a bitch, but she was a beautiful woman," he said softly. "Goddamn." He turned away. I pushed the door shut behind us as we walked back into the living room. With the door closed, it was almost possible to imagine that nothing was out of place; just a small group of men in

180

business suits, getting together after work for some conversation and a few drinks. There wasn't a body hanging in the kitchen. These men weren't cops. God, perception was weird, like owning a home at the beach; as long as you faced the ocean it was vacation, sunshine, cold beer, and good times. The sound of the waves pushed all other thoughts out of your mind, while the sea breeze brought the smell of fresh salt air and the cry of gulls. But out the other windows, the ones facing inland, the highway, there was the reality of uncut lawns, peeling paint, rust, and another hot, unrelenting summer day. Samantha Craig was dead. Murdered. Her body hung in the kitchen casting an enormous shadow on the clean, waxed floor. But if we chose to never look in there again, if we just kept looking at the ocean, then her death would never have to be dealt with. I could use some time at the beach. Marilyn was right. I needed to get away.

The elevator opened and a lean, quick-stepping man in his mid-fifties bustled in. His attitude was businesslike, his manner was take-charge. Florio broke away from his group and the two men became the focus of the entire room as they met outside the kitchen door.

Dr. Timothy Ellerton, associate medical examiner for the City of New York, sensed the attention that his arrival generated, and he came to a stop.

"Well, I don't know if I remember ever having been so eagerly awaited," he quipped. "Is this a surprise birthday party arranged by my ex-wife? About her style, I'd say." He slipped on his half-glasses and asked conversationally, "So where's the cake?"

Marston cleared his throat and motioned toward the kitchen. Ellerton walked through, letting the door swing shut behind him. Nobody followed. It was as if we expected him to scream and come running out with his hands in front of his face. Instead, his head popped back into the living room showing no signs of emotion. He looked at Florio.

"I'll need some help getting her down in a minute, Captain," he said.

181

The spell broke under Ellerton's precise hammer tap, sending cigarettes into designated ashtrays and everyone to work.

Ellerton had been in the ME's office since before I worked there. He was an assistant when I first met him—capable, hardworking, and enthusiastic. He still was all those things, but the years of broken bodies in almost incomprehensible volume had taken their toll on his once jovial nature, leaving a dry, acerbic wit. He wasn't a cynical man; rather, he coupled bemused observation with a special knowledge of the city that he served, a city in which the human condition was slowly, inexorably, corroding.

At this point in his career, he was set on retirement-coast; doing his job and doing it well, just a little detached.

I followed Florio and a couple of his men into the kitchen. Ellerton seemed more nimble than his years should have allowed as he hopped onto the countertop, medical case in hand. He stood well over six feet and his slim frame now towered above Samantha's dangling body as he probed her neck with his equally slim fingers. Her body spun clockwise under the pressure of his inspection, a movement that made all but the most seasoned officers blanch. I glanced at Florio and even he seemed pale. I couldn't have looked much better.

"OK, let's get her down," Ellerton boomed from above. "Just hold her legs and lift slightly so I can slip this knot."

Samantha's weight came down into my arms as the ambulance attendants pushed their stretcher through the door. One of the medics stepped up to catch the body around the waist and together we laid her onto the white sheet. Her skin felt cool. Her legs, bloated and soft.

Ellerton jumped down with a just little too much energy and good health for me.

"I'll have to wait until I get her downtown for a more extensive examination," he said, straightening his jacket. "But after a cursory review, I'd say she's been dead about two hours.

Excellent light up there," he remarked, glancing back toward the ceiling.

"What killed her?" Florio asked.

"A severe blow to the neck with a piece of half-inch pipe."

I looked at him in comic disbelief.

"Pipe?" Florio repeated.

"Pipe," he said confidently.

"I thought you were a medical examiner, not a construction foreman," Florio said.

"True, Captain. A fireplace poker will substitute nicely," he said, smiling. "How's that?"

"Better, thanks Tim."

"Welcome. You guys come visit the plant some time. Get Ham, here, to bring you down for a tour. We've had some nice changes since you left," he added to me.

"Still the best coffee in town?" I asked.

"You bet. Makes it worth coming to the office. See you."

"They do have good coffee down there," I said to Florio as Ellerton left, "he blends it himself."

"Makes you wonder what the secret ingredient is, huh?" he said, trying for humor, but his thoughts were somewhere else. "Marston!"

"Right here," John said, stepping into the kitchen.

"Have we located Banks Reid?"

"Not yet."

"Any word from the unit we sent down to Sharp's?"

"No, they haven't checked in."

"Find them!"

"Right."

"Hey," I said, lights coming on for me, "I have some information about Sharp and his alibi for Peters' death."

"What's that?" Florio asked, turning to me without excitement.

"It's a piece of shit," I said. Florio's expression didn't change and I wondered if he'd heard me. "I finally got in touch with the stage manager who covered the *Macbeth* production when Sharp

183

sent his guy home. He said Sharp didn't spend any time at the theater after the show that night. His movements are totally unaccounted for. Plus . . ." Florio looked at me expectantly, "Sharp and Peters have been lovers for a long time."

"Still no word, Captain," Marston said, coming back.

"Goddamn," the big man grumbled. "Goddamnit to hell. Bunch of fuckin' faggots. John, if you have to, send another car down there. Get to the theater. If Sharp's not there try his home address. After that," he looked at me, "any suggestions?"

"Car rentals, Grand Central, LIRR, the D train to Brooklyn maybe," I said, counting on my fingers. "Christ, Marc, he could be anywhere. He's got to know he's the man of the hour."

"He'd be crazy not to run," Marston added.

"He's crazy all right," Florio said, "but I don't think he'll run."

"Why?" Marston asked.

"Because he's crazy," Florio told him. "He's going to die at home, in the comfort of known surroundings, like a rat in a hole. That's where we'll find him. So let's get somebody down there."

I looked at the two men facing me. Young, successful professionals digging trenches across their foreheads a little deeper with each day; adding to the spread of their crows' feet. I wondered if they saw the same changes in me. I didn't carry the responsibility that they did, or the weight of accountability. I could always go back to Roseman and say I crapped out. But they had commissioners, the press, and public opinion coming down on them, questioning their performance, their ability. Perhaps they didn't think about it, consciously anyway. Suddenly, as they wheeled Samantha's body out the door, I felt a helplessness deep within me that cried out, "What's the fucking point?" and for the first time I wanted to throw up my hands and quit.

I'd busted my ass from the get-go on this case, withheld evidence from Florio, kept all my leads to myself, been shot twice, thrown up on a new suit, dragged myself out of a hospital bed that I never should have left, and all of it in defense of a man

184

I only knew in passing. A man whose innocence I'd taken as gospel on the word of someone else, Arthur Roseman.

I glanced over at Florio, remembering how, standing in this same room, I'd promised him I wouldn't get underfoot. Jesus Christ, what a joke that had turned out to be. I'd lied to him, misled him, and slipped around behind him always with the intention of letting him know . . . later, when it was more convenient. It hadn't been an easy thing to do, but I believed it had been necessary, again, because Roseman was so desperate to keep Leonard stress-free and out of jail.

Florio had never gotten the chance to interview Bergman; I took care of that for him at the Velvet Mace. I knew Marc had checked out the bar while I was in St. Vincent's, but that didn't count. The place was closed by then and the only thing the financial records showed was a low-budget tax write-off. Florio needed the chance to mingle with the crowd, pass around some pictures, hobnob with the patrons; that would have been worth seeing. But he'd never had the chance because of my being underfoot.

Florio could have pressed Reid harder for information. Maybe if he had he would have found out about Lane and Sharp being lovers, assuming of course that Reid knew about the relationship; even if Reid didn't, he was the weakest link among the suspects. Christ, that was the problem, every fucking body involved was a suspect. It wasn't like you just had one possibility, one leading candidate for the warrant; they all had motive. And lie, graduate degrees for everybody in that department.

But what did any of this have to do with Samantha's body lying under that sheet? And why, in the name of God, did I feel like such a shit?

I took a cigarette from Marston and drew strength from the smoke as I pulled it into my lungs. Feeling taller, more confident, and pushing the questions from my mind, I reentered the world around me.

"Who found the body?" I asked, breaking the silence.

"I did," Marston said softly. "When I got your message that

Reid was here, I came back. Samantha let me in and she said he'd come and gone, but I didn't take her word for it; I looked around. He wasn't here. Anyway, I thought it would be worth checking back in later. You know what?" He looked sick at the recollection. "I thought he might have slipped back upstairs using the service elevator. Nothing like being right, huh?"

I groped for something to say that might comfort him but came up empty.

"What do you think, Ham?" Florio asked.

"I think Banks Reid is innocent," I said flatly.

"Really?" He seemed to consider the possibility. "Maybe not."

"There's no other way to figure it, Marc," I said, stepping back against the stove to let one of the lab techs through. "Reid was here less than three hours ago. You couldn't have missed him by more than a couple of minutes. He might have been hiding in the bathroom."

"We checked," Marston said.

"You look under the bed, too?" I countered.

"No, we didn't do that, and we didn't check the outside windowsills either," Florio barked. "What makes you think he's so lily-white?"

"The guy is crazy about her," I said. "He's turned selfless devotion into an art form. Believe me, that's not a man who is going to club his intended with a fire iron, drag her into the kitchen, tie a cord around her neck, and then hoist her up in the air." They couldn't disagree with that.

"So tell me what happened," Florio said. "You're on a roll, keep it going."

"Simple. You guys leave. Reid comes out of his hole and slips out the back, Sharp arrives, fights with Samantha, and kills her. Then, because he's secretly a demented, vicious, spiteful, hunchbacked piece of slime, he humiliates in death the woman who cut off his balls in life, by stringing her up like a sack of oats."

"How'd she get his short hairs?" Florio demanded.

"By fucking Peters," I said. "And by persuading him to go

186

straight, give up Sharp. That's got to be the crux of it right there. The tug-of-war between Sharp and Samantha for Peters."

"Homosexuality is a biological, not a sociological . . ." Marston withered under Florio's gaze.

"It doesn't matter why he decided to swap beds," I continued looking at Florio, "but he did. Samantha won, Sharp lost, and Sharp wasn't going to let her enjoy her victory."

"So Sharp kills Peters, hoping to pin it on Samantha," Marston mused. "He must have shit when Leonard showed up."

"Yeah, it might have worked except for that," I said. "Then later, as the case against Craig starts to fall apart, Sharp tries to shift the focus back to Samantha."

"Of course," Florio scoffed, "that explains why you ended up in the basement of a leather bar with Randall Bergman on the other end of a pistol. How stupid of me. It seems so logical now."

"Listen," I said honestly. "I don't know what I'm talking about. It just rolls out. I'm trying to help for Christ sakes."

"You're a big fucking help," Florio said, his exasperation getting the better of him. "Where's Reid now? How's that for a simple question?"

"I think he's looking for Sharp," Marston said.

"Ham?" Florio asked.

"No, I think he doesn't know she's dead."

"Here we go again," said Florio, rolling his eyes.

"You're suggesting he comes back here, sees the body, and takes off to find Sharp and wring his neck?" I asked them.

"What's wrong with that?" Florio wanted to know.

"Mainly that he leaves his beloved hanging out in the kitchen and she's not watching Julia Child pound a chicken breast."

"OK, so as far as we know, Reid isn't aware that Samantha's dead. He's at the club having a drink, working out some tension in the weight room. Or maybe," he said with obvious sarcasm, "he's gone home to change clothes before picking up the lovely, dead, but still enchanting, Mrs. Craig for dinner. That about round out our choices?"

"You've had this fucking job too long, you know that?" I told him, getting edgy.

"Yeah, I know that," he said. "John, try those guys downtown again." Florio looked at me and smiled faintly. "Then we'll call the transit police and see if they've got an officer on the 'D' train in Prospect Park."

Marston came back with a negative.

"No sign of either man," he reported. "One officer's waiting at the theater while the other checks Sharp's residence."

"Shit!" Florio said.

Then we began to laugh. It started small, a chuckle by me at Florio's complete frustration; then grew as Marston joined in, covering his face with his hands to try to blunt the effect in front of his superior but still unable to stop himself. Finally, Florio himself let loose. Stress, tension, traumatic death—it all had to come out somehow. With no immediate access to alcohol, release took the form of steam from a pressure cooker, forcing its way through the valve with a hiss, sounding like laughter and smelling of tobacco instead of green beans.

I left Florio and Marston searching lower Manhattan via telephone for Reid and Sharp. They promised to call if either showed up. I needed to get back and tell Roseman about Samantha's death. When possible, the news had to be passed on to Leonard, and I didn't envy Arthur the prospect of that delivery. About the only thing keeping Leonard alive was his imagined reconciliation with a woman who had never loved him and who was now dead. If his little world of make-believe couldn't handle that reality, it just might kill him.

CHAPTER SEVENTEEN

Kripp was coming down the hall from Roseman's bedroom as I entered the apartment. He was carrying a tray piled with dinner dishes. Roseman was opting to eat in his room, which was not that unusual an occurrence. If I had a bedroom like Roseman's, I'd eat there, too. Actually, it was a combo bedroom/office with the bedroom section first. Coming in off the hall you ran head first into a high redwood bed with posts that shot toward the ceiling like the spires of St. Andrew's. A couple of rush-backed chairs next to the bed faced the fireplace. I had often sat there and reported to a pajama-clad Roseman while he finished his first morning coffee, or folded away his glasses in final preparation for the night. Bookcases covered two walls and a patterned burgundy oriental covered the floor, ending a few feet short of Roseman's rolltop desk.

The work space near the windows was light and shared the same view as my apartment below: Central Park in all its seasonal glories. Many times, especially since the death of his wife, Roseman would have Kripp serve his dinner in this room. A small room table opposite the rolltop was always set for the day's final meal, complete with crystal and Irish linen.

As I came into the room, Roseman was seated there finishing a cup of coffee and pushing small pieces of cherry pie around his plate with a silver fork. He looked up, smiled, and set the plate aside.

"I've lost my taste for sweets, I suppose," he said by way of explanation. "I don't know that I ever really liked them, but they were a favorite of Marjorie's. Some spouses drink to keep their partners company, I think I did the same with pies and custards."

"I know she set a high-calorie table for tea," I said, "enough to send your blood sugar level out of sight."

Roseman seemed pleased with the shared memory and motioned for me to sit. He rang the kitchen but Kripp was a couple of steps ahead of him, entering with a second cup and saucer and a carafe of coffee.

"Is it my short-term memory loss," Roseman began, "or have I not seen you since you came home from the hospital?"

"You're right: All day on the road and I'm not going to be home tonight either."

"That, I assume, is a song lyric."

"Close. Actually, it's six days on the road and he gets the girl, but for me that's a vacation, not a work interval."

Roseman chuckled and sipped his coffee. "You are often amusing, David. Not funny exactly, but amusing. How is your injury?"

"Fine, without being well. I keep the pills handy and haven't had much trouble. I can't deny that I'd feel better in bed. You could use some sleep yourself."

"I am weary, David." He thought for a moment. "I think Leonard is not going to live much longer. The doctors sell their special brand of optimism, but personally I believe he's lost to me." He glanced at me, his eyes tired, kind. "I apologize if I've pushed you too unfairly. I appreciate what you've done. It was entirely necessary. Not only for Leonard but for me as well. My own peace of mind. My affection for the man, his importance to me as one of my few remaining friends, has, I'm afraid, blurred

190

the lines of distinction between my personal and professional life."

"Forget it, Arthur."

He looked at me closely, finished his coffee, and turned to the window. "You can also be quite deceptive," he said. I laughed. "Seriously, you dissemble well."

"Dissemble, now there's a good Shakespearean word."

"Exactly, and with your ability to memorize, you could have been a convincing performer. Did you ever consider the stage?"

"Yeah, for about ten minutes and two productions in college. I've always thought that in order to do well in a profession like the theater, one that deals so heavily in make-believe, you needed to be able to separate yourself from reality with some facility. My last few jobs have taken the luxury of mental escapism away from me. Too many toes with tags, you know?" Roseman reached for the coffee. "I'm too deeply rooted in the chaos of man to pretend I'm an English king."

"I see," he said. "Well, I appreciate your taking the time to share feelings with an old friend, but I feel this visit is more than social. Have you brought additional news? Bad news, perhaps?"

"I don't think it'll break your heart, but it may hasten Leonard's departure."

"Oh yes, well, perhaps I understand already."

I braced myself. "Samantha's dead. Sorry."

"Sorry? Why sorry, David? Sorry she's dead? Please."

"Sorry I had to tell you," I said, feeling a strange pinch of discomfort at his words. "Sorry because now you may have to tell Leonard and that won't be easy."

"I daresay you're right. I daresay I may never have the opportunity. Here, have some more coffee. You're neglecting yourself."

Roseman poured out the thick black liquid that smelled of French roast. I mixed in cream and sugar, stirring slowly. We sat without speaking. My cup was almost empty when he cleared his throat.

"You'll need to tell me about it."

"I know. Somehow it's difficult this time. I got to know her a little, I think. It's . . ." I paused, words failing me, emotions rushing in. "It's not the same this time."

"Never is, really. Conditioning helps, but it's . . . well . . . I don't have to explain it to you."

"She had her neck cracked by what Tim Ellerton thinks was a fire iron. The police are checking those in the apartment, but any piece of straight pipe would have worked. Then she was hung from a beam in the kitchen." Roseman winced and set down his cup. "Sorry."

"Indeed."

"Florio is looking for both Reid and Sharp, but the only one he needs is Sharp."

"Why is that?"

"Lane Peters was homosexual . . . well, bisexual I guess is more accurate."

Roseman lost his sleepy look.

"Bisexual?"

"You got it. Care to guess who his lover was?"

"Shelton Sharp, of course . . . do you think Leonard knew?"

"My guess is he did. It might have been what he was paying blackmail for."

"How foolish. I don't believe that for a moment."

"Don't you? Think about it, Arthur. Leonard's older than you, he would react differently. To him, it was just one final embarrassment he couldn't stand, or thought he couldn't."

"You present a good argument, but I remain unconvinced. Do you suppose Samantha knew of his bisexuality?"

"Probably, I don't know. Anything's possible with this crowd."

"What a sordid little mess this has turned out to be."

"I agree."

Neither of us spoke for a long time.

"I'm tired, Arthur."

"I imagine that you are," he said, keeping his gaze out the

192

window. "I know Kripp would like to have you take your old duties back. He gets lost in the federal building. And, of course, there are several other 'items' I need you to check. Let the Captain finish this one."

"Sounds good to me; at this point, I'd rather read about it in the *Post*," I said, standing up, knowing that I didn't mean what I was saying but feeling too tired and disgusted to stop the words from coming out.

"Excellent. I'll see you in the office Monday morning." And he walked me to the hallway.

CHAPTER EIGHTEEN

I caught her eye immediately as I came through the door. Her hair was brilliant and reflective under the restaurant's light. Her crew-neck sweater covered a shirt with its collar flipped high, making her look like a sophomore at Columbia. The place was packed and it took me a minute, and some tight maneuvering around outstretched drinks and waving cigarettes, to reach the table that she shared with Jordan.

"You ought to be in pictures . . ." I said, coming up to the table.

"Really?" she inquired, taking my hand.

". . . you're beautiful to see." The line finished, I kissed her cheek.

"Sometimes I think your every waking thought comes straight out of Burbank, California, or an Alec Wilder songbook," she said lightly.

"I know what you mean," I said, sitting down. "It's a little disquieting to realize your major frames of reference are limited to a Casey Kasem countdown and the MGM film catalogue." Jordan moved to leave, but I stopped him.

"No, stay put," I told him, "unless you've got to do

195

something. I'd like your company." Jordan sat back in his chair, and after a brief pause to gather my thoughts, I told them about Samantha. As wet blankets go, it ranked right up there with unanesthetized amputation. Jordan handed me his drink and I sipped the brandy with pleasure.

"I don't know if I care much about the movies anymore," I told Marilyn honestly. "Even if it is William Holden."

"It might help take your mind off what's happened," she said. "Let's at least walk in that direction. We can decide something once we get in the neighborhood. Come on." Taking my hand, she stood up.

"She's right," Jordan said. "You should get out. Take some fresh air, away from the smoke and the noise. Hold hands. Watch the people. If you skip the movies, come back, say you know the owner, and they'll give you a table. Do what Uncle Jordan tells you," he said, shooing us toward the door.

We passed through the bar crowd out onto the street. The cold night air felt refreshing. Marilyn slipped her hand into the pocket of my overcoat. Her fingers found mine and I pulled my hand free long enough to transfer the Mauser into the other pocket. Together we eased down 18th Street toward Seventh Avenue and turned south to the Village.

"What are you thinking about?" she asked after several blocks of silence.

"Dead women, I'm afraid." I squeezed her hand, feeling uncomfortable with the admission.

"Can't dwell on those things," she advised. "They'll make you crazy."

"I understand that, and generally it's not a problem. I guess in this instance I feel"—I drew a deep breath—"I guess I feel . . ."

"A little extra responsibility?"

"Yes. That's it. I feel I should have done more. Moved faster. Thought quicker."

"Read minds, maybe."

"Right, the Vulcan mind probe," I said lightly, adding, "I'm supposed to be the great investigator; the man with insight, knowledge, X-ray vision. If I'd thought about it, I would have realized that Samantha was logically the next victim. But because I didn't exactly like her values, or her life-style, or her attitude, I didn't follow through. I didn't do enough."

"I don't believe that for a minute. You're not as cold-blooded or inept as you make out." I appreciated her support.

We walked on toward Sheridan Square in silence, then headed east to Sixth Avenue, took 8th Street across-town, and turned south toward Washington Square Park. People took the place of conversation and we stopped often to laugh at, talk about, guess, and comment on the different characters who played, postured, juggled, sang, and sold drugs around the empty fountain at the park's center. We strolled back to 8th Street and continued east. In a very short time we found ourselves standing on the corner of Second Avenue and St. Marks Place.

"This has been nice," I said.

"Told you so."

"Yes, you told me so. I still don't think I'm up for sitting through a double feature."

"It's after nine," she said, checking the time. "We've already missed the first one."

"All the same, I'd just as soon not."

"My place? We can microwave some popcorn and see what television has to offer. David, you're not listening to me. David!"

"What? Sorry, I was just thinking that you can see it from here."

"See what?"

"The New Reach Theatre. It's just up there. Thirteenth Street."

"Is that where *Macbeth* was playing?"

"Yes."

"I've never been there. If it isn't west of Broadway between Forty-fourth and Fifty-first, I don't go."

"There's not much to see. It looks just like the exterior of a

1950s movie house, which is what it was before Sharp converted it into a legitimate theater."

"Let's walk by it anyway," she said. "I'd like to see it."

We stayed on the east side of the avenue to get a perspective on the building as we approached. I was pointing out the darkened marquee when I saw a man come around the corner on 12th Street and disappear into the stage entrance of the theater. He wore an oversized coat with the collar turned up, hiding his face, but he had the general shape and movement of Sharp. My body tensed. Marilyn felt the change.

"What's wrong?" she asked, looking up.

A city bus roared by clattering and grinding through the low gears, forcing us to turn our backs to escape the noise and exhaust.

"A man just went into the theater," I said, moving farther up the avenue. "It may have been Sharp. I couldn't tell for sure."

Her hand tightened on my arm. "You're not thinking about going in there by yourself," she said without making it a question.

"I have no illusions about being the great American hero, Marilyn; besides, there should be a policeman inside already. Come on, we need to hurry." And taking her hand we dashed across the lanes of traffic to the corner opposite the theater. We walked down even with the stage entrance—a cream-colored metal door illuminated from above by a single bulb.

"Listen, Marilyn," I said, feeling my heart rate starting to climb, "give me five minutes and then call Florio; there's a pay phone and here's a quarter. It's possible I'll walk in there and find the stage manager or a member of the company and nobody else."

"This is a stupid, stupid idea," she protested. "The instant you cross that street, I'm calling for help."

"Marilyn, whatever makes you feel comfortable," I told her. "Just stay over here. OK?"

She looked at me, her head tilted slightly to one side, considering what I'd said. Her face was strangely orange in the light from the street lamp above. I couldn't resist the temptation and stole a kiss, then ran across the street, turned the knob, pulled the door open, and shut it immediately. A scream tore out of me, and I tried to rub the image of what I'd just seen out of my mind. It wouldn't go. I took a breath, opened the door again, stepped inside, and knelt down. A uniformed officer lay on the floor of a small cubicle just inside the door. He was bleeding heavily from a wide gash in his lower abdomen. Blood pulsed from between his fingers with every heartbeat as the semiconscious young man tried to keep his intestines from spilling out into his lap. His face was pasty white and spittle rolled from the corner of his mouth. He gave no response as I pushed his head back, lifting each eyelid in turn and checking his pulse.

"Will he live?" It was Marilyn standing behind me. I was so absorbed in the cop that I hadn't even noticed her come in.

"Possibly, if we get him out of here fast enough. He's lost a lot of blood. We need to get plasma into him, and check for leaks," I said, pointing to his intestines. "It's a matter of time at this point."

Marilyn reached for the phone that was on a desk just inside the door and pulled it down to the floor while I moved the officer's hands away from his belly. Then, taking off my coat, I folded it into a tight square and pressed it against the wound. Using considerable force, I held the coat in place, undid my watch band with my teeth, dropped the timepiece to the floor, grabbed a wrist, and rechecked his pulse.

"We need to get him to Bellevue," I said as Marilyn lifted the receiver.

"Should I call there directly or 911?" she asked.

"Call 911. If Bellevue's busy they'll know and dispatch the nearest available ambulance. It's electronic," I said, looking at her as if she were a wayward first grader, lovingly, but with mild consternation, "and faster than dealing with the emergency room."

Both of us had been whispering like conspirators in the dimly lit cubicle as though we expected Sharp to leap out of the shadows slicing the air with a bloodied scimitar and vowing death to the infidels. The image would have been worth a nervous laugh if it hadn't been for the kid lying in front of us. He was barely able to suck shallow breaths as he bled steadily onto his new uniform. He couldn't have been much more than twenty years old.

The phone clicked and Marilyn relayed the essential information of problem, location, rate of heart. Her manner was calm, matter-of-fact, almost casual. It was a voice I'd never heard before. She read the phone number off the dial and hung up. I pulled out my automatic and extra clip.

"They'll be here in a few minutes," she said, looking at the gun. "The doctor at Bellevue is going to call and the operator said she'd notify the police."

"I'm sure Florio will get the message. If not directly then he'll pick it up off the radio."

"What are you doing with that?" she asked.

"Counting bullets," I answered, sliding a clip up into the handle and forcing a shell into the chamber.

"You can't leave," she said, suddenly plaintive. "I need your help."

"Marilyn, you're doing fine," I said in a confident voice, but her eyes told me she wasn't buying it. "This door behind us isn't the only exit; there must be four or five others. If Sharp gets back on the street, we may never find him again."

"But it's pitch black in there."

"Against union rules. There's always a light on stage. It's not much, I admit, but it's light. I think where I need to go first is down there," and I pointed to the staircase. In most buildings I'd expect to find a basement at the end of those steps, but from what I knew of theaters, there were often dressing rooms, costume shops, offices, and storage behind the stage if not directly under it. There was no light past the second or third step, where the stairs broke sharply to the left and disappeared from sight.

Marilyn seemed ready to make a speech, but the officer coughed and began to choke.

"If anyone needs help, he does," I told her. "Stay with him."

"What do I do?" she pleaded.

"Hold his hand, keep the coat pushed in tight. You'll do fine." The officer coughed again; when Marilyn turned I was down the steps, immersed in darkness. I counted the steps, taking each one slowly, holding the handrail almost as tightly as the pistol grip. The seventh step brought me to a level floor. The air was cool and musty. My guess was that Sharp had come back for something in his office. Personal effects, something he couldn't live without. Hell, maybe it was the theater itself and he needed a last visit. His office was probably near the front of the theater—I'd check that in a minute. But there was a good chance he also had living quarters, and most likely his private space would be here in the basement.

My hand left the railing and began to search the wall for a light switch. I couldn't see anything in front of me, yet my senses were at ultra-high pitch. I was aware of being nervous but outwardly calm, wide awake, and walking on eggshells. Adrenaline is a great high—a thousand times better than speed. A fortune could be made off the late-night television market, advertising Essence of Adrenal right along with the vegetable choppers and seventeen individually wrapped Korean carving knives.

My hand found the double light plate and brought my free association to an end. I snapped the first switch upward. The sound of the click exploded in the dark like a gunshot. No light. My fingers inched over to the second switch and flipped it up. Again nothing, only darkness. Either the power was off or I was turning on lights in some far away bathroom. I stuck my arm out, feeling for the opposite wall, found it, and stepped across the short distance made greater by my lack of sight.

Suddenly there was light, in flashes accompanied by booming sound. The real gunshots went off like heavy ordnance in a confined space. Bullets ricocheted off the smooth cement floor and cinderblock walls. Both shots were in the direction of the spot I had just left. The brief patches of light from Sharp's gun

201

had shown no definite shapes, only an instant's worth of black and white shadows. I had direction and image, but he had surely moved by now.

"David!" Marilyn screamed from the top of the stairs. I didn't answer. I told myself that my reason for not answering was so as not to give away my position on the floor, where I'd thrown myself with the first shot. But the dryness in my mouth told another story. Besides, Marilyn couldn't have heard me above the crashing of my heart. As my pulse rate slowed from accelerated to medium high, I felt the subtle movement of air as a heavy door slowly, quietly slid shut. Gone, I thought to myself. He's left. I got off the floor and stood with my back to the wall, feeling for another light switch. I found it on my left.

"David, answer me!"

"Marilyn, I'm all right," I yelled, filling the room with light at the same instant. "Don't come down here." This time, she didn't answer. I took a look around and found that I was standing in the corner of a fairly large room, big enough to hold comfortably eight tables for bridge. In fact, two tables in the center of the room were covered with multiple decks of playing cards in various stages of distribution.

Running the width of the wall on my left were six doors, some open, some shut, which appeared to lead to dressing rooms. The wall facing me held a single door and water fountain, an older free-standing model with a porcelain top. This wall was the mirror image of the one I had my back against. The wall on my right showed two large doors without latches; handgrips had replaced doorknobs and spring bolts. The orchestra pit; I'd bet money on it. Orchestra pit and entrance to the theater. Silent open, silent shut. Easy entrance and easy exit. That's where he went.

I moved to the closest of the two and eased it open. I was careful to keep my body out of the line of sight, using a broom handle to shove the door wide, letting light spill into the dark undercarriage of the stage. Generating no response, I rounded the corner to see metal chairs stacked in neat rows and an assortment of ropes, ladders, and two by fours piled on the floor. Keeping the pistol level, I let the door swing shut behind me. Again, nothing happened; complete darkness, making me itchy, uncomfortable. It took a moment for my eyes to adjust. Underneath the stage, a faint light filtered down from above. A three-foot-high black barrier blocked the pit entrance from the front-row seats. Looking higher, I could see the balcony and boxes, empty, waiting, silent. I could only figure that Sharp left by the same door I had and then disappeared up an aisle. There was nothing to do but check.

I climbed the steps out of the orchestra pit slowly, checking for movement in the shadows around me. As I emerged level with the stage, I turned to see the same set that had been there the day I visited Sharp. A bedroom, sparsely decorated. Lady Macbeth's perhaps, though there were no special appointments that would immediately set it out as a woman's room, no flowers, no embroidered bedspreads, no dress slung dispiritedly over a chair.

If this were Marilyn's bedroom you'd recognize it, I thought, sweeping the stage with the Mauser's barrel. Her style was bright, sassy, and right off the pages of *Self* magazine. I froze. Shit! How could I be so stupid? I ran full speed across the stage and out into the wings. A red exit light showed the way and I leaped down the few steps to the rear entrance. She was gone.

"Fuck!" I shouted and damned myself for leaving her in the first place. Sharp must have doubled back across the stage and grabbed her. He obviously wasn't trying to get away. He could easily have made it out the front or, for that matter, out this rear entrance. If escape were his objective, why take a hostage? It would only slow him down. No, he was still inside the theater and waiting for someone to come after him. He'd made a choice. Florio's right, I thought, this is where he wants to die.

The officer leaning against the wall hadn't flinched at my outburst. I wished that he had raised himself up and wagged a finger, or tisked at my negligence. He just lay there dying. Dead maybe. Without Marilyn's attention the raincoat had fallen away

203

letting his intestines tumble back out onto his lap. I knelt down and tried to rearrange the compress. Then I felt for a pulse and had to search to find one. It was almost too faint to register. At the sound of a siren outside, I opened the door and blinked into the headlights of an ambulance.

"He's here on the floor," I said to the white jacket getting out on the driver's side. "He's not in very good shape, either."

"We'll take it from here," the young, short-haired woman said.

"Pass any cops on your way here?" I asked, as she pushed by me to reach the officer.

"Wasn't looking" was her clipped response and already she was cutting away the sleeve and inserting an IV needle into the cop's arm. I took one more look out the door. Whores and policemen: never there when you need them; and neither was I.

I turned back inside asking myself where Sharp might have taken her. Downstairs again? Did he complete the loop? He must have known that I was under the stage and would have seen him coming back across. There had to be another route. Something down the side aisles maybe. I took a final look outside for Florio and then went back downstairs to the Green Room.

There are a thousand places to hide in a theater. I started my search with the six dressing rooms, all identical, all empty. The door by the water fountain led to a large single dressing room with a second door exiting out the back. This second door led to the costume shop, complete with ironing boards, sewing machines, bolts of fabric, boxes of shoes, lace, buttons, hats, shirts, and racks and racks of clothing from past productions.

Crossing the center area again, I entered the dressing room opposite. It was the same large size; big enough for ten or twelve people to dress in comfortably. This room also had a second door leading to a small anteroom that Sharp, no doubt, called home. Carpet covered the floor and large maroon curtains hung in folds from the ceiling, covering the walls and giving the room a feeling of extreme closeness. The bed was the focal point. It was unmade, the sheets and pillows lying crumpled on the floor.

There was also a desk, chair, nightstand, and books. Everywhere, books were scattered or piled three and four deep. Paperbacks, hardbacks, plays, novels, manuscripts, and loose sheets of paper mixed in with the socks, shirts, and trousers. This room was empty, too.

I went back out under the stage, up the steps, and onto the stage itself. The theater spread before me: two aisles, a balcony, box seats down each side, and four beaming exit signs. Nothing. Empty seats and silence.

"Sharp!" I shouted. "Sharp, answer me."

Nothing.

"Goddamnit, Sharp, make an entrance!"

"Excellent projection, Mr. Hamilton. You might have made a fine actor." I followed the voice to the back of the theater. It was Sharp's voice all right, and he was in the balcony, but I couldn't see him.

"And what part would I play?" I answered into the darkness. "The same one Lane did? An aspiring, yet dutiful, lover. A young man of talent but uncertain temperament in need of a loving hand to guide him?"

"You are very much to the point," he said, stepping down the aisle and out of the shadows. He came all the way to the balcony rail dragging Marilyn behind him. She stumbled twice, nearly falling. "Perhaps you should write plays instead," he continued. "Would you care to tell me how this one will end?"

"It's still in the typewriter as far as I'm concerned, anything can happen. One thing's for sure though," I told him, "all the major characters have made their exit except for you. You're the only one left. In fact, she"—I indicated Marilyn—"hardly qualifies for anything other than a walk-on, and you should hear her try to sing. Jesus, what a howl. Why don't you let her go?"

"Because I'm mad at you."

"Then be mad at me and let her go."

"Ah, a touching thought, but poorly delivered." He brought his right arm up in front of him and for the first time I saw his gun. Marilyn stood motionless beside him. My mind raced. My gut hurt. I wanted to blow the hell out of him, but they were very close together and in the semidarkness I might miss. I was prepared should she make a quick move away from him, but otherwise I wouldn't chance it.

"You have been," he continued casually, "the major disrupting influence in this entire affair. More so than the police or any of my now deceased accomplices. Indirectly, you forced the deaths of several relatively innocent individuals."

"And they were such nice people, too," I said, regretting the sarcasm instantly.

"Drop that smartass attitude or you can add her to the list," he sneered, thrusting Marilyn hard against the railing. She tried to hold back, but he shoved her again and this time she fell, grabbing the rail with both hands to keep from plummeting the twenty feet to the seats below.

Watching her weave and falter at the mercy of Sharp made my chest contract like a balloon under pressure. I was powerless. I couldn't watch any longer and looked away in an effort to steady myself, fighting back the urge to shoot wildly, indiscriminately, into the balcony. After a moment, the urgency passed, my respiratory system returned to normal, and I was able to ask another question.

"Is Banks Reid also on that list?"

"I am afraid so," he said, forgetting about Marilyn, "and he 'died hard' as they said in Dodge City."

"And Samantha, did she 'die hard,' too? She certainly wasn't wearing boots when you strung her up."

"Watch your tone," he said in mock offense, "you're getting an edge to it again. In point of fact, Samantha met her death in the grand tradition of King Charles I, with head held high and regal to the last."

"Except that you broke her neck with a fire iron instead of cutting off her head. I realize a New York apartment is a far cry from an Inigo Jones banqueting house, but still, a poker from the fireplace? Pretty pedestrian for a guy like you."

"Excellent. Really quite good, Mr. Hamilton. Obviously a

man who knows his history. And yes, you're right, I did whack her with that poker. And more than once, too; she was no easy kill, let me tell you."

I felt sick.

"It's a shame you didn't have an audience for your handiwork," I managed to say. "I suppose that's why you hung her in the kitchen? Shock value for the masses?"

"Oh, but I did have an audience," he said slyly. "Banks Reid watched the entire performance."

I was speechless.

"You seem surprised, Mr. Hamilton. You shouldn't be. He wasn't a strong man. He cried appropriately and appeared, several times, to be praying. Very biblical. Was he religious, do you know?"

I hated this man.

"And when it was all over, he came with me very quietly; hardly any trouble at all."

"It doesn't seem to bother you," I said, finding my voice again, despite the thickness of my tongue.

"What?" he asked, his face a blank.

"Killing people."

No response.

"For example, it didn't bother you to kill Lane Peters. You stood less than two feet from him and put a bullet in his head, a man you lived with, purportedly loved, and who was responsible for your theatrical success. You killed him easily enough and then, moments later, stood over his still-breathing body and willingly implicated an innocent third party."

Sharp's voice exploded from the balcony down to me on stage. "What do you know about love? Or death for that matter?" he screamed.

"A hell of a sight more than you do, that's for sure."

"Well, aren't we superior. Perhaps I can give you a short lesson in humility." With that he turned to Marilyn, placing the barrel of his pistol against her forehead. My heart stopped, and I, like Banks, began to pray.

"I was simply stating a fact, not trying to be superior," I said, unable to keep the tremble from my voice. "I spent years as a clerk in the medical examiner's office. I was also a cop reporter and I've interviewed moms, dads, brothers, sisters, neighbors, boyfriends, wives, husbands, anyone connected with the body in question. So, yeah, I've seen a lot of death, Shelton. I've been around it a long time." The gun slowly dropped back to his side. When he spoke again, his voice was normal, even unhurried.

"You never knew Samantha Craig did you?" he asked.

"No, not really. Tell me about her, Shelton."

"She was a hateful woman. Didn't give a damn about anyone but herself. I went to see her you know, after Lane told me he wanted to leave the theater and move uptown with her. I told her the whole story, everything about how we only wanted her connection with Leonard, the money, I told her Lane and I were lovers, but she didn't care. I remember she laughed, said the royal order was changing: the old queen was out, the new queen was in. I was furious and let me tell you the ladies had it out. Bitch fight of the year. Tony nominations all around.

"I thought that would have settled the matter, but the next day, when I saw Lane, he told me they had talked about his past. His past! That stupid little git referred to me as his past, God. So they had talked about his life with me, and Samantha said she didn't care—the present was all that mattered for them, or some silly shit like that." He stopped, seeming to consider what he had just said, perhaps going back over it. "She had Lane confused," he continued, still thinking, talking out loud. "She had him believing he was someone he wasn't, someone he could never be, until, at the end, he didn't know who really loved him."

"So you turned on her out of revenge? Spite? All of these people have died because of common jealousy."

"There was nothing common about my love for Lane, but yes, you're right, my motivation was simple. I thought at first the police would ferret her out on their own. Then I would be forced by conscience to step forward and testify to having seen her holding the murder weapon. But, unfortunately, Leonard's ar-

208

rival complicated matters. Your involvement made them worse. Finally, I had to kill her myself."

"How did you know Lane was going to be there that night?"

"Ha!" he said sarcastically, "it wasn't very hard. They spent almost every night together and Lane was never very good at deceit. I knew he'd be there."

"And after you arrived at the apartment there was another fight?" I asked, prompting him, stalling him for time, waiting for Marilyn to make a move.

"Yes, we'd been arguing for weeks, months, longer." He paused again. "I was so surprised to see the gun. I knew he was upset, but he didn't need a pistol to keep me away. I loved him. I tried to reason—the work at the theater had to continue. His place was here, with me, on the stage, not with her. Not with Samantha. Lane couldn't see that she would suffocate him. Without his art, he would dry up inside. He needed me."

"Maybe money meant more to him than you realized."

"He had everything he needed. There were no wants in his life."

"Did you know he was blackmailing Leonard Craig? Using his relationship with you to bleed him for cash?" Sharp seemed overwhelmed by the statement and it took him a couple of seconds to absorb it all.

"I don't believe you," he said simply. "Lane wasn't that kind of person. You didn't know him."

"But we both know something about Randall Bergman. They were in it together. If it makes you feel any better, you can believe it was all Bergman's doing, but facts is facts."

Sharp's anguish became visible in his face. The surprise was genuine; the confusion real. I caught myself smiling, much as Bergman might have; I was sure that he would have enjoyed this, too. A lot.

"Yes, that would have been Randall's little revenge," Sharp said faintly.

"It was you who arrived in the basement just before I shot him, wasn't it?" Sharp dropped his head without answering and waved my question off with his hand. "I couldn't figure out why he was so anxious; he kept looking down the hall. I thought he was waiting for someone who would do the dirty work. Now I realize he wanted to have the note back before you got there. He didn't want you to know about the blackmail or Lane's involvement, not yet anyway. He was probably saving it for a Christmas present."

"Oh, stop it, stop it," he shouted. "I loved Lane . . . he . . . he wasn't that kind of person."

"Did you shoot him intentionally?"

"No, it was quite accidental." The voice had changed again. He was distant now, not paying attention. A vacant quality had entered his speech. "I was trying to shake some sense into him; force him to come back with me. But he wanted to stay. He shouted at me, pushed me away, threatened me. Him! Threatening me! When he pulled the gun from the drawer, I simply took it away from him, slapped his stupid little face, and shot him. One. Two. Three. It was just like that."

Just like that, huh? I thought. One, two, three. Jesus. Something had to happen here soon. Marilyn wasn't holding up well; neither was I for that matter. She still had her grip on the rail and was crouching, cowering actually, next to him. I drew a long breath and started.

"OK, Shelton," I said placidly, "why don't you let her go and then you and I can play Gunsmoke; face-to-face at thirty feet. I'll be Matt Dillon and you can make the first move."

"I think you will remain more agreeable," he said, "as long as I have . . . Miss Kitty, shall we call her? . . . by my side."

"Then I want to point out, respectfully"—Sharp nodded, pleased with the amenity—"that if you push her off that balcony, I'll come down on you so hard you won't know if you've been shot, fucked, stabbed, or stomped."

"Oh, how delightfully evil and intimate," he giggled. "The thought excites me."

"It should sober you," I said through my teeth and wished I

210

had a better view of Marilyn's face, but she never took her eyes off Sharp, and I could see her only in profile. Except for the one audible gasp when she thought she was going over, she'd remained silent. Waiting, I hoped, for a chance to break away and give me a clear line of fire.

"If you leave now," I said, "there is still time. Let Marilyn go and . . ."

"Marilyn," he cried out turning to her. "Is your name Marilyn? Lovely name." He stroked her cheek with his left hand. "Lovely skin." Then looking back at me he said, "Lovely girl."

"If you let her go and leave immediately," I repeated slowly, "there is time to get out before the police arrive."

"Really."

"Yes. You do want to get away, don't you?"

"Not particularly. Does that disappoint you?" He clucked his tongue and dropped his voice to a conspiratorial aside, "And I'm unconcerned about whom I take with me."

The guy was bozo and I was running out of dialogue. A noise below caught my attention and I glanced down to see Florio signaling up from the orchestra pit, one hand giving me the "keep him talking" motion while the other one waved and flapped to imply men were coming up behind Sharp. He looked like a third-base coach for the precinct softball team, only in a business suit. Italians and their hands, Jesus. I came back to the scene on the balcony.

"I'm willing to help, Sharp. I'll try to get you out of here. But my wanting to isn't going to get it done. It's up to you. What's it going to be? Talk to me."

He considered for a second and was about to answer when he shifted quickly to his right. A noise, a motion, a creaking step, something had drawn his attention. He spun a quarter turn and fired. At the same time, Marilyn tried to jerk free and I squeezed off two rounds at Sharp. With my eyes on Marilyn and my gun on Sharp, it wasn't surprising that I missed him. The cop with the heavy tread wasn't so lucky; Sharp's bullet caught him chest high.

He pitched forward into the dim light and rolled down the aisle, vanishing from view between the seats.

Sharp came back around firing toward the stage. Rolling right, I kept him in view and watched in muted terror as he put his weight and rage into Marilyn. She flipped helplessly over the balcony, grabbing for one of the metal braces directly below her that supported the klieg lights. One hand caught briefly but momentum carried her down. She was silent as she fell. Even when she crumpled into the seats with a sickeningly dull crash, there was no cry, no scream.

I was on my feet and moving to her instantly, firing twice more in Sharp's direction, but my divided attention kept him alive a second time. I was certain I had hit him once because he bent forward and swore, but the second shot was wide right and did no more than tear stuffing from the chairback next to him. At that point, I disregarded Sharp totally, my mind overcome with the fear that Marilyn was dead. I heard another shot from above, but I guessed that it wasn't directed at me. Running feet and more shots told me others had reached the balcony.

Florio and I got to Marilyn the same instant. She was alive but unconscious and breathing with difficulty, like a child in need of a humidifier. She lay on the floor, her right leg folded underneath her in such a way that it had to be broken. It was eerie, unreal: a strawman thrown unceremoniously from his post. She had also taken a vicious blow across the side of her head in the fall, but except for a tiny trail of blood that eased past her temple, she might only have been asleep. God only knew what her insides looked like.

Though her body looked tortured, wedged miserably into the small space between rows, we decided not to move her.

"I'll get one of the med techs," Florio said and was gone.

"Hey!" It was Marston in the balcony. "He's not here. Is there another way down?"

"I don't know," I yelled, my mind racing as I checked the exits visible from my position. "He can't go far, he's got a bullet in him, somewhere. I know I hit him."

Florio reappeared on the stage with a paramedic close on his heels.

"Careful Marc," I shouted. "Marston can't find Sharp. He's still loose." Florio slowed and changed direction. The medic came down off the stage looking left and right but moving quickly toward me. When he got to Marilyn, I headed for the right rear corner of the theater. Pushing aside the heavy crimson drapes under the exit sign, I found myself in a corridor running the length of the building from lobby to stage. I went left to the front of the theater.

Reaching the end of the corridor, I rounded a corner and stopped. The whole lobby lay in front of me; red carpet underneath an ornate ceiling led to a staircase rising to the balcony. An identical stairway rose to my right. Nothing to see. What to do? He couldn't have gone far. A back passage or a drop elevator would be the perfect solution, but there was nothing immediately evident, except a door, and it opened directly into the stairwell; storage no doubt. I turned to the wall behind me. It was covered with darkstained oak paneling.

I stepped up close and began fingering the joints, looking for anything unusual that might be a catch or spring point. I ran my index finger vertically down one panel to the floor. As I pulled it away, I noticed the blood, moist and red, on the tip. I straightened up and backed off a few steps. Remember, Ham, I said to myself as I leveled the Mauser at the center panel, he's wounded, armed, and crazy. Blast the fucker and call it self-defense. Better yet, think of Marilyn and call it justice. The urge was overwhelming, my hand trembled.

"Sharp, come out now," I said, not knowing why—good rearing and the Donna Reed show maybe. "No bullshit, Sharp. Now or I shoot."

The pop of his pistol, though muffled, made me jump. The bullet splintered the wood paneling and ripped past me.

"Goddamnit, Sharp, you stupid fucker!" And a second bullet tore out of the wood.

Without firing, I turned and reached for the small closet

213

door and jerked it open. My intent was to use it to deflect Sharp's next shot. To my horror, I found myself facing Banks Reid. He was as dead as a bag of rocks and standing bolt upright next to a Hoover vacuum cleaner. He tilted slowly, picking up speed until he fell full force into my arms. I was nonplussed. He weighed a ton and I had to stagger backward to keep my balance.

As I was dancing across the lobby with my stiff, the panel in front of Sharp slid back to reveal an unhealthy white male bleeding badly from a hole in his upper chest. His mouth fell open at the sight of Reid in my arms and he fired instantly, involuntarily, emptying his revolver into the dead man.

I don't know what came over me in the next few milliseconds. Perhaps the lunacy of my position—cradling a dead man whose lifeless body had just absorbed four bullets meant for me—was more than my shock-weary circuits could handle. Having watched Marilyn fall, I was working on emotional overload anyway; the blow to my psyche as she hit the metal back of that seat had been tremendous. Or maybe it was just the sight of that swaggering egotist still clicking his empty revolver at me, thinking maybe I'd disappear like the image from a remote-control television. I only knew he deserved to be hurt.

Oh, he was bleeding and in pain, but help was close at hand, the danger wasn't serious. This guy had shown no pity, remorse, or compassion for any of his victims. Especially Marilyn, a woman he didn't know, whose life or death was of absolutely no consequence to him. Sharp deserved to be really hurt and I was the one to do it. Why? The question rang like a bell clap. It wasn't that I would suffer the most of those surviving, or even that I felt a sense of greater violation. The man was cruel, evil, and unrepentant. In another time, he would have been hanged, but we'd progressed since then. Today, with the right lawyer, a few tears, and an agreeable district attorney, this piece of shit that passes as a life form could end up in Bellevue doing five years with a chance for parole in eighteen months. I could hear the judge explaining his reason for the mild sentence: a first offender, mentally unstable at the time of the crime, and mitigating circumstances, meaning that the family minister got up on the stand and said a few words about the boy he once knew.

No, I was the one to do it because I had the opportunity and a swelling in my chest that was going to blow me wide open if I didn't relieve the pressure.

Enraged, I charged him, keeping Reid's body between us and slamming Sharp into the rear of the elevator. He gasped, cried out, and weakly waved his revolver, firing empty chambers. I vaguely heard a wild, gutteral scream and realized that it was coming from me. Sharp gave a last wounded yelp and flapped his arms like a waterfowl at takeoff. My right hand came up, jamming the Mauser into the soft flesh of his jowl. For a brief, horrifying second his eyes registered the knowledge that I was going to kill him; that, truly, his life was about to end. I couldn't stop. I didn't want to stop. I squeezed the trigger just as Marston came over my back and grabbed my arm, pulling downward with enormous strength. The bullet exploded into the wall less than an inch from Sharp's skull, the muzzle flash scorching his skin and singing the hairs across the back of his neck. I could hear Marston's voice beside me screaming, "Stop it, stop it!" but I barely felt the automatic in my hand as it bucked over and over and over, each shot moving farther down the wall as he kept the pressure on my arm.

I must have blacked out for a second. Time stopped. The next thing I remember was Marston tearing at my shoulder, shaking me hard and yelling my name. As he manhandled me out of the tiny elevator, Banks Reid hit the floor like a felled Georgia pine. Marston and I watched him drop, bounce once, and lie there. Sharp, moaning, bleeding, but unmistakably alive, slid down the wall like an elevator arriving on the main floor. I could even hear the ubiquitous department store bell sounding "Ping! ping! First floor, men's wear, cosmetics, ladies shoes and accessories." I was losing my mind.

"Ham," Marston said, shaking me again, "snap out of it for Christ sakes. Hey!" he shouted, peering into my face, "you in there?"

215

"Yeah, I'm in here. I'm fine."

"You're not fine," he said, easing the automatic from my hand, "but you're OK."

"Have they moved Marilyn?" I asked.

"I don't know. Come on, let's find out." He turned without releasing his grip on my arm. We walked across the lobby to the top of the center aisle where Marilyn was being laid onto a rigid steel frame. I stood there, watching, unable to comprehend as she was lifted onto a stretcher. It could have been the second feature at a revival house.

The other part of my brain was considering whether or not I should ride with her to the hospital. Of course I should, and I started immediately for the ambulance. I wanted to touch her, hold her hand, stroke her hair.

Marston tugged at my arm and I turned to notice that he was still talking. An actor in a silent movie, a TV star with the volume off. I put a hand on his shoulder and watched his lips say, "You can't go, Ham. Sorry."

"Where are they taking her?" I asked him.

"Lenox Hill."

Florio stepped up and gave me the same worried-look inspection that Marston had earlier. Everyone was having a turn at staring into my eyes.

"You take a course in holistic medicine recently?" I asked him. He didn't smile.

"Doc," he said over his shoulder. Tim Ellerton walked up, he, too, peeked inside.

"Mild shock," he said curtly to Florio. "Send him home, unless you plan to arrest him, and then send him home anyway and arrest him later. I wouldn't let him drive, either." And with that he adjusted his glasses, turned to me, and said, "Brandy, three fingers, like this," and he held up his hand in a horizontal fashion with his fingers spread wide. Then he winked and was gone.

"OK, John," Florio said, "get him uptown. I'll be along as soon as we clean this up."

216

"Will do, Captain."

Florio started to add something else but didn't get it out. "Ham . . ." he stopped again. "I'm sorry about Marilyn."

"It wasn't your fault," I answered in a voice that seemed to come from someone else, someone far across the room, someone I didn't know. "There wasn't anything more you could have done. I made the mistake. I brought her here."

"There's no question she'll live," he said. "Ellerton was definite about that, no serious internal injuries." He paused, uncomfortable. "See you later."

Marston led me out to his car. I went easily, luggage to the airport, and we headed up Third. We were both silent. At 32nd, he offered a cigarette that I accepted. I cracked the window and watched the storefronts pass. Each one reflected Sharp's face in those last seconds: frightened, comprehending. Had Marston not jerked the gun clear, Sharp would be dead. I would have murdered him. Jesus save me. I closed my eyes but the thought didn't go away. The cigarette tasted awful; its smoke burned my throat and coated my tongue. I pushed it out the crack, and rolled the window tight.

When we arrived at 61st Street, Marston left the car at the curb, showed his badge to the doorman, and we got into a waiting elevator. The light above the door flashed at the twenty-second floor before I found my voice again.

"I want to thank you for stopping me back there," I said. He didn't answer, but studied the tassels on his shoes. "I couldn't have stopped myself. I'd have killed him."

"Don't think about it, Ham," he said, looking up. "In fact, it never happened. OK?"

"Maybe Florio really should charge me with something."

"Shit no. Christ, forget it. OK?"

We were both silent for another moment. The elevator hit the forty-third floor and we got out.

"You know," I said, just as we were about to walk into Roseman's, "I don't know what bothers me most: almost killing

Sharp, watching Marilyn come off that balcony, or catching Reid as he fell out of the closet."

He looked at me with what I thought was admiration. I realized then that to Marston I was just the package clerk at Bonwit Teller, wrapping things up all nice and tidy. Oh, he liked me, sure, I liked him, we'd probably grow up to be friends. But at the moment, I was nothing more than a convenient solution to a nightmare situation, the hand of God, a lanky kid from North Carolina who had put a hard fast one into the left-field bleachers for the winning run.

It was a role that didn't feel right, things just happened that way. Maybe after retirement I could take over the Mister Coffee ads for Joe DiMaggio.

CHAPTER NINETEEN

Kripp came from the kitchen when he heard us enter the apartment. His day over, he was dressed to leave, but stopped short at the sight of us.

"What's up?" he asked. "Ham, you look terrible. Are you OK?"

"Maybe you should go get Mr. Roseman," Marston suggested over my mumbled response.

Kripp disappeared down the hall and came back in a moment removing his coat.

"I'll have some coffee in a minute. Mr. Roseman will be right out."

"Bring some brandy, too, will you Kripp?" Marston said.

"You got it, Lieutenant."

To my relief, Marston did most of the talking when Arthur came padding into the living room in slippers and wrapped in his aging silk robe. Roseman listened intently, as always, with an occasional glance toward me. I moved to the couch, grateful for a comfortable place to sit, one that didn't bounce and weave and smell of stale cigarettes.

The coffee arrived as Marston finished his update, and he

was still busy answering Roseman's questions when Florio showed up. The conversation turned three-way at that point with Florio informing us that the disemboweled officer at the stage entrance was holding his own and, though critical, would probably recover. The second patrolman was pronounced dead on arrival at Bellevue.

The body count had stopped at seven.

For my part, I still wasn't fully connecting on any conscious level. Voices faded in and out, my attention span was incredibly short, and the brandy did little to help. Roseman, Florio, and Marston stood nearby with Kripp coming and going, but no one spoke to me directly. I was the bereaved relative who was talked about in the third person, patted and patronized and pitied.

"Does he want coffee?"

"No, I don't think he does."

"Maybe later he'll feel up to a cup."

"Some more brandy? He should have something."

"Right, some more brandy would do him good."

I simply stared into the glass, rerunning thoughts in my head, replaying those closing moments again and again, watching her fall helplessly, wondering if I could have prevented it. The impact of almost killing Sharp had faded completely. I found myself mentally watching a 1940s newsreel, or it might have been promos for John Garfield's latest gangster movie. Vivid black and white pictures filled with action showed Tommy guns blazing away at dumpy men in suits and straw hats. The words, Law! Justice! Loyalty! overlaid scenes of the American work ethic as they flashed across the screen. None of the familiar symbols, or the pat responses, justified Marilyn's crumpling into those seats. The memory made me startle. My brandy glass hit the floor. The room immediately became quiet.

"David," Roseman said softly. "David, perhaps you should retire. Lie down. I can send for a sedative."

"Mild shock, according to Ellerton," Florio repeated.

"He'll pull out of it," Kripp said, picking up the glass and scrubbing the spot on the rug. "Just leave him alone. You'll be all right, won't you, Ham?"

I knew at that instant that I did, indeed, need to pull out of it. Not for my sake—hell, I could go on feeling sorry for myself forever—but because I owed these men an explanation. Explanation was really the wrong word. A sign, perhaps, that I was OK. These were my friends. Their concern warranted consideration. I needed to come around. Ask for help. End their confusion. Let them know my state of mind, where I'd been, and how far below the surface I was. The longer I paddled around in these mental depths, the more worried they were going to get. Next thing you know, their wives would have me holding some chicken dish in my hand, not good quality liquor.

I emptied the fresh brandy Kripp had poured, gave a strong kick, and came up for air.

No one moved. I commanded center stage and their silence.

"Could I have another brandy?" I asked.

Suddenly everyone was talking at once: Roseman grabbing my arm, smiling, saying how relieved he was; Florio thundering something to do with not worrying about charges or indictments or anything criminal; Marston telling Kripp he'd have that drink now; and Kripp not hearing him because he was too busy telling Roseman, who wasn't listening either, that he'd been right about me all the time.

"He's just down there thinking," Kripp was saying. "He's been walking along one of those back roads, just thinking. Didn't I tell you that?"

I never thought four men could create such pandemonium.

"Forget the brandy," I said loudly. "I need a drink. Gin! Anyone want a gin?" I asked.

"Yes," Marston said emphatically. "Large, extra dry, straight up, and quickly."

On that note, we all moved over to the bar like extras in an Italian western. All we needed was a footrail. The doorbell rang, and without waiting for anyone to answer, Jordan came in.

He looked at me questioningly, as the others had. I smiled,

handed him a glass, and said that Marilyn was going to make it. I couldn't talk about it, but she was going to make it. He turned to Florio with a compliment on his tie—"Armani, no?"—and they were off into the small-talk of men's clothes and where to buy it wholesale. Jordan, of all people; Mr. Casual, wear it until it unravels, talking fashion with an Italian twice his size, while he stood there dressed in a bright Hawaiian shirt, penny loafers, argyle socks, and draped in a full-length, threadbare cashmere coat. Jesus, what a pair.

"I called Jordan." It was Kripp next to me. "I knew he'd want to know about Marilyn and how you were."

"Thanks."

"I knew you were OK, just shock like they said, but I also figured that if anybody could talk to you, I mean, if we needed somebody, it would be Jordan. You know?"

"I know. You were right, too. Listen, Kripp," I said, deeply touched by his concern, "I have a confession to make about all those songs I pretend to know. . . ." He cut me off with a laugh.

"Shit man, I knew about those books you bought six months ago."

I paused trying to place the sensation that had come over me. "Could I have a sandwich? I'm starved."

"You bet! Turkey, corned beef?"

"Either one would be great; both maybe."

"Trimmings?"

"Everything. Anybody want food?" I said to the others. "Arthur, I've opened your kitchen."

"You're most welcome. Please, everyone into the kitchen."

"I'll go with you to the hospital," Jordan said as we all came together moving out of the living room.

"Thanks, I'd appreciate that."

"Kripp," he said, approaching the black man at the refrigerator door, "shall we turn this into a Jewish deli or what? Roseman's. Has a nice ring." He slipped off his coat, wrapped an apron around the waist, and started taking out jars of assorted mustards and pickles.

"So," Florio said, back to business. "Think it was Sharp all along, by himself?" I paused before answering, trying to focus, and it seemed to make him nervous. Probably even he was concerned that it was too soon to question me, that I couldn't handle it. I dove in.

"Yes, I do think Sharp acted independently with regard to the murders. He had a preexisting relationship with Bergman and he drew on that for the automobile, a place to lock me up—they'd been lovers up until Lane's appearance and after that were at least business partners, which was probably Bergman's way of hanging on, being there." Florio's head bobbed in agreement. "And for Sharp it was convenient to keep Bergman around—to tag along with Reid."

"So you think it was Sharp that Bergman was waiting for down there?"

"I do. They were together in wanting me off the streets, but for different reasons. Bergman just wanted to rough me up, frighten me so I'd keep quiet about the blackmail. I think he wasn't planning to kill me—I couldn't picture him in prison and I bet he couldn't either; so, I didn't figure him for murder."

Everybody was listening to our conversation, silently awaiting their sandwiches. Even Jordan alternated his attention between the chopping block and what we were saying. He wiped the knifeblade against a towel, set it down, and asked how come nothing about the blackmail story was in the papers. I looked at Florio.

"Until we could get Leonard on his feet and talking, there was nothing to report," he said. "So I never released anything, and the press—meaning Ira Katz," he said in my direction, "didn't know to ask."

Jordan gave a satisfied nod and went back to making sandwiches.

"Have you thought about how your final report is going to read?" I asked Florio.

"That's a problem," he said bluntly. "Well, not a problem exactly. But I hate dangling threads and we've got some here. I'd like to have a halfway plausible sequence of events to tie these ends together." This last bit he said with a sideways glance at Marston. I pulled a cold beer out of the fridge and handed it to Florio. He took a bite of corned beef and popped the aluminum tab.

"Do you have a reasonable explanation, David?" Roseman asked.

"Nothing that's precise," I said, "just some random thoughts I haven't had time to connect."

"Such as?" he prompted.

"Well, Arthur and I disagree about this," I said to Florio, "but here's my theory on the blackmail: Suppose Bergman goes to Leonard with the story about his pretty wife humping a homosexual. That's bad enough, but what if he threatens to announce the fact publicly unless he sees some cash. Leonard pays up."

"I tend to agree with your boss. Ham. It's not much of a reason."

"Maybe not," I said, "but anyone who could say different is dead. Sharp, never knew about it, I'm certain of that; and Leonard I don't count because—I'm sorry Arthur—he may never recover, and even if he does, I'm sure not going to be the guy to put it to him. He's been humiliated enough."

"He might be right," Marston said, coming to my defense. "By telling the old man, two things are accomplished: he gets some money, maybe, which he needs, and he also gets the opportunity to involve Peters in a situation that he can use to his advantage later; which is what he really wants, right, Ham?"

"Bergman wins either way," I said. "Blackmail money or the pleasure of wrecking Sharp's well-laid plans to get himself financed all the way to West Forty-fifth Street. Also, I don't think Lane was ever part of the deal," I added. "Bergman probably just used his name to turn the knife a little farther into Leonard." Florio still looked doubtful, but I kept going anyway. "Faced with Bergman's accusations, Leonard confronts his wife and delivers

224

an ultimatum: stop seeing Peters. Not because she's screwing around—he almost expects that—but because Peters's peter isn't the kind of peter he wants petering his wife."

"Rather selective morality to my mind," Roseman stated.

"You're right about that, Arthur," I agreed, "but Leonard's outburst also gives Bergman a back way of letting Samantha know she's porking a homosexual. Something he couldn't do himself without losing his relationship to Sharp."

"Wait a minute," Florio said. "From what we know about Samantha Craig, do we actually believe she would blanch at having a bisexual lover?"

"No, she wouldn't," I agreed, "but she'd hate like hell to be led around by the nose and Peters and Sharp had been doing it for almost a year." I took a bite of my sandwich and Marston got up to put water on for coffee.

"Now, Shelton Sharp's dream was to build a theater," I continued, "and it might have remained just that, a dream, if it hadn't been for Lane Peters. He was the catalyst for a remarkable chain of subsequent events. Young, strikingly handsome, and possessed with an unusual desire: to play the classics. I picture the day Sharp saw him in that showcase production—it must have been the theatrical equivalent of Cro-Magnon man showing up at Margaret Mead's office. I mean, after his arrival, the New Reach was off and running. In time, they were getting better reviews, drawing larger crowds, selling subscription tickets—and the next thing you know they have a couple of smash hits. Then came the front-page story about Sharp, the theater, and his leading man in the Sunday Arts and Leisure section of the *Times*."

"The beginning of the end," Jordan said drily, drawing a short laugh from Roseman.

I stopped talking and worked on my sandwich. After a gin chaser I started up again.

"Suddenly it becomes easier to raise money, interest patrons, expand the budget, pay salaries, and give parties that the right kind of people want to attend."

"Enter Samantha Craig," Marston interjected.

"Exactly," I said to him. "She turned out to be better than the National Endowment, too. Maybe she liked theater, maybe she even liked Shakespeare."

"But she definitely liked Lane Peters," Roseman surmised, "and despite Sharp's claims to the contrary, he must also have liked her."

"Without question," I tagged.

"I bet there were plenty of fights with Peters trying to convince that old fag he wasn't having too much fun seeing New York from the penthouse suite," Florio said with a laugh.

"How come you guys missed the homosexual bit?" I asked him.

"Good question," Marston answered. "When we went back and interviewed Brock Leland—he's the stage manager—a second time, he said Lane and Sharp had been chewing ass for the past six or seven months." And he added, in an aside, "We figured that wasn't a sexual term."

"The reason Leland hadn't mentioned their relationship during our first chat," Florio said, "was because nobody asked, and it probably didn't seem important to him."

"Well, whether Lane was bisexual, trisexual, or simply confused and ambitious, is anybody's guess," I continued.

"You know," Marston mused. "Peters is the one I keep coming back to. He was playing everybody with a different tune: Sharp, Leonard Craig, Samantha. His ambition must have been awesome."

"The vaulting kind which o're leaps itself and falls on the other."

"Pardon me?"

"Nothing, keep going."

"Right, so this guy is humping his producer, the company's leading patron, and maybe even Bergman. That's a lot of sex, even for someone his age."

"He was shrewd, no question about it," Roseman said. "In retrospect, it's not surprising he got shot."

226

"What I want to know is when did Peters and Sharp actually split up?" Florio asked, his frustration getting the best of him.

"They split," I said, "about three seconds before Sharp took him out. That was when Sharp realized Peters was serious and he was being replaced permanently by Samantha. But initially, I think it was nothing more than a plan to milk money. Somewhere along the way, it went wrong."

"In the bedroom, I should think." Roseman said, touching the corners of his mouth with a napkin.

"Which brings us to the night the Lavender Laertes died," I said.

"*Macbeth*," Roseman groaned. "The play was *Macbeth*."

"Sorry, I couldn't resist. Anyway, that night, Samantha arranges to meet him after the theater. Leonard overhears, realizes she had no intention of standing by his ultimatum, gets fed up, and confronts her at the Carlyle. Peters arrives at the penthouse first, orders some Chinese takeout, fluffs the pillows, and waits for Samantha to finish with Banks Reid."

"What about Leonard?" Jordan asked incredulously. "They all sleep in the same bed and get kinky, or what?"

"Leonard is out of the picture at this point," I told him. "They have separate suites in the same penthouse, and they occasionally meet at breakfast. But that's it. Besides, after she latched onto Reid, and his money, she had neutralized Leonard's only real leverage over her. So, expecting Samantha, Peters gets Sharp instead. One pleads, the other plays tough, and their discussion turns into another argument."

"It wasn't premeditated then," Florio asked. "You don't think Sharp went there with the intention of killing him?"

"No," I said simply, "he went there to get his boyfriend back."

"And, if he had decided on murder," Marston said, giving me a chance to eat some more, "there were easier ways and better opportunities than a penthouse on Eighty-second Street."

"Yeah, I'll buy that," Florio said.

"In any event," I went on, "Peters pulls out the gun, Sharp

relieves him of it and 'bang!' A French jury would let him go in an instant, if he'd stopped there," I threw a wink at Roseman. "What I can't believe is that Sharp didn't call for help."

"That is a difficult and delicate position for any person," said Roseman. "He might have been too frightened, or in shock. It's not surprising he didn't have the presence of mind to make himself stop and reflect on his actions, much less check for a pulse."

"Killing the take-out guy wasn't an accident," Florio snapped.

"You're right there," I agreed with him, "and it wouldn't have mattered if I'd gone down, too. Harwood must have seen Sharp at the apartment when he delivered the food. He could have identified him, so once Peters was dead, Harwood had to go, too. I'm certain Sharp simply checked the take-out order, got the restaurant's address, and went looking for him just like I did."

"And Samantha comes home to find the body," Jordan said. "Incredible."

"Right. After she goes upstairs, Reid follows her. He's not stupid, he knows hanky-panky when he sees it, and we all remember how discreet Samantha was." I drifted mentally for a moment as I flashed back to her gently swaying, half-clothed body in the kitchen. "Randall Bergman goes up with Reid. Sharp, who's watching from somewhere close by, must think it's Grand Central Station. He also notices that nobody has called an ambulance. No sirens in the distance, nothing. He starts to worry: Maybe Peters isn't dead, maybe he's regained conscious-ness, maybe he's telling them how his estranged lover just tried to murder him. A million possibilities are going through Sharp's brain, none of them good. So he girds his loins and goes back upstairs to find out what's happening."

"That took some balls," Marston said.

"You bet it did," I agreed. "He walks in, sees Samantha with the gun and thinks, 'Wonderful.' But before he can play the outraged lover, Leonard rings for the elevator and he, too, wanders in. The answer to all of their problems. Deus ex machina. The perfect patsy."

"Almost," Florio said, moving back to the chopping block and picking up loose strands of corned beef, "because Sharp knows the take-out fella is going to have to die. Then you"—he pointed at me—"started nosing around on Leonard's behalf and Bergman figures you're on him for the blackmail."

"It's all too much for me," Kripp said, getting up to leave. "I'm going home. You white jockeys are always in some kind of shit and this time it's more than I can deal with."

The phone rang.

Kripp's voice from the hall said, "I'll get it." A short pause and he was back in the kitchen. I was already on my feet and moving. The clock on the wall said 10:45.

"Marilyn's out of surgery, Ham," he said to me. "She's stable, but not conscious. Prognosis is good."

"Great! Gentlemen, I'm out of here. Jordan? Will you come?"

"Right behind you."

"You will, at an appropriate moment, give her our best, won't you?" Roseman asked.

"Yes, of course."

"Kripp and I will be down in the morning," he continued. "Leonard's there as well, remember?"

I had my hand on the doorknob when the phone rang again.

Kripp answered immediately and looked to me. I exchanged glances with Jordan and waited. Kripp covered the receiver and said, "It's Rachel Carlson. Do you want to talk to her?"

Rachel. She seemed light years away. I didn't know what to say.

"Tell her I'm on my way to the hospital," I said. "Tell her . . . it's been a very long night. Tell her, tell her . . . I'll be in touch." And I closed the door behind me.